To My Friend Jay,

May the muses smile
upon you
with generosity
& grace.

Jay L. Lawrence
6/17/2019

BAFFLED
and other stories

Gary Lawrence

Gary's Write Stuff

Copyright © 2013 by Gary Lawrence

ISBN: 978-0-9882497-3-8
Library of Congress Control Number: 2013947915

Printed in the United States of America

Publisher: Gary's Write Stuff

Design: Soundview Design Studio

The stories in this book are fiction.

All rights reserved. No part of this book may be transmitted in any form or by any means, electronic or mechanical, including photocopying, recording, or by any information storage or retrieval system, in part, in any form, without the permission of the publisher.

Requests for such permissions should be addressed to:

Gary's Write Stuff
Visit us online at www.garyswritestuff.wordpress.com

CREDITS

An earlier version of "Why I'm Here" was first published online at www.shortstoryamerica.com (March 2012), and subsequently published in *Short Story America, Volume Two: 47 Great Contemporary Short Stories* (September 2012).

ACKNOWLEDGEMENTS

I have many people to thank for making this book a reality:
- My teachers, family and friends who have encouraged me throughout my life.
- My parents, for living the lives they did and for giving me the experiences and opportunities they did.
- My uncle, Tom Lawrence, who never finished high school, but literally reached into his wallet and gave me a handful of money for books for Rockford College without question or a moment's hesitation at a time when I really needed it.
- All the people at Rockford West High School, but especially Coach John Vitale, and Ernie Stokes and my other English teachers.
- All the people at Rockford College, but especially Dr. Dain Trafton, Dr. Peter Stanlis, Mr. John Glass, and my other English teachers.
- All the people at Vermont College of Fine Arts MFA in Writing program, but especially my workshop leaders and groups, and my beloved advisors: Christopher Noel, Ellen Lesser, Robert Vivian, and David Jauss.
- My friend, fellow writer, final reader and Greek chorus all rolled into one, Mark Teismann.
- Finally, and far from least: My friend and wife Linda, for her constant faith in me and her stalwart belief that you can not only live your dreams, but that you owe it to yourself to do so.

Production of this book would not have been possible without the skills and assistance of Tim Johnston and the organizations he created: Short Story America and Short Story America Press.

ABOUT THIS BOOK

This book is my debut collection, a compilation of twelve short stories written over the last thirty years. The kernels of these stories vary widely. I originally wrote them around the time they first came to me. Over time, I attempted to pound them from the merely real to me into decent literature for us.

Some of these stories won awards and contests; most didn't. Only one of these stories was previously published: "Why I'm Here," at www.shortstoryamerica.com. The oldest story is "Garage Sale;" the most recent is "Throwing Snowballs at Cars." All of these stories, in earlier forms, were part of my education at Vermont College of Fine Arts.

Many or most of these stories are set in Rockford, Illinois, the town where I grew up and raised my family. Many of them overlap in theme. Some also overlap in characters, and can be read as sequences. But read them alone first – they need to stand alone, too. The sequence is icing, like an overtone in music – something that's there, additional, but nobody's literally playing it.

Many or most of these stories deal with "men" issues – whatever that means. Hopefully many or most also touch on issues we all may be "baffled" by from time to time, at one time or other.

This book can be used as a textbook or guide as well as a short story collection. Some of you will read the stories first; others will go straight to the back to read more about the author, or check out the study guide and the author commentary on each story. Use the book however you want, for individual or group enjoyment, enrichment, and/or study. Creator and critic – that's me, that's us. Feed both here – this book's a one-stop shop.

But mostly this book is about my love of the short story and my attempt to honor the short story form. Start with the stories.

Read them more than once. End with the stories. Re-read them once every few years. See if they stand up. It's all about story. Story is all there is.

    Enjoy. Think. Understand. Relate. Share.

    You could do worse.

Gary Lawrence
Phoenix, AZ
June 2013

PRAISE FOR GARY LAWRENCE:

Writing

"Gary Lawrence's fiction is crisply and meticulously written, with a kind of quiet and straightforward lyricism, and it is always emotionally, intellectually, and morally involving. He writes excellent dialogue and description, and his stories are chock full of compelling characters and events – and a good measure of subtly-expressed wisdom to boot."
> – David Jauss, author of the award-winning collection *Black Maps*

"At their best, a Gary Lawrence story shows ordinary folks struggling to find their own place in the world and their own voice… [they're often] stories [that] touch on timeless and universal themes of male relationships and initiation, though they do so with a touching frailty disguised as toughness…"
> – Robert Vivian, author of *The Tall Grass Trilogy*

"Compelling material."
> – Ellen Lesser, author of the collection *The Shoplifter's Apprentice*

"Gary Lawrence possesses a gift for storytelling, for hooking the reader and moving the plot, and it shines…"
> – Christopher Noel, VCFA faculty

"Testosterone stew, with an estrogen sauce."
> – Mark Teismann

Literary criticism:

"Gary Lawrence is a wonderfully astute reader and articulate analyst, never losing sight of that dimension in which concrete technique and meaning or vision coexist in mutual, inextricable service."

– Ellen Lesser, VCFA faculty

"Astute, incisive…Gary Lawrence should be commended for writing and presenting one of the most enjoyable, instructive, and valuable lectures I've seen during my twelve years on the Vermont College of Fine Arts faculty."

– David Jauss, Contributing Editor, *The Writer's Chronicle*

TABLE OF CONTENTS

Baffled 1
Showtime 9
Famous 21
Trinity 35
    You Just Had To Do It (1963) 35
    The Wait (1983) 39
    Dreamer (2003) 42
Throwing Snowballs at Cars 49
Wrestleback 67
Why I'm Here 79
Garage Sale 93
The Sum of All Fears 103
Working Class 129
Turnabout 141
Coming Home 157
Gary's "Extras" 179
    How to Get More Out of Any Short Story 179
    Interview with the Author 183
    Author Commentary and Discussion Questions 193
    Failed Poet's Society 205

*We don't have to live great lives,
we just have to understand
and survive
the ones we've got.*

– Andre Dubus,
Voices From The Moon

For my family
For my teachers
For my friends
For the short story
For me

BAFFLED

Up until Summerfest, I thought things were going pretty good with Ann and me. My buddy Paul's girlfriend Tammy Rae introduced us one Thursday at karaoke night at Spanky's Bar and Grill downtown. Ann was a looker: blonde, blue-eyed, short and petite mostly, but big in all the right places, you know? She was also a mama's girl in the best sense, one of those girls that will stick with you through thick and thin, a real keeper.

Like that night I left her house in a hurry after the Cubs lost another extra-inning heart-breaker to the Cards. I got to thinking about how hard it was going to be to get up for work the next day, I guess, and gave her a peck on the cheek on my way out. She called me on my cell a few minutes later—made me turn my pickup around right then and there and come all the way back. She met me at the door with her hands on her hips and a look that could kill. "Comings and goings are important, you know. Let's make sure we do it right—every single time, okay?" Then she reached up, wrapped her arms around my neck and kissed me hard, deep.

I had a hell of a time getting to sleep after that.

Imagine me, Mike McGority, the pushing-forty good-for-nothing high school dropout from the wrong side of town, still swinging a 32-ounce serrated-head Estwing hammer fifty hours a week building friggin' pole barns for cows, hooked up with a girl like this. So what if I was four-F and couldn't go over to Iraq just to get all blown to hell on I.E.D. Alley like my dumb-ass little brother Mack? If only the old man could have seen me with Ann!

Loser, my ass.

Ann and me had been together a couple weeks then, and we wanted to do something special together. We decided to go to Summerfest up in Milwaukee for the July 4th weekend. We both liked live music a lot, and catching the local day acts was fine with us. We weren't really interested in the big-name, high-dollar commercial acts that came at night. "We'll be worn out by then and ready for bed," Ann said, and I swear she blushed when she said it.

Actually blushed.

So we both took Friday off and drove the hour and half up to Milwaukee that morning. We took her car 'cause it used a lot less gas than my truck. To get a general feel for the place we paid a few bucks to ride the elevated tram. From up there you could see it all; you could even smell the popcorn and brats cooking when the breeze blew right. Lake Michigan was on one side; seagulls floated lazy there, rode the thermals. The Summerfest grounds ran along the lake, full of exhibit halls, tents, picnic tables, rest areas, restaurants. And lots of music stages – one for every different type of music there was, looked like, and one for every brand of beer brewed in Milwaukee. That's a lot of music and a lot of beer.

It was only noon and the wide black asphalt paths were filled with people laughing and pointing, kids running here and there like hungry seagulls, diving in and out two or three times for every step their parents took forward.

Ann had on this green-and-brown camouflage suit like the soldiers wear, baggy pants and shirt with lots of Velcro'd pockets, except she had a big-brimmed straw hat with a yellow ribbon wrapped around it that hung down her back, and she wore—what do they call those sorta-short pants things? Pedal pushers? Before we even left home this morning she'd gone through and marked her program in yellow highlighter with the acts she thought we might be interested in so we wouldn't miss anything. She didn't move her hand from the map, even when she touched me on the shoulder and pointed to one of the buildings with names with her other hand, like she was afraid she'd never find her place on the map again. Back on the ground, she charged off the El and led the way. I just tagged along.

School teachers, I tell ya.

We spent a couple hours just strolling around, stopped when we wanted to stop, grazed our way through the food stands. The crowd was a rainbow of people of all shapes and sizes and colors, except every once in a while you got the paranoid parents and kids all decked out in the same color outfits like some sports team looking for a better sponsor. My family had gone to the county fair once when I was fifteen, but the old man spent all our money on beer for himself before we got to go on any rides, and got so drunk that he picked a fight with a rent-a-cop and my mom made Mack my baby brother and me carry him out to the parking lot where he leaned over and puked into some guy's brand-new Malibu convertible. We had to beat it out of there fast after that.

Wandering through Summerfest that Friday with Ann, seeing all these happy families in one place, I caught myself staring more than once. I thought about what it meant to be here with people you worried about, what it was like to take care of them in a crowd. I wondered if it was an adventure or a nightmare.

Whenever Ann and me came to a music stage, we stood there and listened to a song or two. Pretty soon she'd say to me, "Are you liking it?"

"Eh...take it or leave it," I'd say.

"You're right. Life's too short," Ann would say. "Let's keep moving."

Then she'd take my hand again, give me a smile and a little tug, and we'd move on.

After hearing a couple tunes from Ernie and the Po' Boys at the Miller Genuine Draft Rhythm and Blues tent, we nodded at each other. Then we found some white plastic lawn chairs in the back of the tent and sat down.

Ann pulled her chair next to mine, close. We watched for a while and then she leaned over and pulled her sunglasses down her nose just a little and looked over at me, her big blue pupils and the whites of her eyes shining just above those dark wide frames. "Check out the bass player. I haven't seen him breathe yet, have you?"

I looked. "Nope. I figure he's dead but still standing. Ya think?"

She laughed, then pulled up another chair in front of her and turned it backwards to put her feet on. This time when she sat down she reached over and laid her hand on my thigh and left it there.

We sat like that for a half-hour or so until the band took a break. Ann leaned her head into my chest and said, "Are you liking it?"

"Yeah, I'm good," I said. "Real good."

She patted my leg. "Why don't you go get us a couple cold beers?"

People filed in and out of the Rhythm and Blues tent while the roadies milled around the stage. Taped music played in the background from several big black floor speakers. Nobody was in any rush. By the time I got back with the beers, a young family was taking their seats around a table just in front of us.

The mom looked Fortune 500 in a dark blue two-piece suit with a beige silk blouse. She looked tired and hot. She wore a pendant necklace with a silver chain and a pale blue stone that made her eyes stand out. The baby on her hip, stripped to just a diaper, was red from the sun and streaked dirty from crying. A sleepy-looking five- or six-year-old boy dragged behind, clutching the mom's hand. She sat him in a chair next to her. The boy had curly blond hair and her blue eyes. Cute. The dad, lugging a duffle-sized diaper bag over his shoulder, brought up the rear and plopped into a chair on the other side of the boy.

Mom blew a few strands of long black hair out of her mouth and brushed more hair off her sweaty cheeks with her free hand. They were close enough to us to hear. "I gotta take Ellen over to the porta-potties and change her," she yelled to Dad. "She's soaked. You watch Hank, okay?"

Mom bent over with her face close to the little boy's. "You stay here and be good for Daddy, Hank, and maybe Mommy will bring you something cold and yummy, okay?"

Ann turned to me and smiled. She had that look single women get when they're around little kids. "Yeah, yeah, pretty cute," I smiled back.

"And quit sucking your thumb." Mom yanked Hank's hand away from his face. Ann gasped next to me. Hank froze, fist in mid-air. Mom just grabbed the duffle diaper bag, swung it over her own shoulder, and headed for the porta-potties across the road while she balanced the baby on her hip, all in one fluid motion like she'd done hundreds of times before.

I took a slow sip of beer, and watched. I remembered *my* mom trying to break Mack from sucking his thumb. We thought he'd never stop.

Sprawled in his chair, Hank's dad sighed like he couldn't have walked another step. He had short blond hair and wore dress clothes, like he'd just come from work somewhere downtown, just like his wife. Fortune 500 too, but *Esquire* casual. Short-sleeved dress shirt. Creased slacks. Black socks and wingtips. Made me feel sloppy in my khaki cargo shorts and raggedy old Cubs tee shirt.

Ann was breathing normal now and smiled whenever the little boy turned to look at us. "Isn't he a doll?" she said, loud enough for him and his dad to hear. She scrunched her shoulders and wiggled against me when she said it.

"Sit up," Dad said.

Ann stiffened again at his tone. Hank squirmed slightly in his chair. I waited some more.

"And take your thumb out of your mouth," Dad said, without looking over at Hank.

Hank turned his head and glanced at his dad. He pulled his thumb out of his mouth, but kept it close to his lips. When he saw that his father wasn't looking at him, he jammed his thumb back in his mouth and sucked hard.

Dad sat leaning forward, looking down at the ground, his elbows on his knees and his hands in front of him, fingertip to fingertip. Then with a quick jerk he reached out and caught one of the legs on Hank's chair and yanked it so hard that Hank had to grab the top of the chair to keep from falling out.

"Bet that got your goddamn thumb out of your mouth, huh boy?"

Ann took her hand off my thigh, crossed her arms over her breasts and squeezed herself like she was cold. I put my half-empty beer cup on the table. My mom got so frustrated with Mack sucking his thumb she finally gave up and left it up to the old man to break him of the habit. Left it up to The Boss of the House. To *Mr.* McGority, the assistant high-school principal. Assistant Dean of Bad Boys. Dean of the Dropouts. The Enforcer himself.

This here was nothing compared to that. Not yet, anyway.

I did think Hank might cry, though. He scrunched up his face, and his bottom lip started to tremble.

Dad whipped a pack of cigarettes out of his pocket and had a smoke in his mouth in one swift move, like the tough guys do in the movies.

"You'd better not be thinking about crying, you little baby," he said, pulling a blue Bic lighter from his pants pocket and lighting up. He stared over at Hank. "Baby."

Hank was trying his best not to cry. I could tell. He fought hard, but a couple tears ran down his cheek anyways.

"Where the hell *is* that bitch?" Dad said to no one, looking in the direction Mom had gone.

I couldn't feel Ann breathing against me anymore, she'd gone so still. I looked over and saw her chest move. She was still breathing, at least. I cleared my throat, focused on the big black speakers in front of me, and took another sip of my beer.

"I said sit up right, dammit!" Dad grabbed Hank by the shoulders this time, then picked him up and threw him back down hard on the chair seat. Hank didn't have a chance of holding back the tears now. His mouth got rigid, his lips tightened, and a long wet sob broke out from deep in his throat. At that Dad reached over and slapped him hard across the face. Ann jerked like the dad'd hit *her*. She let out a loud gasp and covered her mouth with her hand, too late. "Shut the hell up," Dad said to the cement floor. "Baby."

The hair on the back of my neck stood on end. I got goose bumps on my arms. I felt a little sick to my stomach, but brushed that off to the beer. I thought about going over and slapping the shit out of that dad, but I knew it would just make things worse – eventually – for the kid.

So I took a couple deep breaths, reached over, grabbed my clear plastic cup, and drained what was left of my beer.

Around us the taped music still blared from the speakers. The roadies were scrambling to get ready for the next set, which would start any minute now. People kept walking by on the hot asphalt paths outside, slipping in and out of the beer tent like nothing had happened. I relaxed some in my chair, figured the worst was over now.

The look on Hank's face was almost funny. His lips quivered, his eyes were shut tight, tears were streaming down his cheeks, and a bright red welt was rising on his cheek. But no more sound came out. Pretty tough kid, I thought with a little grin. A lot like Mack. He'll be okay.

Dad slipped back to his slouched position. He pinched his lit cigarette tight between his thin fingers, then took a drag. Ann turned to me with wild eyes, panting. "Mike—aren't you going to *do* something?" she said, her own face red.

"Geez, Ann," I breathed. "Quiet!" I talked down to my empty beer cup. "The guy's sitting right there."

She jumped up out of her chair and stood over me. "I don't care if everyone *here* hears me!" She looked around quickly, daring someone, anyone, to speak. Her teeth were clenched, her arms were up and her hands were in fists in front of her shoulders, like a boxer's.

"Ann, sit down," I said, standing up too. "It won't do any good," I pleaded. "You'll just make it worse for the kid." I reached for her but she was already turning away from me. "I've seen his kind before," I mumbled after her, stuck between the chairs, but she was already gone.

She took three big steps and stopped right in front of Dad. "I can't believe what I just saw." Her arms hung straight at her sides now, forced. Her lips trembled. Her clenched fists were white.

Dad looked away. Then he took a long drag off his cigarette and blew smoke at her. Hank just stared up at Ann, wide-eyed.

She stood her ground and stomped her foot hard on the cement floor like a little girl throwing a temper tantrum. "You bastard. I can't *believe* what you did." She spit the words at Dad. She looked down at Hank then turned away, tears in her eyes. She bolted for the exit, strutting, not running exactly, walked straight, stiff, hollowed, knocking two lime-green snow-cones out of Mom's hand as she charged past her.

"Watch it – bitch!" Mom yelled after Ann. She stopped in front of Dad. "What's up *her* ass?"

Dad just shrugged. "I dunno."

"Well. Skinny little skank owes me two snow-cones," Mom huffed as she sat down next to Hank. Hank stared at the crystal green liquid pooling on the hot cement floor and stuck his thumb in his mouth. Mom smoothed her beige silk blouse and jammed a bottle in the baby's mouth. I picked Ann's cup up out of the spilled beer where she had kicked it over, and ran after her.

* * *

The Summerfest crowd was changing by then, from the happy family crowd of the early afternoon to the loud, hairy, heavily-leathered Harley crowd of the evening. The streets felt more crowded now, too, harder to move through, dirtier, darker. I caught up with Ann, but she wouldn't stop no matter what I said. I ended up having to take a bus home that night – Ann drove away in her car and left me stranded in the parking lot.

Now, three weeks later, she won't return my calls, my emails, my text messages. Nothing. I thought about going to her house to talk to her, but that didn't feel right. I even went to Spanky's last week on karaoke night, but she wasn't there, either. None of the regulars had seen her in a while.

No, none of them had seen a girl like that.

I wish now we'd never gone to Summerfest. I wish now we'd never sat down in that damn beer tent. I wish now we'd just stayed home.

Wish in one hand, shit in the other, the old man always said. See which one fills up the fastest.

SHOWTIME

The courtroom studio audience was restless. The previous trial had not lived up to its billing. Ratings were down for the third quarter in a row. Asses were on the line. Someone's head was going to roll if ratings didn't improve quickly, the people upstairs said. Mr. Monney, the show's producer, scurried back and forth between cameras, wringing his hands and shaking his head. Every time someone in the audience complained or got up to leave, he took flight to another camera, back and forth, back and forth.

"Not good. No no. Not good."

Out on the brightly-lit set Frank, the director, leaned against the fake stucco wall behind the Judge's seat. *We're in trouble here. Where else can I get a job as good as this? No time to panic now,* he thought, rather weakly. He spoke to the actor standing next to him, the man who played the bailiff. "So what's up next, Charlie?" asked Frank. He tried to talk without his voice cracking, in case the producer heard him.

"A murder case this time. Some guy raped and killed this little guy's brand-new wife." Charlie's eyes grew wider. "Did it at the train station – in broad daylight!"

Charlie could barely contain his excitement. He couldn't keep his hand off the pistol in his leather holster. He'd just found the Colt .45 prop last night in the Western studio three stages down. He imagined that *this* was the gun used by Clint Eastwood in *High Plains Drifter*.

"Well, that last one looked like it was going to be a winner, too," Frank said. "What a yawner. You'da thought a kidnapping case would do better than that." He shook his head. Frowned. "With the little kid involved, and all."

A commotion at Stage Right got Frank's attention. Two real bailiffs pulled a huge man in handcuffs, orange jail jumpsuit and leg irons into the room. The man in the jumpsuit stood a full foot taller and weighed a hundred pounds more than either of the bailiffs, and they weren't small men. One of the bailiffs had a long red welt on his left cheek.

"Son of a bitch didn't want to come up here," the bailiff muttered when he saw Frank staring at him.

"Just a minute, boys," Frank called out, quickly assessing the situation and heading them off. He walked toward the trio quickly, his arm and hand up like a cop stopping traffic. "They're not quite done cleaning up from the last show yet."

Joey the janitor had just wiped the modified witness box down with a pine-scented disinfectant. "How ya doing, Joey? About got that cleaned up?"

Joey looked up and smiled at Frank. He took a long leisurely swipe across the seat of the black leather chair with his wide wet rag. "Can't rush quality, you know." Joey finished wiping down the chair and slapped the rag across the top a couple of times, popping the rag when he swung it. Finally he folded his rag onto itself three times in a rectangle shape and threaded it lengthwise through his belt so that it hung there securely – all while Frank and the others waited. Then Joey bugged his eyes out, opened his arms and yelled, looking right at Frank: "It's show time!" He laughed loudly all the way off the witness stand and through the stage-hand exit door in the back.

Friggin' stage unions. Frank made a mental note to file a complaint. He turned back to the bailiffs and their prisoner. "Okay, boys, bring him on in now. Bring him on in." The bailiffs struggled to get the prisoner to move, until one of them finally cracked him across the back of the knees with his nightstick.

"Wake up, Judge," Frank said softly as he moved past the bench. Judge Wulover was hunched over her hands; a metal nail file at least ten inches long hung in mid-air. Frank could smell the liquor seeping from her skin even from where he was in front of the bench. The judge didn't acknowledge Frank, but she did start filing her nails again.

Frank moved closer to the witness box so he could watch the preparations. The bailiffs locked the prisoner's leg irons to the round polished-steel bar that ran low across the front of the box, and locked his hands in cuffs in front of him on the higher bar at his chest. Charlie the actor-bailiff hung back on the other side of the room. Once the prisoner was safely secured, Charlie hooked his thumbs over his holster's belt and sauntered over to the witness box.

"I'll take it from here, boys."

One of the bailiffs, the one with the welt on his face, gave Charlie the finger and walked off. "He's all yours now, asshole," he said. The remaining bailiff looked briefly at the prisoner and smiled. "Enjoy."

The prisoner made a kissing sound with his lips. "Blow me."

Oh, this is going to be good, Frank thought. *This is going to be real good*. He noticed that the studio audience had quieted down now, settled into something close to silence on the set. An air of excitement and expectation settled in. *A little like when I was a kid and people stayed home to watch the Friday Night Fights*, Frank thought fondly. He remembered sitting up late with his dad to watch the fights, eating popcorn, drinking beer or root beer for him, and munching on chocolate-marshmallow-jelly-pinwheel cookies. Most of the time his dad fell asleep on the couch before the actual fight was finished, so Frank would have to remember who won, and how, and tell him the next morning.

Back at the studio, Frank turned quickly and headed back toward the studio booth when he saw the plaintiff standing just inside the lounge area door at Stage Left. He wouldn't have even noticed the man if the large red "Plaintiff" badge hadn't hung crookedly from one of the lapels of his suit coat. The man was barely five feet tall, balding with thin gray hair, wore wire-rimmed glasses, and sported a suit coat whose sleeves came well over his tiny wrists, almost to his middle knuckles, hiding his small hands when he stood straight. He wore a polka-dot bow tie and white shirt with the gray jacket. The man hung close to the participant lounge door, leaning backwards with his hands and rear end pressed against the door, looking like he was ready to bolt.

"Over here!" Frank yelled loudly. "Over here, sir."

The crowd settled further. They'd seen the show before. They knew the routine. They were ready. Frank gave his best traffic-cop wave to the man who was the plaintiff and walked toward the single wooden table in front of the judge's bench. He tapped on the table. "This is your seat here, in front." *We've got the crowd right where we want them*, Frank thought as he smiled brightly at the small man.

Hurry up, dammit, we don't want to lose the mood.

Frank spoke into his headset. "We're doing this live, people. Live. And we're doing it now. Right now. So straighten up and look smart."

The plaintiff still hung back by the door. "Mr. Monney," Frank said over his headset. No response. "Monney!" Frank yelled to get the producer's attention. Monney looked up at Frank, startled. People didn't tell him what to do, ever. "Go over there and get that guy, will ya?" Frank pointed across the room. Monney didn't move. Frank pleaded. "Will ya? Please?! I don't want to lose them!" He nodded slightly at the audience.

That was enough for Monney. He jumped to life off his perch at Camera Two and shuttled the plaintiff over to the table, one hand on his forearm and the other on his elbow. Monney nearly carried the man. "Glad you're here, sir, glad you're here," Monney chattered as he steered the plaintiff around the cameras and cables and across the polished-wood floor. "Terrible. Yes, just terrible. What happened. Terrible."

Frank too jumped into action. "Get me another mike and a mini-cam down here. I'm shooting this one from the floor, too. Myself." He looked up at the prisoner, who stared at the plaintiff. A slight snarl formed on the large man's lips. "Get me a mike and a camera, goddammit, and get it here now." One of the temp girls from Central Casting, a young blonde intern named Ginger, ran down, pinned the mike on the plaintiff's collar, and gave the hand-held digital camera to Frank.

Frank looked over at Doc, the physician's assistant, to make sure he was ready. Doc sat at the table in front of the bench, where the court recorder sat in the old days. The plungers on the syringes were up and ready, like valves on a trumpet, ready to go. Three colored tubes, red, blue, and yellow, ran from Doc's table into the back of the witness stand, hidden there in the prisoner's orange jumpsuit but connected to the standard state-issued port.

"You ready, Doc?" Frank asked. Doc had on a brightly-colored hospital smock with little blue and pink bunny prints hopping across his chest and back. Doc cracked his knuckles, adjusted his head mike then nodded. "Good to go here."

Frank spoke again into his headset. "Okay then. Here we go, people. Three. Two. One." He pointed to Charlie. On Frank's cue Charlie stood up from the plaintiff's table and strutted to center stage. "All rise!" he said, waving his hands. "All rise for Judge Wulover!"

The judge kept filing her nails, not looking up from the bench. The studio audience scurried to their feet and stood in dumb reverence. *I love it when they do that*, Frank laughed to himself. *Gets me, every single time*. He saw one old lady in the front row clutching a knitting basket and a half-knitted baby blanket as she wobbled to her feet. He zoomed in on her. She balanced the partially-finished blanket and a large ball of white yarn on her right elbow so she could stand; her knitting needles pointed high in the air at her left side, in a little salute, nearly poking out the eye of the man next to her when she struggled late to her feet.

Frank controlled the studio now. He gave a cue to Judge Wulover. She didn't respond. "Sam, get Wulover's attention," he said to Camera Three. Sam covered his mouth with his hand and spoke sharply into his headset. The judge started slightly, but continued filing her nails.

Another moment went by, then Wulover cleared her throat. "Be seated," she said, and the crowd fell noisily back into their seats.

"Who comes here before me today?" Judge Wulover said flatly. Frank winced. Monney wrote that line and insisted that it be used in every show.

"This here's Bob Slack, Your Honor," Charlie said, checking his program notes. He pointed at the prisoner in the witness box as he spoke. "Mad Dog Slack, they called him on the street." The audience booed. The old lady in the front row started her knitting. The steady *click-click-click* of her knitting needles pulsed in the courtroom like a metronome.

The Judge inspected her hands, turning each slowly in front of her. "What's the charge?" she said, on the cameraman's prompt. She touched up a spot on her left middle finger with the long file.

"Rape and murder, your Honor!" Charlie yelled too loudly. As he yelled he swung his arms wildly and turned toward the crowd. "Rape. And murder!" he repeated. A splattering of applause swept across the studio audience. An "oooh" or two escaped.

"And who is it that bringeth these charges against this offender?"

Charlie walked over and touched the table where the little man in the bow tie sat quietly. The plaintiff tucked his legs beneath himself in his chair; they weren't long enough to reach the floor. His folded hands were in his lap.

"Me, Your Honor."

Frank scowled. "Get his volume up. Get the volume up on Mike 8 or we'll lose him, somebody!" Frank hissed into his mouthpiece.

Charlie walked over, leaned down, whispered to the man, adjusted the microphone on his lapel, then stepped back.

"It's me, Your Honor. Axel Trembles."

A man in the crowd snickered.

"Your involvement in this case, Mr. Trembles?"

"I was the victim's *husband*, Your Honor." Axel's voice shook. He swallowed before answering. "We'd just started our honeymoon."

The crowd behind the cameras erupted. "Bastard!" some yelled. "Murderer!" a little girl screamed from under her mother's arm. Mad Dog Slack bent down to his cuffed hands and shoved a long finger up his nose, oblivious to the audience's jeering.

"Quiet in the court. Quiet in the court," said Judge Wulover in her soft monotone. "Or I'll clear the studio."

Over my dead body, thought Frank. But he knew she had to say that. Something about state's liability and the actors' union. In the contract. And judicial tradition, whatever the hell that meant. Monney again.

The crowd settled down after a few seconds. The knitting needles clicked on steadily, their staccato *click-click-click* in the background.

"Tell us what happened…Plaintiff." Wulover was supposed to say his name but she must have forgotten it. *Again*, Frank thought. She tucked her hair over her left ear, then resumed her filing.

"Well, Your Honor...," Axel began. He looked up and Charlie smiled at him. He hesitated long enough that Frank could hear the knitting needles again, clicking rhythmically, almost soothingly now in the quiet pause. Axel took a breath and smiled back at Charlie. "And the court," Axel said, turning slightly toward the studio audience in his chair.

The little guy's getting into this, Frank thought. *Good.*

Axel Trembles cleared his throat and began. "It was a Saturday, of course, and we'd just been married. At one o'clock, in that little stone church down on Broadway." People in the audience shook their heads. They knew Broadway. They knew the little stone church.

"Judy and me, we were childhood sweethearts. She was my girl-next-door, my own little calendar girl. We both loved trains. Model trains. Don't know why, we just did," Axel said, turning away from the judge and facing the crowd again. "It was at one of those model train shows that we got our whistle." Axel hung his head.

"Stay with him, Three. One, you stay with Charlie," whispered Frank.

"What whistle is that, Axel?" asked Charlie, hands on his hips.

"The train whistle. The tin train whistle. An old man at a model train show made it for Judy and me one year. They're usually made out of brass, you know," said Axel, talking mainly to Charlie, "but 'cause we were kids and didn't have hardly any money at the time, he made ours out of some scrap tin he had. 'I'm just making one,' he said to us as he made it, 'just this one, 'cause you two will never be too far apart from each other. I can tell.'" Axel did a good imitation of what an old conductor's voice might sound like.

Everyone was quiet. The methodical *click-click-click* of the knitting needles continued.

Charlie cleared his throat loudly and walked to the bench. He held up a clear plastic bag with yellow tape across the top.

"State's Evidence – Trembles" was printed in bold black marker across the sealed top. "Is *this* that whistle, Mr. Trembles?"

Axel took the bag from Charlie slowly, caressed it. "Judy wore our whistle around her neck from that day until...well, you know. Until the end."

"Screw your little whistle." The harsh deep voice crackled across the still courtroom like so much thunder. It belonged to Prisoner Slack, who stared straight ahead.

"Shut up, asshole!" Charlie jumped in front of the witness stand. He drew his pistol and waved it back and forth inches from the prisoner's face. He got no response from Slack, and slowly regained his composure and put the prop back in his holster. Charlie stared at Slack for a moment longer, then turned back to the table. "Sorry for the interruption, sir. Please proceed, Mr. Trembles."

Cameraman Two looked over at Cameraman Three. Three nodded knowingly and rolled his eyes.

"When we got to the train station after the wedding, I left Judy with the luggage while I went to confirm our seats. I never would have thought she would be in any danger with all those people standing around..." Axel looked up at Judge Wulover, but she was now putting nail polish on and didn't seem to notice.

"Break for commercial, Frank? We're past time," The assistant director's voice broke across the headset into Frank's ear.

"Not if you like working here," Frank snapped back. "Stay with Trembles."

"Then what, Mr. Trembles?" Charlie was on the table now, sitting on the edge, hands in his lap, looking down into Axel's eyes. "Then what happened?"

"Then? I was halfway to the counter when I realized I didn't have Judy's passport with me. I headed back to where I'd left her two minutes before, two tops, and she wasn't there. The luggage was there, but she wasn't." Axel stopped, looked down at his hands.

"Then what, Axel?"

"Then I heard it."

"Heard what?"

Axel hung his head lower. "Heard our whistle."

The room fell dead silent. The old lady stopped knitting. Even Wulover stopped polishing her nails.

"I heard our whistle. Faint – but I heard it." Axel stopped, caught his breath. "I tried to follow the sound. But the terminal was too noisy. And then it stopped." He looked up helplessly at Charlie, his face screwed up tight. Tears filled his eyes. "I looked and looked, but I couldn't find Judy."

Charlie leaned forward and put his hand on Axel's shoulder. "It's okay, Axel. It's okay now." Charlie looked over at the crowd and looked up at Frank. Only Frank noticed his wink. "Then what, Mr. Trembles? Then what happened?"

"Then they found her. Found my Judy."

"What? *Fo-o-o-o-und* her?" Charlie looked around at the crowd wide-eyed. "Where did they find her, Axel?"

"Around the side of the terminal. In the dumpster." Axel's head snapped and he glared up at Slack. "In the frigging dumpster – like some piece of trash!" Prisoner Slack smirked and grinned, then yawned widely, bored with the proceedings.

A moment passed. "And what else did they find, Axel?" Charlie asked quietly.

Axel pulled his legs under himself and then stood up in his chair. "They found her, all right. Beaten to a pulp. And…raped. By *that* bastard." Axel pointed directly at Slack now, his tiny finger barely clearing his sleeve. His hand shook in the air. Then he spoke again slowly, softly. He lowered his arm to his side. Looked down. "They said she might have had a chance to survive the rape, and even the beating. But he'd rolled up her passport and stuffed it down her throat." Axel stared at Slack as he spoke now. "Stuffed it so far down her throat she choked and suffocated on her own vomit."

Charlie sprang to his feet. "Rolled up her passport?" He strutted to within three feet of the prisoner. "Stuffed it down her *throat*?" He turned to face Slack even more squarely. "You bastard!" he screamed, raising a fist. The prisoner looked at Charlie like he was a fly that needed swatting.

Charlie turned to the plaintiff. He took a deep breath, then quietly he asked: "And the whistle?"

Axel moaned and clutched the plastic evidence bag to his chest. "That's how they found him." His face was red. His eyes bulged as he leaned toward Slack, so far forward he nearly fell off his chair. "Caught you in the metal detector, didn't they? Huh Slack? Because of the *whistle*, you stupid bastard. The whistle!"

Then Axel started to laugh hysterically. "Stay on him, Three!" Frank said. The knitting needles rang in Frank's ears, *click-click-click*, clicking faster and faster.

Axel jumped on top of the table in one bound, his little legs stronger than they looked. "Our whistle!" he yelled, tearing the thin tin whistle from the plastic evidence bag. Then he leapt from the table to the floor so fast even Charlie didn't flinch. He covered the ten feet between him and the prisoner in a second, climbed over the short wooden witness gate, and crawled up onto Slack's back. Slack shook his head and shoulders furiously, struggled to get his hands and arms free from the cuffs and chains that held him secure. Axel wrapped one arm around Slack's head, whipping back and forth as the big man thrashed and shook and roared. He dug at Slack's neck with the sharp edge of the whistle, dragging the whistle around Slack's neck like he was cutting the lid off a can of soup. At first only a thin red line showed around the prisoner's neck. But the jagged edge of the tin whistle ripped through Slack's carotid artery, then tore Slack's windpipe open with a sick hiss and a gurgle in Axel's tiny hands.

"Zoom in! Zoom in for Christ's sake, Two!" Frank yelled.

Slack's mouth gaped open stupidly, his lips working frantically, gasping for breath like a fish on land – but no sound came out. Blood squirted out of his neck and throat all over Axel, and dribbled down onto his orange DOC coverall chest between spurts. The small silver chain that had once hung so close to Judy's pale flat chest swung back and forth in Axel's slick red palm as he thrashed. The swinging motion of the chain slowed as the last of the blood flowed out of Slack. The knitting needles clicked quicker and quicker through Slack's death throes, then slower as he died, keeping rhythm with his pulsing blood. He finally quit struggling and sat still.

"I'll stay tight on Trembles! Two, stay tight on Slack! Three, get the crowd reaction."

People in the studio audience were on their feet. They cheered and bounced up and down where they stood, and hugged each other in little groups of twos and threes. A little girl of around eight leaned over the guard rail and puked on the floor, splashing her patent leather shoes and frilly white socks with her soft-pretzel-and-mustard lunch.

Doc sat frozen in his bright bunny smock, his hand set on the lethal plungers, unsure what to do now. Judge Wulover spun in her chair but couldn't find her gavel; she forgot to say her last line—a minor contract infraction. Slack's head rolled back and hung limply to one side by a thin blue-gray thread of muscle tissue. Axel Trembles finally slid down Slack and collapsed and lay like a pile of crumpled laundry on the floor, sobbing. Frank turned and saw Monney sprawled out in a chair in the command booth with his eyes closed, his feet crossed, a broad smile on his lips, and his hands behind his head. Charlie sat on the edge of the plaintiff's table smugly, stroking the top of his fake .45 with his hand, over and over again.

A thick ball of yarn rolled out from the crowd, leaving a thin white tail behind it. It bounced on the polished wood floor a couple of times, then settled sloppily into the pool of blood now collecting at the drain in front of the witness chair. The yarn jumped when the old lady yanked her needles for another stitch, still *click-click-clicking* in the front row in rhythm, and quickly turned rust red as it settled in the muck.

"Cut! Cut!" Frank held the mini-cam high over his head. He danced a jig in a small, tight circle.

"That's a take! That's a wrap, everybody!"

FAMOUS

My dad was Famous. I mean literally. That was what everyone called him. Not just me growing up, but everyone. Famous. My old man could drive farther, faster, better than any other trucker in the world—just ask him, he'd tell you.

At the time I thought he was special. Hell, at the time I thought *I* was special. Probably every dad must be famous to his ten-year-old boy somehow or other, right? Maybe long, long ago even my grandpa was famous to my ten-year-old dad, huh? I'm famous now to my own kids, too, I imagine—for a little while yet.

Staying famous. Now that's the real trick, isn't it?

Dad drove a tractor-trailer truck cross-country and was only home on weekends. First thing that one Saturday in February we headed over to Donut Land for a glazed donut and coffee for him and a cream-filled long-john and chocolate milk for me. I was ten at the time.

Donut Land was a small white cinder-block A-Frame building with big soaring windows and orange-painted wood trim, next to the tracks on Auburn Street. The two huge aluminum-framed glass walls came together at the top like two sides of a triangle leaning on each other. A white Formica counter and orange-cushioned chrome stools surrounded a bunch of tall wood shelves against the walls. The shelves were filled with large wire baskets, and those wide wire baskets were filled with donuts of all shapes and sizes on wide sheets of waxed paper. With its high, pointy-topped, wide-open entrance, Donut Land could've been a church if the windows would have been stained-glass and it was a little bigger maybe, and there were pews instead of stools.

This Saturday, with his tax return money bulging in his front jeans pocket, Dad walked through the swinging glass doors like he owned the place. He strode fast and pointed his hips and feet to the outside a little when he took a step, like he'd learned when he marched in the Air Force, he'd told me a hundred times before. He said it made him look more "official" to walk like that. To me it just made him look like he took up more room than he really did.

"The usual, sweetheart," he said to the waitress, halting at attention next to his stool and drawing his hand across the bristly top part of his flattop before he sat down.

"You got it, Bob. Er, Famous," she said, already pouring his coffee in front of him. "What about you, honey?"

I'd trailed behind. By then I was spinning back and forth on my stool at the counter, thinking about how good that long john was going to taste. It took me a second to figure out she was talking to me. I had a flattop haircut like my dad's. I pushed my black Buddy Holly glasses up my nose so I could see her better. Her breasts jiggled a little in her low-cut blouse as she leaned toward me. "I'll take the usual, too, please." She smiled bigger at me. My dad rolled his eyes and ordered my long john and milk.

He was a natural talker, my dad, a guy people flocked around when he was telling a joke or one of his stories, which was pretty much all the time. He took pride in being able to talk to anyone about just about anything—it didn't matter who they were or what they did for a living.

This time, this Saturday he started telling the story about how he stole Grandpa's brand-new Buick for a joy ride when he was a kid. Even though I'd heard this story a million times before, I still got caught up in it every time because of the way he could tell it.

"Marked the tires on the street with chalk first," he said to the guy across the way from him at the counter, raising his eyebrows. I don't think he'd ever seen that guy before, he was just convenient. "So's the Old Man wouldn't know I moved it."

The guy nodded, like he understood.

"My brother Tommy and me, we drove that Buick around all weekend, cruising for chicks."

The guy dunked his powdered-sugar donut in his coffee. I licked the whipped-cream topping off the end of my long john.

"Cruised the A&W over on Main Street—know where that is?" he said with his arm out, pointing north. "Then a couple hours before the Old Man got home, we filled 'er up with gas and started driving around the block backwards to roll back the miles."

The guy held his wet donut in front of him, ready to eat it but not wanting to be rude.

"But my brother Tommy, he couldn't back up to save his life, the dumb ass, so I had to do most of it. We knew the Old Man would've written down the mileage before he left. He was one cheap son of a bitch, I'm telling you."

Dad leaned forward, shaking his pointy finger at the guy. "So what happens when the Old Man got home? Tommy went right over to him and told him I'd stole the car." He sat back in his stool. "Got smacked good that time, but it was worth it."

Dad saw me listening then, I guess, because he bent down toward me. He hung there long enough for me to get a whiff of his Brylcreem and Old Spice. Then he said to me real loud: "I ever catch you doing anything like that, I'll whip your ass." He looked straight at me for a couple seconds. I fought to stare back at him. Then his face exploded in a big white-toothed laugh and he looked around at everyone there. The wet half of the guy's donut flopped off into his coffee. All the other people in Donut Land laughed too, including a couple construction guys in checkered shirts that had just walked in, like it was contagious. The waitress tried not to laugh, tried to look like she wasn't really laughing, like she wasn't really paying any attention to him, but she couldn't help herself.

I knew the feeling.

After we finished our donuts we went to Bill's Aqualand and Pet Store in the new mall on the East side, across town from where we lived.

"I've been thinking it's time we had a dog around the place. What'dya think?"

I bobbed my head, both excited and scared. So much for Mom's new washer and dryer from the tax return money, I thought.

Dad walked through the store and up to the puppy cages like he'd been there before, straight to those squares in the walls with the windows right next to the big aquariums and kitty litter. He looked the windows up and down slowly, his arms crossed over his chest with one hand holding his chin, one finger laying up on his cheek.

"What kind of dog is that yellow one there?" he asked when a girl clerk about eighteen finally came up.

"That sandy-colored one? She's a cockapoo."

"A what?"

"A cockapoo. A new breed. A cross between a cocker spaniel and a poodle."

He snorted. "Well, I'll be damned. How the hell'd they do that?"

The clerk blushed. "Same ole way they ever get anything, I guess, sir."

My dad laughed and the clerk smiled. She had dimples in her cheeks. "How big will she get?"

"Not too big. Fourteen, fifteen pounds max," she said, making a small box in the air with her hands.

"Cockapoo, eh?" He smiled, thought for a second. "I like that. Wrap her up or whatever the hell else you need to do. We'll take her." Then he peeled three fifty-dollar bills from the silver-and-turquoise money clip in his pocket, and pressed them into the clerk's small hand. "That hold her for now?" He smiled his Donut Land smile, reached up and stroked his flattop back again.

"Yessir." The girl blushed and walked away quickly.

"You know Jeff," Dad said while the girl was getting the puppy ready to go home with us, "I had a dog named Buddy when I was about your age. My old man just brought him home one day, kinda like we're doing now." He picked out a small pink collar with fake diamonds on it. "Buddy was part cocker spaniel, too." He threw a bag of puppy food in the cart. Stopped. "Buddy got himself killed when I was fifteen. " He paused again at the Milk Bones, grabbed a box of "smalls," then got a chrome food and water dish with a wire stand, too. "Same year Tommy and I stole the Buick, come to think of it."

I thought he was going to tell me something more about how Buddy got killed, or some secret part of the Buick story he hadn't told in the donut shop, like maybe his dad had run Buddy over or something. Instead he said, "My old man still had a picture of that damn dog in his wallet when he died. Sixty-seven years old, thirty-five years later, and he still had a picture of that damn dog in his wallet."

Mom told me later when I told her this story that that picture of Buddy was the *only* picture Grandpa had in his wallet when he died. Dad never mentioned that part.

So we went out for donuts and brought home a puppy that Saturday. The pup sat with me in the front seat all the way back to the house. I didn't quite fill up the passenger seat back then, I was such a skinny kid, so she stood half on the seat and half on me with her front feet on the armrest and her back feet on my lap and her wet nose barely reaching high enough to look out, smearing the padded window ledge with dog spit.

Our house was in the middle of a block of look-alike houses on Lawndale, the last block before Ridge Avenue. Across Ridge were the same tracks that went by Donut Land. Across the tracks and that grassy field were the West High baseball diamond and Welsh Elementary, the school my sisters and I went to. We whipped into our driveway going fast, like Dad usually drove, and made a little screech when we stopped. My older sister Carol and my younger sister Ann were doing dance routines in the front yard, even though it was cold out. *CarolAnn* we called either one of them, because they were always together and defended each other to the death. They stood so close to each other most of the time that there was hardly ever any space between them. So we just combined their names, too, to go along with that, and it stuck.

Of course they fell in love with the golden-haired puppy as soon as they saw her, like Dad and I knew they would.

We walked through the back door into the house and I turned right into the kitchen with the dog. CarolAnn piled in close behind me while Dad hung back. Mom was drinking coffee and reading the paper at the kitchen table. I could tell how mad she was right away by how tight her face got.

"You didn't think to talk to me first about this?" she said to me instead of him, like it was my fault. I froze in front of her and clutched the dog tight. She didn't like it that even then I was as tall as she was and I was only ten, so she didn't stand up. But then

Dad took the pup away from me and held her up next to Mom, and she put her front paws on Mom's chest and licked her face. She looked real cute in the pink collar. Everyone was quiet. Nobody breathed. Mom tried not to smile (she was funny that way too, like that waitress, maybe), but then she started talking baby talk and cuddling the tawny pup.

"I think we'll call you Ginger," my mom said, looking around at us. "Unless you've already named her, too?" She snapped her eyes at us, first me, then him, then the girls, daring us all to say something with her thrust-out face and set shoulders. Then she stood up and walked away, swaying her hips in her housecoat and noisily kissing the dog's ears.

You could hear everyone start breathing again.

None of us was surprised when it fell to Mom to train Ginger to go potty outside, Mom least of all. She kept her from barking at every little blowing leaf and made her walk on a leash right too. Dad was gone most of the week anyways, so it was just Mom and us around the house. Mom worked nine-to-five as a secretary, so my sisters and I had a little time to ourselves at home after school usually, but she left us notes every day about the chores we were supposed to get done before she got home.

During the week everyone was serious and quiet and tried not to take up much space. It was like that until Dad got home Friday night or Saturday morning, depending on where his run took him that week.

Unlike Mom, Dad spoiled Ginger something awful, like that was *his* job. Once when I was twelve, after a big Sunday dinner Mom made special for Carol's birthday, he fed Ginger some of his people-food scraps. Mom couldn't stand a dog that begged at the table, let alone one that would *eat* at the table. She snapped her eyes and made her "tish" sound with her tongue. My sisters and I had seen that look often enough to know not to make eye contact and to be quiet. Dad just leaned over and fed another handful of leftovers to Ginger like it was nothing.

Mom slammed her fork on the table, sloshing some milk out of her glass. "You've *got* to be kidding me, Bob." She glared at him, daring him to feed the dog another scrap. My shoulders tensed, waiting for the explosion; my sisters stared at their plates harder. Dad just laughed like he was at Donut Land sipping coffee, and this time slowly set his whole plate on the floor for Ginger.

"That dog's got fewer germs than you do, Barbara. What's *your* goddamned problem?"

Mom got up and grabbed all the plates off the table, as many as she could carry, whether they had any food left on them or not. "I don't *have* any problems. Except *you*." She didn't pick Dad's plate up off the floor. She stood stupidly for a second with dirty dinner dishes piled in her arms. "You're *disgusting*." Her lips curled when she said it; then she slammed the plates hard into the sink and stormed out of the kitchen.

I don't know which of us laughed first – but someone at the table did, and we had all we could do to keep quiet. If Mom heard us from the living room that day, she never said. Of course it wasn't one of those things she'd want to talk a lot about, anyway.

* * *

Besides drying dishes and taking the trash out to the garbage cans and putting them out on the street once a week, my chore was to feed Ginger and make sure she always had water in her bowl. My sisters had to let her out and clean up her house messes, which made them throw dishes and groceries and pillows and whatever else they could grab around for a while whenever Mom told them to "do their jobs." They said I was the "favorite" in the family because I was the boy, that I was "the lucky one." Days like that, Carol would dump all the silverware out of the drawer into the dishwater just so I had to rinse and dry it.

Of course, my sisters were never around when Dad got on *my* case, it seemed. Like that time with the dog food, when I was thirteen.

"Jeff, got a question for you," he started one day.

"Yeah, Dad?"

"You eat today?"

"Yeah, sure. Why?"

"You drink anything today?"

I looked at him, crinkled my nose. "Yeah?"

"That a question or an answer?"

I swallowed hard. "An answer."

"Then tell me again. The whole thing."

"Yeah…"

"Yes."

"Yes, I ate and drank something today. So?"

He nodded his head. Then he stood up suddenly, wrapped his fingers around the back of my neck, shoved my head toward the empty dog dishes and pointed, like he was rubbing a dog's nose into a wet spot on the carpet. "Then why in the *hell* are Ginger's dishes empty?"

Soon as he let go of my neck, I opened a can of dog food quick at both ends like he'd taught me, pushed the meat into Ginger's dish whole from the can, then chopped it up with one of the thin sharp lids before I set it down. He stood there and watched me until I filled the water dish too and crushed the can and threw it and the lids in the garbage. Then he turned and walked away without another word.

I wish he would've just smacked me and been done with it right then. But that wasn't his style. Not Famous.

* * *

It was on a sunny mid-June Saturday that Ginger got herself killed. I was fourteen then. My sisters usually let her out in the morning. That day, though, Dad was home and up first so he let Ginger out himself. From my bed upstairs I heard him walk across the living room, open the door, and let her out.

Half a minute later he was yelling out the door: "Ginger, goddammit, get back here."

He must've been in his underwear when he let her out or he would have gone out and got her right then. I heard him walk back to the bedroom, heard the change in his pockets jingle as he tried to slip his pants on quick, heard him hop on one foot and bang into the wall. "*Son* of a bitch."

I imagined Ginger streaking across the street over to Hollands' to see Happy, their nasty old basset hound, like she did when my sisters let her out the front when they were too lazy to walk her around the block on her leash like they were supposed to.

I heard my dad yell her name again, then right after that I heard another sound, like the smack of a wooden bat on one of those brown leather mush balls with the red lacing from gym class that don't hurt when they hit you. That day it sounded like the mush ball popped when it got hit and those thin red seams all came undone.

Dad exploded out the door and I jumped out of my bed, pulled my jeans on and crashed down the stairs.

When I got to the door I saw a long green Ford Falcon wagon stopped crookedly across our street with its left front tire on the curb closest to our house. A pretty blond girl who didn't look much older than me was sitting in the driver's seat. A tall man on the passenger side of the car—her dad, I guess—had already gotten out and walked around to the front grill. He had a flattop like my dad's, but his was gray around the ears.

I saw Ginger lying in the street by the curb under the car's high chrome bumper. She was on her side, her legs and feet sticking straight out. She was panting, the tip of her tongue hanging out on the dirty tar.

Dad knelt, shirtless and shoeless with both knees on the pavement, staring down at Ginger. His hair was mussed and wild-looking, not all slicked in place like usual. All I had on was a pair of old jeans, not even zipped. I fell to my knees next to him. I was dizzy and a little sick.

"What do we do, Dad?" He'd always bragged about seeing plenty of accidents on the road. This was nothing. He'd know what to do, I thought.

Dad didn't say anything. He slid his hands under Ginger to pick her up. But she whipped her head around and bit him on the forearm. Two bright red holes appeared suddenly on his tanned arm. Then for the first time I saw a puddle of darker blood on the street under Ginger's tail. Even though I was kneeling, for a second the whole street got black and I thought I was going to topple over.

"Ran out." The man from the car said softly, both hands out from his body, his palms up. "From over there." He pointed at Holland's across the street. He was talking to my dad, I guess, but my dad didn't look up, so he turned his eyes to me. "Just ran out in front of us. No time." Behind him the girl sat frozen in the driver's seat, tears on her pale cheeks, eyes wide, fists white and still clutching the steering wheel at the 10-2 position like she was taught.

"She has her permit," the man said.

"Get me a towel," Dad said to me.

I jumped up and ran back toward the house. Mom stood halfway down the porch step in her short white house coat and silver-sandal slippers, one hand over her mouth, elbow in her other hand. Her blue eyes were wide and the whites showed, like the girl driver's did. With her streaked hair up high, wrapped in toilet paper and hair pins to hold its shape, she looked like that statue of the Egyptian queen in Miss Winter's History class.

"Get a towel, quick!" I yelled at my sisters huddled in the doorway. Carol turned first, then both she and Ann disappeared into the house. Finally they brought out a dark green towel. By then I was pacing back and forth.

"That isn't one of my good towels, is it?" Mom said.

I took the towel and ran back. Dad was still on his knees where I'd left him. He'd managed to pick Ginger up by then and held her with her back against him, holding her half on his lap, half against his bare chest. She whined weakly. Her feet stuck straight out, and her body jerked once in a while in his arms. He stood up, took the towel and covered her head, then walked stiffly toward our garage behind the house.

The man from the Ford wagon followed him a few steps, saying again how sorry he was. I got up and followed, too, but glanced toward the house as I went.

Mom stared at me from across the yard. Snapped her eyes at me in that way she had. Then she turned and I heard her say, "Go on inside, girls. It's over."

The man from the car stopped at the curb. He put his hand on my shoulder and squeezed, and didn't take his hand off for what felt like a long time. I could only look in his eyes for a moment, then had to look away. Then he walked back toward the driver's side of the Falcon. He crouched down next to his daughter at the open driver's door; her hands still gripped the steering wheel tightly. Tears streaked her cheeks. The man peeled her hands off the wheel, helped her out, and walked her gently around to the passenger seat. He practically put her in the car, had to pick up her long legs to tuck them all the way in so he could close the door, then walked quickly back to the driver's side and drove off.

By the time I got to the garage Dad was headed for the house without Ginger.

"Where you going, Dad?"

He strode through the back door without answering. I stood there wondering what to do with myself. I worked my way over and looked at Ginger lying in the front seat. Her head was still covered with the towel, and her chest didn't seem to be moving anymore. I slowly reached in through the window and touched her. Her body jerked and I jumped back. I could see her shallow breathing then if I stared right at her chest and the towel and the seat all at once. I remembered the day we brought her home four years ago, when she stood on my lap and bounced on my leg and slobbered dog spit across the same window I leaned through now.

Dad came out wearing a wrinkled shirt, shoes but no socks, and different pants. His hair still looked wild. I could see the two red holes Ginger gave him in his forearm when he climbed into the car. He didn't say anything to me.

"Where you going?" I asked again.

He started the car.

I was close to him then. I looked him in the face, thought for a second about reaching through the open window and grabbing *him* and squeezing *his* shoulder like that other father had grabbed me…but I didn't.

Couldn't.

He put the car in reverse and turned past me to look out the rear window.

"Take me with you." He backed the car down the driveway . "Dad! Take me with you. *Please?*" I yelled.

He bounced out of the driveway, squealed off down the street. He didn't look back.

I watched the car until I couldn't see it anymore. I stood there in the empty yard for a full ten minutes. I wondered if we had any pictures of Ginger, where they were. Maybe the girls were already getting them out? Then I wondered about my dad, about whether he had a picture with him, a picture of Ginger stuck in his wallet like my grandpa had had a picture of Buddy stuck in his.

I didn't doubt it.

* * *

He came home an hour or so later. Alone. Not looking quite so Famous. Nobody said anything about Ginger's accident all that day. Later, when I did my chores, I saw the bloody green towel in the garbage can. Mom got rid of Ginger's dishes and leash somewhere else, I guess…they were gone when I got up to put food and water in them around suppertime.

After that morning we never talked about Ginger in our house again.

Ginger's pink collar lay on the kitchen counter, where Dad had put it, for a couple days. Nobody wanted to touch it. On the third day I took it and hid it in my room under my bed in the box with my baseball cards.

Things went on for a while after that, but they were never the same. Later that summer Dad took a load of truck parts to Washington state on a Monday morning like usual, but didn't come back. Mom acted like that was a normal thing for him to do. She said that going on was the normal thing for us to do. So we believed her and we did it. We went on.

We never talked about *that* in our house again, either.

* * *

Ten years later I saw my old man again. A call out of the blue after all that time; he'd finally found one of our messages,

I guess. My wife Jenny and I got a call from him at nine p.m. on a Wednesday night. He was still driving trucks. "All I ever knew how to do," he laughed on the phone. He was just passing through, had to run a load of apples from Washington state to Detroit and pick up some engine parts to bring back. Even though it was February then, below freezing, windy, a 60% chance for snow, Jenny and I hurried as fast as we could, piled the kids in the car, and drove the sixty miles north up there from Rockford.

We met him just off Interstate 90 at a truck stop in Sun Prairie, Wisconsin.

Once we got to the truck stop I called his cell, and he talked us over to where he was parked in the large gravel lot by the rest of the tractor-trailers. When we pulled up, he swung down out of his dark-blue Peterbilt using the chrome side bar. Even after all those years he looked the same. I got out into the cold and walked toward the truck. Jenny stood by the car and held baby Rob in her arms; three-year-old Angie hung at her knee.

My dad hadn't met any of them before. I'm not sure he knew they existed.

He stepped closer and took my extended hand. "You know the difference between pussy and parsley?" he yelled out in the truckers' parking lot. He waited a tick. "Nobody eats parsley." His face exploded in laughter.

I froze, my hand still in his grip, wondering how long he'd saved that one up just for me. I knew he'd practiced it to himself plenty of times in the truck. He laughed so loud in the cold night air that I was sure he could be heard across the gravel and above the idling trucks.

A shiver flared up my spine and settled cold across my shoulders. I thought, decided, then swallowed hard. "You were wrong, you know."

He stopped short, a frown quick to his face. He tried to pull away but now I held his hand tight. He recovered in an instant. "Me? Wrong? Never!" He grinned and tried to shake his hand loose.

I hung on.

Baffled

"About the cars. Grandpa's Buick." I paused. "The mileage doesn't come off when you back up."

He thought about that for a second. Looked down at his feet, looked back up at me. "Yeah, well, I never said it did. What the hell did we know? We were just stupid-ass kids."

I let his hand go then. We stood still. "Come on over and meet the wife and kids," I said, sweeping my hand toward our car. "We brought baby pictures of our little guys, pictures of Carol, and Ann, and their families, too."

He looked at me with his mouth hanging open, like I'd just asked him what his name was. "Do I look like a picture-kind-of-guy to you?" Then he marched over to Jenny and the kids, heel toe, heel toe, feet pointed out every step, covering the open ground between them swiftly.

He stopped at attention in front of my wife and kids, brushed the bristly part of his flattop back with his hand, then smiled his Donut-Land smile and said, "So…who the hell are you?"

TRINITY

You Just Had To Do It
(1963)

You just had to do it, didn't you?

I could have told you she was in a pissy mood today, if you would have asked me. Saturdays are always like that with her. Saturday is her cleaning day. I used to look forward to Saturday mornings like the other kids do; then I learned, and tried to escape those Saturday mornings by going to the Junior Bowling League up at Reitch's. But she caught on to that quick and just left my chores for me to do later and got all over me if I didn't do them right. But even that was better than having her follow me around while I cleaned and her yelling at me for not doing something right.

Of course, she doesn't really yell at me with words, she just shoves me aside and redoes the chore I've just done, silently, like if I got close enough or watched long enough or enough times I'd eventually "get it." It must be a girl thing…a guy would call you a dumb shit and maybe smack you on the side of the head and talk you through what you were supposed to do instead of just pushing you aside and glaring at you.

You would have said it like this: "Jesus, Jeff. You take this rag like this, see? In a square, not all crumpled up like you got it. Not a rag from the goddamn kitchen drawer, one of the rags from in the closet above the towels, you know where. Then you spray some of this lemon shit on it and wipe the coffee table down. Don't spray the shit all over the floor and waste it. Don't put too much stuff on the rag, either – this lemon shit's expensive. And make sure you go back and forth, back and forth, like this, see? Back and forth, like mowing the yard. And turn the goddamn

Baffled

rag over once in a while or all you'll do is smear all that shit over there over all this shit over here. Get it?"

That's how you would have said it.

If you would've ever been around to say it.

No, instead, today of all days, you just had to ask her about her secret savings accounts, didn't you? You know how she is about money...you're not much help there, to be honest. You, you get a paycheck and you cash it and spend it quick, on only the best stuff, steaks not hamburger, till it's gone, then what the hell—then you starve the rest of the week until you get your next paycheck and do it all over again. Her? She buys only the stuff on sale, stocks up on it in case we might need those dozen rolls of toilet paper or that ten boxes of macaroni and cheese or that extra 24-can carton of Van Camp's pork and beans for when we get stranded in a snowstorm or tornado or tidal wave in Northern Illinois sometime in the next decade or so.

So what if she's as tight as a crab's ass, like you say? You still shouldn't have said that. And man, you shouldn't have laughed at her, either. I could've told you that too. And she doesn't like to be called crazy. You know that. You know that for sure.

So here we are, now, at home, her and me and the sisters, me wandering the smoking battlefield among the stinking piles of dead and wounded. *No one left in headquarters to report to, sir. No one here I really want to talk to anyways, sir.* Slicing across the lawn from the street to cut her Bonneville convertible off at the driveway with your big bad cop-car Fury was a cute trick, but the whole neighborhood saw that one and me and Carol and Annie, *we're* the ones who have to still live here so maybe that wasn't so cute after all, huh? I saw ole lady LaManche too, out dusting her mailbox while you and Mom had your screaming match in the front yard. And D'Angelo next door, he peeked around the house to see what was making his dog bark so much, just spun around, wasn't there for a second, but he pretty much saw it all, too. They all saw it all, and as usual now we're the ones who have to stay here with her and live with it.

Not you.

Did you want her to kick you out? Why didn't you just walk

away, then? What, you couldn't stand that you guys hadn't had a knock-down-drag-out fight in a while? Things going too smooth for ya?

I think Carol peed herself, she was so scared. Her eyes nearly popped out when you slapped Mom. She didn't run, but she probably should have, for her own good. Annie just curled up in a little ball inside herself while she stood there watching. I saw it, when she went. She didn't flinch on the outside, but I could see her pupils fade then glaze over when she clicked off; I knew right when she checked out, the moment she went.

She didn't know whether to shit or go blind, you would've said.

Guess what? She didn't do either.

And me? I'm supposed to take it like a man, you would probably say. But which kind of man am I supposed to take it like? You never showed me how to do anything but crack a joke and laugh or get mad and swear or just shut the hell up and leave. Or to do all three if I ever got the chance, like you, just for added effect.

Really, though, you aren't very good at the shutting up part, and neither am I, so I guess we do have that in common.

I'm staying out of her sight for now, sitting with my back against the far end of the garage, picking grass and watching ants climb up on my jeans. I'm looking at the rusty remains of the burning barrel, remembering how I used to burn papers back here in the days before we got the natural gas incinerator downstairs. I remember how in the winter it was hard to light the trash because my hands were so cold but then the match finally took and the red and orange flames gobbled up the papers and garbage and snow around it, turning the garbage to black and the snow to water just as quick, leaping for more but killing itself even as it leaped across the mouth of the barrel by eating its own fuel so fast. I wonder if the fire knew what it was doing to itself, and did it anyways, or if the fire did it because it just couldn't act any other way.

It's been a couple hours since you left this last time, and she still hasn't got to go through her fit, maybe throw a few more things around before she's done. Then she'll probably sulk a little, crawl inside herself like Annie did, maybe cry some more, maybe not. If it's really bad, she might call me in to watch me redo a few chores, just to make sure someone is there to feel her being silent, to hear her long heaving sobs, to see how wronged she is, to know how many chores it falls on her to do over and over again in her suffering.

But me, I'm the boy, so she says with eyes big and wet and snapping at me, "Is he gone for good this time?" *How the hell should I know?* I wanna say. But I don't. She never asks the girls any of those questions – just me. I don't think she trusts me, like just because I'm the boy I'll turn out like *my goddamned father*, like it's already been decided by someone, somewhere, my fate is all decided for me just because I have a penis.

Then finally she'll get tired, collapse to the floor if anyone is around to see it, and crawl to the couch and watch *Mutual of Omaha's Wild Kingdom* or something else about long ago or far away or not-from-around-here. That's when the girls will come out of hiding, slink around, ask her if she needs anything Mommy, then maybe ask her if it's okay if they fix something to eat, Mommy, or have the last of the secret stash of Little Debbie snack bars up in the cupboard, or like Carol sometimes does, get the dust rag out (something quiet, not the vacuum cleaner) and do some of my chores again to suck up as long as Mom can see her doing them.

Depends on how brave they feel.

You? You never get to see this part because you're already gone. I wonder if you even know it happens. It seems now like you weren't here today at all, it was so long ago we had breakfast together and laughed at the dog when she chased her tail around and around in circles, biting herself and getting madder and madder about being bit all at the same time.

"What a dumb shit," you said then, laughing at the dog. "What a dumb shit."

The Wait
(1983)

The drive home from Chicago wore on. Rob and Jeff'd had a great father-son weekend together. Two nights at an Embassy Suite in Schaumberg with the soccer team. Saturday and Sunday – the Club's last three games of the year. All weekend long he'd wanted to pull Rob aside for a talk, but it just hadn't worked out. He thought about talking to him several times on the hour-and-a-half drive home too, but he couldn't. His tongue was too fat; his breathing, too hard. He felt it most in his throat, a quick rising and catch. He held his emotions in his throat, something about himself he knew too well, something he hated. He felt stranded and alone in the car, even though Rob was only feet away from him.

He turned onto Shaw Street from State. Two blocks from home. Her home, now. Time was running out.

"Rob." He laughed at how loud his voice sounded in the dark car, at how it cracked just a bit. He cleared his throat quickly. "Rob," he said again. He reached over and shook Rob's knee.

Rob pulled his ear phones out and looked up from the passenger's seat. "Yeah?"

Rob was fifteen, five-and-a-half feet tall, one-hundred thirty pounds, flat crew cut and stringy smooth muscle. Wore sandals and thick white socks, T-shirt and blue silk soccer shorts still, even in the late autumn cold. For a moment Jeff thought of a time when he was with his dad, back when he was fourteen. It must have been Rob's white socks that triggered this memory, a big deal back then: finally being able to NOT have to wear white socks everywhere anymore.

They'd never had this talk, Jeff and *his* dad. Not then, not ever. His father, like most fathers, waited, stood or sat back and waited for their sons to meander through life and stumble their way through it. As if the boys had taken out the garbage one afternoon and got lost. Somehow, to these dads, the boys would come back; they'd magically find their way back home all by themselves.

Come around, come to their senses, come back. Back home to where their fathers sat, waiting…and then everything would be okay.

Or not.

Jeff never had come around. Never had found his way back, not to his dad, anyway. And he didn't want that to happen to his son. So they had to have this talk. Now.

He squelched a tickle with a cough. "Rob. There's something important we need to talk about."

Rob sighed and stared down at his knees. "Now?"

"Yeah. Now."

They'd stopped in front of the house. Her house now, he reminded himself again. Pulled up to the curb so that the passenger door was closest to the house. He put the car in park. He'd given the house up without a fight; his lawyer thought he was out of his mind. It took Jeff almost two years to figure that out – figure out what mattered, what didn't in his new divorced life. He reached down and flipped the headlights off, left the dash and parking lights on, and kept the car and heater running against the chill October night.

Jeff looked out the windshield, thought. He didn't want Rob to think that what she was saying about him was true. He wanted to tell him that he'd never cheated on his mother. Ever. He wanted to make sure Rob knew the truth. Wanted to set the record straight.

Jeff glanced over at Rob to see him inspecting the volume on his Walkman, eyebrows stitched tight together in concentration, real or fake he couldn't tell.

He sighed. He wanted to tell Rob that the divorce had nothing to do with him and his sisters, that it wasn't their fault. He turned in his seat to face him. Rob squirmed, slumped further in his seat without looking over. Let out a small whimper like a trapped animal.

Jeff thought about putting his hand on Rob's shoulder, but didn't.

Started to tell him, then checked himself.

Grunted.

Looked away.

Jeff put a hand on his knee and thought some more. He felt like telling Rob that he and his mother had just grown at different speeds, grown apart. Not like they'd planned, like they'd hoped once. Grown away from each other instead of together. Once they started sliding apart there was no stopping it.

He looked out his side window. No good. He hadn't figured out exactly what had happened yet himself.

Jeff looked at Rob one more time. Felt a tug at his throat. This time he did put his hand on Rob's shoulder. Waited a second. "I'll always be your dad, you know."

He expected Rob to say, "And that's why you left us, right?"

But instead Rob just shrugged. "I guess."

"Good." Jeff smiled and leaned back in his seat a little. He realized he'd been holding his breath. He relaxed his throat. "Got any questions?"

Rob shook his head.

Jeff squeezed Rob's shoulder again, harder this time. They both laughed, and then managed the best hug they could over the car's console, slipping in the smooth leather bucket seats. Then they sat up, and Jeff swatted Rob's back twice, hard, quick, like he was swatting a baby to keep him from choking.

Rob stretched over the console to the back seat, grabbed his duffle bag, and was out of the car and on the curb quick. The dome light shone bright between them until Rob shut the door. He didn't look back as he walked down the driveway to the house.

Jeff rolled down the passenger window and yelled out. "I'll call you. Tuesday, maybe, okay? Or you call me for once. Alright?" He pointed his finger at Rob like a pistol, then flipped his hand and held it to the side of his head like a phone.

Rob turned, smiled, then paused and put his earplugs back in. He walked to the bottom of the driveway to the garage door, then up the ten cement steps and through the solid outer door. Light burst out from the hallway when the door opened, enveloping everything it touched, in the yard and beyond to the street and to the car and on Jeff. Then Rob stepped into the light and was gone.

Darkness swept over Jeff like so much fast-tumbling water, black and cold and hard enough to take his breath away.

Dreamer
(2003)

"Jeff'll be here. He promised. He probably just had to work late." She slammed her wheelchair into the nightstand, trying to steer around the hospital bed in the small room. "It's my 70th birthday. He wouldn't miss it for the world. He wouldn't dare. Now get down my purple dress. The pretty one." She snapped her good eye quickly at the aide. Since the stroke the other eye was taped over. "I want to be ready when he gets here. I don't want him to have to wait for me."

"Si, senora."

She waved a curled crooked hand toward the closet. "No, not that one! The other one."

"Si."

She sat fuming in her baggy grey sweatsuit, shoulders hunched, her arms folded as best she could in her lap, her bright white K-Mart canvas tennis shoes propped on the foot pedals of the wheelchair. The help around here is getting worse and worse, she thought. You have to yell at them all the time just to get them to do what you already pay them good money to do. But what can you expect from someone who doesn't even speak English? She snorted. The damned colostomy bag needs to be emptied again; I can smell it. Can't they smell it? Disgusting.

Once she was dressed they headed out the doorway to the dining room. A much younger eight-by-ten black-and-white picture of her hung on her door. She was doing a pirouette in her performance uniform at the Ing Roller Skating Palace in 1950 – the last year she lived on the family farm.

Since she arrived at the nursing home ten months ago she'd been dreaming about the farm more, more than ever before. Last night she was a ten-year-old girl hanging on the tire swing in the shade of the large walnut tree in the front lawn of her childhood house. They had horses and cows and chickens and pigs and a hay mow and a grain bin and a corn crib and a windmill that looked like an oil derrick that pumped cold water to the small milk house next to the yellow gravel driveway. The bus from her consolidated school had just dropped her off. Her mother Edna waved at her friend Meg the driver; Edna was out in the vegetable garden cutting rhubarb so she could make them sauce for ice cream. Her dad was coming up from the big barn after milking the cows. He shuffled his open rubber boots in the gravel and the buckles rang in her ears like so many spurs. He leaned forward into the rectangular yoke of the wagon and pulled the old wooden cart behind him, loaded with the tall gray steel milk cans that weren't shiny anymore. He put the filled cans into the water tank in the milk house, where they'd stay cool till the driver picked them up next morning. The windmill blades spun loudly, she remembered, banging the cage slightly against its vertical stop in rhythm with the Midwestern summer night's wind.

She lay back across the tractor tire swing until the ends of her hair touched the ground. She tried to make her hair move to the same rhythm as the wind, pushing her hips and legs against the tire, up and down, up and down, push once, wait, bend her knees, push again. Now, anytime she closed her eyes, she was there at the farm. It was like marching to a song she'd heard once and just remembered that moment, something from long ago, lost in her mind until just then.

At the nursing home the other patients were already done with their evening meal. They had put her in the dining room at a table with a bunch of old people while the others finished, but she didn't like that and wheeled herself out into the hall.

"My son *is* coming," she said. "He just had to work late."

The nurses and aides smiled and kept walking. A few glanced back over their shoulders and smiled at her. She saw them duck their heads and whisper to each other about her.

"Bitches," she hissed.

Her feet moved in ragged steps, crab-like as she made her way along the hallway wall from the dining room to the street entrance of the nursing home. It was dark outside. Since the stroke her left arm hung useless in her lap. She pushed as much as she could against the narrow wheel with her right hand to move herself along. Surgery on her neck the year before repaired the whiplash from a long-ago auto accident. The doctors'd prescribed steroids for the arthritis, which puffed her up like a sausage, and the Bell's Palsy had left her once-beautiful face in a constantly-twisted expression that made half of her cheek hang over her mouth and made her one good eye droop.

A man strode up the long asphalt driveway, holding his jacket over his head in the sleet. He carried a large bouquet of tulips, hard to get in winter here. At first she thought this was Jeff, and smiled; it was just like him to bring her flowers. But then she saw it was some other man she didn't know, coming to see someone else.

"Cold out there," he said as he stepped through the sliding double doors and saw her.

"My son is coming. For my birthday," she said.

"Well. Happy birthday to you!" the man said, and gave her a smile and a quick pat on the shoulder as he walked past her.

She folded her arms on her lap and watched again out the nursing home's sliding entry door glass. Her one hand didn't lie flat on her lap anymore. She tried to hide it with her pink shawl in case anyone else came through the door, and got most of it covered.

The night before last night (or was it last week sometime?) she dreamt of the year they had lambs on the farm. She had been out in the barn when most of them were born, helping Bill and her mom pull the kids out when the ewes needed help. So far thirty kids had been born just that night. They were cute on their short wobbly legs. They bleated loudly when they couldn't find their mama's teat, and then punched that same teat and bleated again whenever they didn't get enough milk. Barbara knew not to get too attached to them; she tried to ignore them all she could, but it was hard for her. Bill went from lamb to lamb, circling endlessly that birthing week, and nearly exhausted himself. They'd already sold the kids for Passover, and it was good money they needed badly. Bill did everything he could to keep them alive, even fed a few of them by hand from a bottle when the mothers didn't have enough milk; but he'd never done it before, with sheep, and they lost half of the ewes and ten of the lambs to fever anyways.

They only raised lambs once, Depression or not. In the end it just about killed Bill to give the lambs up, and he sold all the grown sheep to old man Rittmeier down the road for way less than what they were worth, her mama said.

"Hey Mom. How're you doing?"

Jeff stood by her suddenly, one hand on the handle of the wheelchair, the other holding his Blackberry, answering email. He had a London Fog trench coat on over a nice grey suit and red tie. The top button of his shirt collar was undone. He focused on his phone.

He didn't have any flowers in his hand.

"Hello, son," she said, looking up and smiling as best she could. "Where…are your gloves?"

"Thought they were in my pocket, but I guess they aren't," Jeff said, shrugging. "Probably dropped 'em somewhere getting in and out of the car. Oh well. There's more gloves where those came from."

She adjusted herself in her chair. He dropped his Blackberry into his coat pocket and then grabbed the handles of the wheelchair and pushed her back toward the dining room. His steps echoed lightly in the quiet halls and the tiled floors were shiny from the many coats of cheap industrial wax. The walls were pale green – the color of dried-up grass in fall, almost white. Every once in a while Jeff had to steer around the Nurse's Station, or a cart with dirty food trays, or the nightly medicine chest with black-and-chrome wheels and red-and-blue plastic drawers all around like those old roll-top desks, or some thin dry crumpled person in dull clothes in a walker or another wheelchair.

To Jeff the whole fluorescent corridor smelled like antiseptic wash. She hoped her feet weren't dragging too much or Jeff would get upset. When they got to the dining hall, he asked, "So where do they have us set up for dinner?"

"They were supposed to have…a separate place set up for us…outside the dining room…but they… probably… don't."

Jeff called and waved to one of the aides, smiling brightly. The aide strolled over and they talked easily for a second like they'd known each other for years, like men always do. A few of the other patients still sat in their chairs around the dining tables, finishing their meals. Some, already done eating, waited to be pushed back to their rooms. A few were already asleep. Those who could go back to their rooms on their own and were still awake stared openly at her and Jeff as they went past. She sat as tall as she could in her wheelchair and stared straight ahead.

Jeff weaved between the tables as the aide led them to their spot. They stopped at a table by the picture windows looking out onto the patio. Jeff pushed his mother's wheelchair to the table and nodded a small thanks to the aide. "Sorry I was late," he said, sitting. "Conference call with the west coast. Time zones. Couldn't get out of it."

"You've done well...there." She had been a secretary for several top executives throughout her career, and she knew the ins and outs of business politics and power plays. She knew all too well how secretaries lived and died with the daily fortunes of their bosses. Loyalty had little or nothing to do with it. It was all just business. Nothing personal, just business.

Music from the boom box in the kitchen blared into their small alcove as the clean-up crew moved in after dinner and took over. The Muzak system also played over the dining room, an old Andy Williams Christmas tune competing with the Motown rap blaring from the workers' radio in the kitchen.

One of the other aides brought Jeff a plate of spaghetti and vegetables, and a bowl of the same pureed for his mother, along with her vanilla milkshake. A straw stood in the blob of clear gelatin that served as her water in her other glass.

"So what's the therapist say about your throat muscles? Getting any better?" Jeff had to speak loudly to be heard over the boom box.

"They say I'm... doing much... better," she lied. She kicked the speech therapist out of her room last week for telling her that she'd probably never eat solid foods again, snapped her good eye at him and told him to get the hell out of her room and never come back.

"Good, good." Jeff nodded. She looked away. They slid back into their silence. The music played on. Jeff finished half his food, pushed his plate aside, checked his Blackberry and tapped out a quick message.

She couldn't get much of her food into her mouth, but she didn't want to have someone feed her in front of her son. The Christmas tunes made her think again of her dreams. Bill, her dad, always had the radio on when he milked the cows. She remembered that old radio, although she couldn't reach it herself way up there in the rafters with the spiders and cobwebs and dust. The glow from its vacuum tubes filled the corner of the barn by the half-door entrance with a dull yellow light. The barn always smelled like sweat, leather, sour milk, fresh straw and chalk from the lime disinfectant Bill sprinkled in the shit troughs every night. "Music keeps 'em calm," he told her once. "Makes 'em make better milk," he smiled. She could barely hear him over the sputter and cough of the old lawn-mower engine driving the compressor hooked to the chrome milking machines. Every few minutes Bill would grab a suction cup and rearrange it on one of the cows, or move one of the milkers from one cow to another cow stanchioned in line, or dump the warm milk out of the milker into one of the tall gray steel cans. He moved constantly, never a wasted motion. Bill always talked to the cows as he moved, she remembered now, calling them "ladies" and "missy" and clicking his tongue. She wondered if he did that to keep from getting kicked or did it to keep himself company out there in the barn?

"I have to get home to let the dogs out." Jeff was standing at her side. It startled her. "Gotta run. Sorry."

"We didn't have…cake yet…" she whispered.

"Oh yeah," he said. "Happy birthday."

"Tell them…we want our cake." Jeff sighed and sat down, waving to get the attention of an aide. A short lady with smooth brown skin and dark brown eyes brought over a small cake with a lit candle on it. She placed it in front of them with two clean plates and forks, then at Jeff's suggestion, she blew the candle out.

"Can I get a coffee to go, please?" Jeff asked the lady.

"I've been dreaming… a lot… about the farm… lately."

"Oh yeah? Good dreams or bad dreams?" She was still thinking about that when he added, "What, no dreams about life on

Lawndale?" He laughed loudly, making a few of the remaining patients turn and look. Lawndale was the home he grew up in, where he and his sisters were young, the last place the family had lived together before the divorce.

She thought about the house on Lawndale while they ate their cake. Jeff was jumpy as he ate. "I wish they could turn at least two or three of those goddamn radios off," he said, waving his fork toward the kitchen doors and dining room.

"Shit," he finally said, throwing down his fork. "This is driving me nuts. Sorry. The dogs...I gotta go."

She looked over at him and set down her long-handled spoon as best she could. Bits of milk and cake and blended spaghetti and green beans dribbled down her bib and squeezed between her fingers and the spoon handle like so much glue.

Jeff tapped the handles of her wheelchair two quick taps. "I'll call you next week," he said, and then he was gone, headed for the exit.

She sat there, silent, still. She couldn't turn herself enough in her chair to see him go. She was stuck under the table. She thought about pushing herself away and calling after him, but realized she couldn't do either of those things now, either. A sickening smell rose from her side, and she knew the seal on the colostomy bag had slipped.

She thought once more of the farm, about the fields this time, when the green winter wheat was waist-high. The stiff stalks, smooth grain, and bristly-thick tassels tickled her fingers and brushed against bare legs under her skirt as she ran. She sucked the cold clean air in deep, filling her lungs nearly bursting, then sang an old Celtic prayer at the top of her young, still-innocent voice while the sun struck her face and warmed her.

THROWING SNOWBALLS AT CARS

We'd seen some pissed off people in our time, but this guy was in a class all his own. He left his beautiful bronze-and-copper '68 Hurst Olds 442 sitting in the middle of the dark and snowy December street, red air scoop shuttering to the *chug chug chug chuuug* beat of the four-barrel carb and oversized cam, barely over the train tracks on Custer Avenue, our favorite snowball target range.

To us, throwing snowballs at cars was like a winter baseball league: Conditioning for the real thing in the summer. Not all drivers saw it that way, apparently.

The Hurst Olds driver's door flung open and the guy came at Anderson, Holland, and me, slipping and sliding, screaming at us in the snow and slush. I caught a glimpse of someone else in the passenger seat—a quick flash of the dome light, a girl in a white-colored coat. The hopped-up Olds sputtered and coughed again like it was going to die, but then caught itself and kept idling. The three of us stood behind the lilac hedges for a moment longer and stared with our mouths hanging open, when we should have been running. We thought the twisted, thick hedges would hide us, but no. It was like the guy had a heat seeker in his hands or was using his outstretched arms like divining-rod boy-catchers, coming right at us down the hill off the street from fifty feet away. He moved fast for a guy that big, in his dress slacks and trench coat and fancy shoes.

Why we were all laughing so hysterically when we should have been scared shitless I didn't have time to figure out just then. I started slipping and sliding and falling in the snow trying to get away from Hurst Olds Guy. It skipped through my head that maybe my scholarship offer from St. Francis might not hold up if I had a police record, and it's that thought, I think, that snapped me out of it and finally made me run.

"I see you, you little bastards!" Hurst-Olds Guy yelled. I

doubted he could see me. I looked over my shoulder to check it out. Hurst Olds Guy was breathing hard through his mouth, standing on the other side of the lilac bushes, hands on his knees, lit up by the streetlight while he stood there panting from his slipping and sliding. I could still hear his Olds behind me and above us on the street, *chug chug chug chuuug, chug chug chug* as the four-barreled carb sputtered and the cams barely rolled over again. "I know where you live, you little shits!" he yelled from behind me. "Your old man's going to beat your asses black and blue! Your mama's gonna cry her eyes out over your pathetic bloody bodies!"

I wasn't laughing as hard as I had been before, but I was still smiling even though my sides hurt now from running. The guy did have a way with words. I made my way to Cassaro's garage, the designated meeting point. We'd split up like we'd agreed ahead of time, running through the dark back yards in three different directions, like foxes chased by hounds. Besides being young we had the advantage of knowing where we were – this was our home territory, after all. Hurst Olds Guy was out of his element, out of his private little world of a souped-up car and tan leather seats and Fender eight-track tape systems, wandering blind out here in the snow and frozen grass and maze of fences and garages and tool sheds and houses where we all grew up.

He was just another foreigner to us.

As I came around the corner of Cassaro's garage, I saw Anderson half-way up in the willow tree that let us climb on the roof. Cassaro had a mean-looking German Shepherd named Babe that lived out here; a picket-fence dog run wrapped around the side and back of the garage. A square hole cut out of the garage wall at the corner let Babe inside when he got real cold. You had to go over the top of the dog fence on the willow limb to get on the garage roof, usually with Babe pacing below. No driver would ever climb up and catch us up here, and the garage was far enough behind the house that Cassaro would never hear us here, either. Ed worked for the city so was gone half the time, anyway.

I climbed up next to Anderson, already squatting on the roof, hoping to think of something cool to say, but all we could do was look at each other and bite and nearly swallow our fisted gloves to keep from laughing out loud and giving up our hiding place. I could feel the tears freeze on my cheeks. The breath frosted over our thin throwing gloves as we nearly banged heads together rocking back and forth. Then we lay on our stomachs so we could look back over the peak of the garage and see where Hurst Olds Guy was now.

Anderson was smaller than me, quick as lightning on his feet and on the mat. He wrestled 98 at West High School, a couple blocks over. He wore his red-and-black wrestling tunic around the neighborhood on meet days, just to piss me off 'cause I was a year younger and not in high school yet. I rubbed some of his strawberry ointment in his headgear last time he did that, and that seemed to cool *that* shit off, since I already outweighed him by thirty pounds and was a head taller and he didn't want to mess with me.

"Where the hell's Holland?" I whispered.

"He knows the plan," said Anderson. "Probably got his fat ass stuck in a fence or a bush somewhere."

I thought about that for a second. Holland was what you'd kindly call husky; we enjoyed teasing the shit out of him about all of his baby fat – his bulging baby belly and his baby face. He was a freshman like Anderson, too, officially, even though he'd been held back a couple times. But for all that Holland had soft hands and good feet, was a decent catcher and good hitter when he stayed focused and got a jump. Holland's the guy you'd want blocking the plate for you in a close game.

"His hardest problem will be keeping his goddamned mouth shut," I said to the cold air on the garage roof, "what with Hurst Olds Guy still snooping around." Anderson grinned. Holland's mouth *was* famous in the neighborhood.

"Holland's one thing," he said. "Where the hell is Hurst Olds Guy?"

"Good question." I looked around and spotted Hurst Olds Guy going back down Custer to his car, wetter, colder, madder. He stomped his feet and grabbed the door handle. Then, for sure, when the dome light came on, I saw that there *was* a girl in the right bucket seat next to him, cute little white parka on, fluffy fur hood folded down over on her shoulders, filing her nails or something while Hurst Olds Guy got back into his car.

"Wish he had a feather up his ass and I had that car," Anderson croaked next to me without moving his eyes. "Then we'd both be tickled."

"We gotta watch to see that he leaves for sure," I said. Hurst Olds Guy gunned the engine, popped the clutch and spun away from the curb. He rolled through the four-way stop at Ridge, turned left and then left again, and drove down our street, slow. I could imagine him in the Olds, pissed off, smelling his own wet dog smell when the heater blew hot air on him, rolling down his window in the cold, breathing hard, whipping his head from side to side looking for us.

I wondered what kind of air freshener he hung from his mirror. I wondered what his gear shift looked like, factory or custom chrome – custom chrome probably. I wondered if the girl said anything to him or just kept quiet there in the soft glow of the Olds' dash lights. If she kept quiet, I wondered if she did it because she was scared or because she was smart. She didn't look like much of a talker to me. But then again she couldn't be any too bright now, either. Couldn't be too smart and still be dating Hurst Olds Guy, right?

Although that car was pretty cool, I'll give her that…

Behind us the limbs scratched loudly on the stiff shingles. My heart jumped, even though I was just looking at Hurst Olds Guy. But then I realized it took a lot of weight to push that willow branch all the way down in December weather like this; it had to be Holland. It had been nearly ten minutes since we'd bombarded the Hurst Olds Guy with snowballs at the railroad tracks.

"Did you see him? Did you see that little dandy?" Holland's bare white head and wide eyes popped into sight as he crawled over Anderson first then over me and collapsed with a thump on the garage roof at my side. He didn't do himself any favors in the looks department by keeping his hair cut so short. He had a nervous habit of running his palm straight up over his nose and then back through his hair, which gave him a slicked-back look like

Woody Woodpecker. The more nervous he was, the more often he'd do that swipe over his nose.

The whole garage shook when Holland plopped with his arms and legs sprawled wide, trying to catch his breath, breathing hard. Steam rolled off his bare head as he lay there. He did the hand thing again and dragged snot up over his head. "Jesus, I thought I was going to piss myself when that guy came outta that car!"

"Yeah, yeah. We were there too, Lardass," Anderson said.

"Shhh. The guy might still be driving up and down our block, looking for us." I said. "Unless he's back out of his car, knocking on doors again."

Holland got up on all fours like a dog and crawled to the peak. "No shit? He's knocking on doors?"

"I shit you not," I said, waving my arm a little. "Must've picked up your hat somewhere in the bushes." Holland's hand jumped to his head. "Started down by Ridge and knocked on all the doors." I pointed that direction. "I bet he showed that hat to everybody that answered their door." Holland's eyes grew even wider. "Went to your house, Holland," I added, shaking my head, looking down. Then I looked right at him: "I couldn't hear all they said, but your old man was peeee-issed from the sounds of it."

"I'm screwed," Holland said. "I'm screwed, screwed, screwed for sure."

Holland's sputtering sounded a little like the Olds' rough idle. I almost felt sorry for him then, tried not to laugh, but couldn't hold it in anymore. He stared, caught on, then roared and lunged, smothering me in his coat, pinning me to the roof and slamming his fist into my body over and over, although I could barely feel it through the heavy clothes I had on. The more I laughed the more pissed off he got.

He pushed himself off me. "Screw you," he said, digging at his nose. He was a great nose picker too, anytime, anywhere, it didn't matter who was there or where he was. Anderson and I both gagged loudly.

"What the hell happened to your pants?" I said, getting up to my elbows and pointing. Holland's bright white briefs shone through his blue-jean crotch, catching the street and house lights while the legs of his pants flapped in the cold breeze.

"Caught it on LaManche's cyclone fence, going over. One of those pointy things on the top?" I nodded. He went on. "Thought he had me for sure, but then I thought what the hell: I was more worried about losing my nuts than I was about getting caught by that dandy."

I imagined Holland trying to straddle LaManche's fence in his panicked and adrenaline-steeped state of mind. Hung out to dry, flopping like a fish on a hook, ripping his own pants nearly off to get away, like a wolf chewing through his paw to free himself from a hunter's trap.

"Yeah, and I was on my way down to climb in his car and drive off in it too," Anderson said.

After a couple more slugs all around, we climbed down off Cassaro's garage. Holland went home to change his pants. Anderson and me headed to his house to mooch some hot chocolate from his grandma.

"You coming over?" Anderson yelled to Holland.

"Nah. Figure I'll go beat off as long as I got my pants down." He snickered. "You boys wanna come help?"

We'd seen Holland beat off before. Not a pretty sight. "No way!" we yelled at him in unison.

We walked in opposite directions for a few steps, me and Anderson headed to his house for hot chocolate, Holland headed home. I stopped and turned. "Tomorrow night?" I yelled to Holland, holding my hand up in a high-five salute.

He returned the salute. "Tomorrow night," he said. We grunted and shrugged, leaving each other for now.

* * *

Walking the short distance home after a quick cup of cocoa, just kitty-corner across from Anderson's house, I stopped in my front yard. My house was dark, like I knew it would be, except for the flickering light of the TV that showed around the bottom of the shade. I wondered what the mood was inside the house, but then I already knew that answer. My dad's car wasn't in the driveway, not that I expected it to be in the driveway; he hadn't been home for the last three weekends or called to tell anybody where he was, not since that Thanksgiving fight of theirs. So how did I *expect* the mood to be inside?

Instead of thinking about all that any more, I turned toward Holland's house across the street.

My mind wandered and flew. Why was the Hurst Olds Guy here in the first place? Was he driving home himself? Was he just driving through? Maybe he was driving to or from work, although I couldn't imagine anywhere around here that would pay enough for someone his age to have a car like that. Why was he on Custer Avenue, way over here on the west end? Was he picking his girlfriend up? Dropping her off? Did she live over here? I'd never seen her before, would have remembered that for sure. What were they doing before they were so rudely interrupted by snowballs smacking the side and top of their car like so many icy hand grenades? Now that he knew there was a good chance he'd be pelted with snowballs whenever he ventured into our neighborhood, would he ever come back? Would he and that girl still go out, or would they break up because of our snowballs? Or break up maybe just because Hurst Olds Guy thought she was bad luck? Or break up because she'd seen his temper tantrum and saw him chasing us like some maniac, and she didn't want to put up with any more of his shit?

The thought that I could have thrown the snowball that hit the Olds that caused their breakup that ruined their wedding and eliminated their children from ever being born made me smile.

I realized then that I was still standing in my own front lawn. I went over to Holland's and knocked on the door. His mom answered, an older German woman with a kind face and slow, quiet motions. "Why hello there, Jeff," she said, opening the door and stepping back. "I'll see if Bobby is in." As she was walking back to Holland's room, I stood in the door and did a little wave to Mr. Holland. His emphysema was worse in the winter – the air was thinner then, I guess. He was on oxygen tonight, having trouble breathing even while just watching "Combat" on TV. A green metal tank sat at his side, a plastic hose leading up to a clear mask that was rubber-banded to his face like a cheap Halloween mask.

"Hey, Mr. Holland."

"Jeff, how the hell are you, son?" His voice echoed a little in the mask. He stuck out his hand and I took it. He squeezed hard. He was always doing manly shit like that to me.

"I'm fine sir, thanks. How're you doing?"

He waved off my question, gesturing toward the oxygen and pills on the table next to him, shrugging his shoulders as if that was answer enough. Stupid question, but he didn't seem to mind. "Sit, sit right there, take a load off," he waved. His beagle, Happy, growled at me as I passed from his spot between Mr. Holland's thigh and the chair cushion. Mr. Holland slapped him across the nose hard. "Shut the hell up, Happy," he grunted, taking off his mask. "You know, Happy, if I'd a known you were gonna turn out to be this worthless I never would have gotten your sorry ass in the first place," he said. The dog looked sorry enough then, I guess, because Mr. Holland rubbed him behind the ears.

"So how's your mom these days?" Mr. Holland asked, straightening in his chair some and raising an eyebrow twice, quickly. He had commented more than once on how sharp my mom always looked going to work and all, usually when Mrs. Holland wasn't in the room.

"She's doing fine sir. Working hard, as usual."

"Yes, yes, I bet she is." He held his finger on his chin for a moment. "And your dad – how's he doing? Where's he at these days?"

I coughed in my hand to buy time. "Well, it's Wednesday… so that means Wyoming," I said, smiling, avoiding his real question. "If he's running on schedule," I added.

"Huh. Still trucking to the west coast and back every week, eh?"

"Pretty much, sir, yes sir." I wondered if Mrs. Holland had got lost between the living room and Bobby's room, or if maybe she'd walked in without knocking and caught him jacking off like he said he was going to. I wondered what that might be like. For her to see it, I mean. Holland'd be pissed at me for sending her his way if that was the case. I almost laughed out loud at the thought.

"All that driving," Mr. Holland was saying, "screws up your

body big time, boy, even if you can manage not to crash into all those crazies out there or get run over by one of 'em. Bad enough here in the city, can't imagine it at eighty on the freeway," he said. "How long has he been doing it now?"

"Twenty-three years, sir. Since he was seventeen, pretty much full time since then. 'Don't know anything else so I'm stuck doing what I know,' is what he says," I said, making my voice low like a man's. "That's what he says whenever anyone asks him."

Mr. Holland lifted his mask and took a long swig from the dark brown bottle of Schlitz on the coffee table next to his big overstuffed recliner. Holland stuck his head around the hallway corner. "Hey, what's up, Miller?"

"Nothing going on over at my house," I replied. "Boring. Wanna come out?"

"Sure, I ain't doing anything here." He pumped his right hand up and down from a spot where his dad couldn't see him. He rolled his eyes. "Be right there." I guess Mrs. Holland must've gone to the bathroom or something, or maybe went to her bedroom to recover from seeing Bobby messing up his sheets, if that's what she saw. I shook my head and stood up to go.

"Good chatting with you, Mr. Holland. You take care now," I said, and shook his hand again. Happy just lay there while Bobby and I went out the door.

"What the hell do you and my dad talk about, anyway?" Holland said once we cleared the porch. He punched me in the arm. "He never has *anything* to say to me."

"Nothing much," I said. "You know. Baseball. White Sox. Who's gonna play where next year, who's gonna whip the Yankees. Shit like that." Mr. Holland coached our Little League team. Gave me my first first-baseman's glove when my mom couldn't afford one for me. When Bobby and I played wiffle ball in our back yards almost every day in the summer, I was always the White Sox; he was always the Yankees.

The snow was still good for packing when we headed back to our spots at the snowball hedges. I found myself still looking over my shoulder for the black-and-gold Hurst Olds as we walked across Custer, like the guy might still be hanging around looking for us. I was in this quiet world, focused on the next car that came around the curve, whatever it might be, when Holland cleared his throat and spit.

"So'd you get the letter?"

I stalled. "What letter?"

"You know what letter!" he yelled, shoving me.

I was messing with him. I knew what letter. "Yeah, we got the letter."

He stopped. "And?"

"And what?"

"And what did your old lady have to say about that? Huh? It's not every day someone gets a baseball scholarship from friggin' St. Francis, man!"

I shrugged. "She hasn't seen it yet."

He waited. "You're shitting me." He thought for a moment. "What do you mean, she hasn't *read* it yet, or she hasn't *decided* yet, or *what*?" He did that swipe thing on his face again. "What's to decide? Jesus!"

"No...she hasn't *seen* it yet. I took it out of the mail box when it came so she wouldn't see it."

He snorted. Stared at me. "So'd *you* read it at least? What'd it say?" Another hand-wipe thing. "How much of that Catholic shit you got to put up with to go there? They give you your own rotisseries?"

"Rosaries, dumbshit. Catholics use rosaries, rosary beads, not *rotisseries*."

St. Francis scouts had been at the last of our Little League games, because their team stuck together all summer as a Club team, an All-Star team. The scouts really only came there to watch their own kids win. We were just a bunch of kids from the poor side of town thrown together by zip code by the league.

I was playing first base for most of it, and Holland was catching. I begged Mr. Holland to let me pitch one inning. He finally caved in the sixth when things were too far gone. I threw twelve straight strikes to retire the side, three more than I had to because Bobby dropped one third strike and the guy got on, so I had to strike out the last guy from the stretch. I never threw anything but a fastball that whole inning. Anything else Bobby called, I shook off. Even though I went two for three with a double, and Holland went one for three but brought me in, we only scored the one run and got our asses handed to us by those St. Francis snobs.

Best team money can buy, Mr. Holland said afterwards.

While it *was* true that I got a scholarship letter from St. Francis Central Catholic High School, it wasn't in baseball, like I'd told Holland before I swore him to secrecy – the offer was based on grades and a letter from my eighth-grade English teacher, Miss Wilson. But I wasn't going to tell Holland that. Much more exciting for him if he thought the scholarship was baseball. Let him think what he wanted to for now.

I tossed a lazy shot at a U-Haul truck going by. Bobby lobbed in two more before the panel truck was out of range. "The letter was what I expected, pretty much," I said. "Full boat tuition, yeah, that's the good part. But I doubt my mom can pay the books and fees that go with it."

Holland whipped an iceball at me. "Shit, you gotta go, man!" he said in my face, his own face red and sweaty. "Someone from our neighborhood, someone I know in person, playing ball for St. Francis…Showing up those rich little pricks on the field, showing them what it's like to play baseball *right*, to play the game the way the game was meant to be played. Damn, they need that, man!" Holland stopped and jabbed me with a pointed finger. "That asshole that chased us tonight? That Hurst Olds Guy? I'll bet *that* bastard goes to St. Francis!"

I was about to correct Holland, to tell him that there's no way even some spoiled little rich kid from St. Francis would be driving a car like that, when we heard a short loud bang. An explosion. Close. Holland was facing me and had his back to LaManche's garage.

"What the hell…?"

In a second we'd dumped our extra snowballs and were running toward our houses.

We ran hard for the second time that night. "Aww man," Holland panted, next to me. "It's *my* house. Shit!" Black smoke billowed out of the front window. We pounded and tugged on the door until our hands were numb and smudged black, but were driven back by the heat, choked by the smoke and the smell.

A minute later a cop car sat in the middle of our street. His red, white and blue lightbar flashed. A fire truck joined him in another minute. Guys in black raincoats with their names stenciled in bright yellow fluorescent letters on their backs poured out like ants. Three firemen broke through Holland's front door and dashed inside. Two other firemen broke out more of the front window with their axes. Smoke poured out, but in the dark we could only see the smoke rise for a second from an indoor light still on. In another minute spotlights were trained on the house, one on the door and the other one sweeping across the roof.

Then a fireman came out of the house carrying a body over his shoulders. He laid the body out on the snow at the curb. He held his hands under the head. An EMT started working on the body; I saw him put his ear to where the mouth would be, then lay his head on the body's chest.

"Dad!" Holland coughed, running over to his father and sliding on his knees at his father's side.

The fireman that had carried Mr. Holland out bent over with his hands on his knees and breathed heavily through his mouth. The chief in the white hat came over and crouched next to him.

"Good job, Pete," I heard. "Is he alive?"

"Hope so," Pete gasped.

"Anyone else in there?"

"Tassone and Mack have a lady in a back bedroom. Knocked around pretty good but seems okay. Looks like an oxygen tank blew when the guy was grabbing a smoke, the dumb shit. The damn foam in the armchair caught quick – got him pretty good. Third's all over his arms, I'll bet."

"Go take a breather, Pete. Good job." The chief clutched Pete's elbow and handed him off to one of his other firemen. After that he turned away from me and talked into his walky-talky and I couldn't hear anymore.

Another cop arrived and set up a perimeter line to keep people out. I just stood there, not knowing what to do with myself.

The cop came up and pushed me back. "Behind the line," he said, nodding at the roll of yellow and black tape in his hand. "Behind the line!" A few other officers set up sawhorses in the yards next to Holland's and made yellow-and-black tape lines too.

By now most of the neighbors had come out to see what was going on, and were huddled together in groups of two or three. Bertha LaManche came out in her bathrobe and slippers. The cop that pushed me out of the way had gotten rid of his roll of tape and was working his way through the crowd, leading everyone back away from Holland's house. I saw Anderson walking up and down, spinning away from the officer, peeking over and around the people and the cars and the trucks in the street and driveways.

He ran over to me. "I heard someone died," he said quickly. "Who died?"

I stared at him for a second. "Nobody's dead!" It came out too loud. "I mean...they don't know for sure if anyone is hurt or not," I mumbled.

Anderson looked at me funny, his eyes dancing to somewhere behind me. "I'm gonna go find out who died," he said, and left.

I turned around and saw my sister Carol standing across the street in our yard. She had on a hooded sweatshirt. She shifted from foot to foot with her arms crossed over her chest to keep warm. I walked up to her and she smacked me on the arm, hard.

"That's for belching into my phone again, you pig," she said. "It's a wonder Tommy keeps calling me." I just stood there, frozen. That was earlier tonight. Ancient history. Then she moved in front of me, looking at the commotion as if she'd just noticed it, and looked into my face. She used to babysit for Bobby back when he was a kid, back when Mr. and Mrs. Holland still went out on dates. "Is it bad?"

"Could be," I said, looking away. "Me and Bobby were out back, throwing snowballs." I looked down. "We tried to get in but we couldn't," I said, showing her my blackened hands. "I saw a fireman carry Mr. Holland out. One of those EMT guys started working on him." I took a breath. "I think he was smoking with the oxygen on again."

Carol stood there nodding her head. She knew about Mr. Holland's emphysema, about the oxygen. "Mrs. Holland is so nice," she said, shaking her head. "Hope they'll be alright." She put one arm in the small of my back and one on my shoulder and turned me toward our house. I saw my mother briefly at the window, the bright flash of a hair clip, a blur of silver-highlighted hair wrapped in mounds of white toilet paper and wide blue eyes and the silky edge of a blanket as she spun away from the window.

"Hey, maybe we'll luck out and that stupid 'Happy' dog of theirs will have choked to death in the smoke, huh?" Carol said.

I had to smile.

* * *

Christmas came and went before the Hollands were back in their house. You couldn't see anything different, really, but the whole neighborhood looked like someone had painted all the houses with oil or something, and it stunk like banana skins burning in our rusty trash barrel every time you stepped outside.

Carol and I went to the visitation but not the funeral. Carol drove; Mom stayed home, said she wasn't feeling good. Most of the other neighbors came; Bertha LaManche had on a low-cut dress with bright orange flowers.

Mr. H would've appreciated the dress.

I hugged Mrs. Holland and she hugged me back like it was the last hug she had left in her body. "He thought a lot of you," she whispered in my ear. I stood by Bobby a while at the visitation, but didn't know what to say and didn't know what to do with my hands, so I went and sat down where the chairs were all in rows, but that didn't last long 'cause I didn't want to sit with the family, not being family, and didn't want to sit over *there* while Bobby had to stand over *there* with his mother, so we didn't stay long.

New Year's Day, Bobby and his mom came back home. Sadly, Happy the stupid bassett hound survived. Mr. Holland must have kicked him out of his chair or forced him away with all his beer farts before he lit up his cigarette that night. I waited until just after dark and knocked on their door. Mrs. Holland answered and invited me in.

"Oh Jeff, so good to see you…Can I get you some hot chocolate? Let me see where Bobby is."

I stepped into the house and closed the new front door behind me. It clicked shut loudly with hardly a push. The furniture was new, but to me it was pretty much the same design and colors as the old stuff. The window in the front room had been replaced, and the trim surrounding it was painted a clean bright white. An overstuffed armchair sat where Mr. Holland's recliner had sat, empty now. I didn't see Happy anywhere.

I sat on the couch under the window trying not to look at the empty chair. Mrs. Holland sat on the loveseat across from me. The TV was off. The room was quiet. Bobby came out of the hallway.

I stood up. "Hey Bobby. How ya doing?" I said. How stupid that must have sounded. My cheeks went hot.

"I'm doing okay, I guess. Considering." He started to sit in the recliner, then thought better of it and sat on the other end of the couch from me.

"Wanna go outside, hang out?" I leaned forward in the couch and wrung my hands in front of me.

Mrs. Holland looked back and forth, from me to Bobby and back again. Bobby hesitated. "Why don't you go on out and play with Jeff?" Mrs. Holland said. "The fresh air will do you good."

He sighed. "Okay, okay. I'll get my coat and be right back."

I smiled a thin smile at Mrs. Holland, then looked down at my boots. Mrs. Holland stood up and came close. She leaned over me, put her warm cheek against my cheek and ear again like she had the night of Mr. Holland's visitation. I could smell her old lady perfume, that and bread or something from the kitchen. It wasn't a bad mix.

"Thank you for being Bobby's friend," she whispered. She kissed my cheek. Then she stood straight, turned, let her hand drop from my arm, and walked away from me into the kitchen.

She didn't look back.

I let myself out and met Bobby on his porch when he came out.

We walked without talking, moved slowly toward the back yards, to the snowball spot. On the way there, we ran into Anderson.

"Hey," Anderson yelled, running toward us. "Guess what?"

Bobby and I looked at each other and shrugged. "Okay, what?"

He stopped and smirked. "I'm going to go to friggin' St. Francis next year."

Bobby glanced at me, his eyes wide.

"No shit," I choked out. My own scholarship papers sat under my bed, unsigned, never to be returned. I stared at Bobby hard.

"No shit," he said to Anderson after a moment.

"My dad's company donated them a ton of money for the new gym, so the bishop's giving me a scholarship. Everything's paid—books, tuition, fees. Hell, even hot lunches probably, I don't know." Anderson could hardly contain himself. "All I gotta do is show up January 5th."

Bobby drew a deep breath, then placed a finger over one nostril and blew out hard. "Not me," he said. "I wouldn't go to friggin' *Saint Fran's ass* if they paid me." He hawked up a wad of phlegm and spit. "Best sports teams money can buy."

He looked at me. "I wouldn't go there if they begged me. You, Miller?"

"No way," I said, relieved. "I wouldn't go there if they fricking *paid* me. Especially now that Anderson's gonna be there." I slugged Anderson in the arm.

"You're just jealous, the both of you," Anderson said. A little pout flashed across his face.

By then we'd reached the back of LaManche's yard, that familiar corner pocket of hedgerow we usually threw from. We bent down and packed three or four snowballs each, held onto one in our throwing hand and put the extras in our big side pockets. Anderson had to move down the hedge away from us to be able to throw over the shorter, lower part. "Just in case," he yelled, studying the road in front of him. "Just in case that crazy mother in the Olds shows up again. Same runaway plan, right?"

Bobby and I grinned at each other.

"Yeah, same plan," I said.

Bobby and I leaned into each other, shoulder to shoulder, *wish-*

ing that Hurst Olds would drive by so we could pound him with iceballs again and see him throw the door open and run toward us again with his arms all stretched out like Frankenstein. We both knew that this time, this time, we would stand our ground, we wouldn't move an inch.

Neither one of us.

WRESTLEBACK

Sure, the School Board wants to promote school spirit and encourage greater participation by the student body or some other silly bullshit, but who would have thought they'd actually tell us to stage a *fight* at West High in *those* days? A wrestling match? As a school assembly? Come on. Half the people in Rockford don't know what real wrestling is. All they know is that fake WWF crap.

Who really gives a shit, anyways?

That's what we all thought when Coach Germano gave us the word. Imagine how I felt when he told me I was going to be one of the wrestlers.

West High School in the early 1970's was a lit stick of black-and-white dynamite ready to explode. West had the highest minority population of any Rockford school, about fifty percent. So what did Coach Germano do for the assembly? Why, he matched me up with Malcom Tanner-Murphy: "Miller. Malcom. You're it."

Except I'm white. And Malcom's black.

We thought at first that Coach was just screwing with us again. But not so.

The day of the assembly, we got out of third-hour class so we could get ready. Coach said I could have someone out there with me (it wouldn't be right for him to show favorites), so I picked "Fish" Kelly, my best friend.

I was wearing home tights for the assembly, the black ones with the warrior's face on the hip. Malcom had lost the coin toss and was wearing visitor tights, plain red. My home tights and muscle-man T-shirt had a wide diagonal black stripe from one shoulder to the opposite leg.

"You remember what Coach said, right?" Kelly asked while I was getting dressed.

"Which part?" I said. "Coach talks a lot."

"I'm telling him you said that." Kelly smiled, playing with the jar of strawberry balm, smearing it on locker handles. "The part about half-speed drill. You know, like practice, so we can show everyone in the crowd all the moves."

"Oh yeah, that part," I said, smiling as I laced up my wrestling shoes. Wrestling shoes look pretty weird. They're like plain ole Converse tennis shoes, high tops, but the bottoms are flat, with no treads, to grip the mat better, I guess.

"Shouldn't be a problem. Malcom and I are workout partners, so we're used to half- speed, you know?"

That's when Malcom came into the wrestling locker room with *his* coach for the day, Danny Brown. Danny was star point guard for Coach Demitri's champion basketball team. I'd apparently not gotten the memo, because Malcom and Danny were dressed to the hilt. Malcom had on a suit and tie. And Danny? Not only was he wearing a three-piece suit, he also had on a crisp-edged top hat and carried a chrome-topped walking stick, like a New York pimp.

"Geez. I don't even own a *regular* suit," Kelly whispered.

"Hey Malcom. Hey Danny," I called out.

You would have thought someone farted in their faces, the way they curled their lips and flared their wide brown noses.

"Hmmp" was the best I got from either of them. Malcom started undoing his tie to get undressed. He wouldn't look up at us. Danny stood with his back to me, tapping his cane on the wooden bench in front of the lockers.

"We'll see you out there in a few, then," I said. I rolled my eyes at Kelly, who grabbed a pile of white towels on his way out.

"What the hell was that all about?" Kelly asked when we got out on the stairs.

"Beats me."

Normally we took the hallway and bike ramp down to the wrestling room for practice. No one had ridden a bike to school in twenty years, but everyone still called the long slick concrete slab down to the furnace room "the bike ramp." Coach Germano liked to practice down there because it was next to the big boilers that heated the school, which made us sweat more.

Today we took the stairs up from the locker room to the gym

on the second floor. Kelly and I were jostling each other as we came up the stairs, play fighting, our feet making loud squeaking noises on the cement steps. He had my headgear on his head like a dunce cap, sitting high.

"Don't you be screwing no pooch out there today, boy," he was saying.

"You're the fish, son. I won't be doing any flopping," I fired back.

Then we both stopped, frozen at the doorway. The gym was packed. Absolutely packed. The polished wooden bleachers, normally folded up to make more room in the gym, were unfolded today to hold the crowd. Two teachers were posted at each of the long cement aisles on the third floor above the bleachers by the steel-pipe railing. Four teachers were standing at each of the double doors on the second floor. They all looked nervous. Mr. Erickson, the principal, was at the scorer's table, in front of the microphone. The bright red wrestling mats were laid out on the floor in the center of the big room. At one end of the gym was the balcony that held the pep band. At the other end were the scoreboard and clock.

The bleachers were full – with a twist. All the white students were on one side of the gym. All the black students were on the other side. As the crowd saw Kelly and me, they let out a whoop and clapped loudly.

The white half, that is. The black side booed.

Kelly and I looked at each other, laughed, and, as if on cue, we ran out onto the gym floor and continued our play fighting. He got a laugh for his head-gear accessory, and I decided to go for my best "Incredible Hulk" imitation: Flexed my arms, bulged my neck, clenched my teeth and roared as best I could. The crowd erupted. Then Kelly chased after me with a loose towel, snapping it at me as I ran around in circles.

Three large rectangular wrestling mats were shoved together to make one big center mat. The freshmen wrestlers had just finished taping the seams together. A big black warrior silhouette sat at the center of a white circle on the middle red mat. The freshmen lined up and made a gauntlet for Kelly and me to run through; we slapped as many hands in high-five fashion as we could. Finally we sat down on the mat, me stretching and Kelly relaxing with his head on his hands.

"Weird, huh?" he said.

"Huh," I said, reaching for my toes to stretch out a hamstring.

Coach Germano walked over to us from his spot against the wall. "Who'd a thought?' he said, waving to the crowd. He was smiling, something we didn't see that often. I saw him tip his head to someone, and looked up to see Coach Dimitri up by one of the third-floor doors. Coach Dimitri had his arms crossed on his chest, and had his game face on, but he nodded slightly in our direction. Coach Germano whispered "Still pissed this isn't a basketball game" through his smile.

About then we heard shouting from the other side of the gym, and looked toward the stair entrance we'd just come through. Malcom Tanner-Murphy was coming into the gym in a gold silk boxer's robe, hood up, and Danny Brown was trailing slightly behind him. Malcom was shadow-boxing as he walked. The first row of black girls stood up as Malcom passed and shook red and black pompons in front of their chests and then over their heads. Not to be outdone, Dave Leske, the Warrior quarterback, grabbed a couple stocking caps from people and did a cheer and a passable split on the white side.

Danny looked and walked like he was bored to be here. He tipped his hat and twirled his walking stick once, but that was all.

"Coach," I said. "How come I didn't get a robe?"

Coach Germano slapped my shoulder. "Gotta go," he said, and walked over to greet Malcom and Danny.

The boys' gym teacher, "Wild Bill" Stoglitis to all of us, had been drafted to referee the match. He came over to me now.

"Let's see 'em."

I showed him my hands and fingernails. He grabbed a couple of fingers, turned my hands over, and grunted.

"Shoes."

I had to stand up and lean against Kelly when I showed Wild Bill the bottoms of my shoes.

"Headgear?"

I pointed to the top of Kelly's head.

"Jesus H. Christ," Wild Bill mumbled, then left to go check out Malcom.

High school wrestling matches at that time consisted of three two-minute periods. You both started standing up in the first period. The last two periods, you alternated positions. The "down" position had you on all fours. In the "up" position, you put your chin in the middle of the down-position wrestler's back, your finger and thumb in a "u" on the elbow closest to you, and your other arm wrapped loosely around his waist.

I got my headgear back from Kelly and was ready to go. Malcom too seemed ready, and we met at the middle of the mat, both standing on the warrior's face, about six feet apart. Wild Bill stepped between us in his black-and-white-striped referee shirt and black pants.

"I want to see a nice clean match here, boys. Got that?" He looked at each of us and waited till we nodded back. He caught our eyes and held them a second. Then he blew the whistle and snapped his open hand up between us as he stepped out of the way.

I was ready for a nice leisurely run-through, ready to practice a single-, maybe a double-leg takedown, but Malcom shot out of his opening stance and basically tackled me. I had reflexes enough to throw my legs back and put my weight on his shoulders as I dove forward. His momentum carried me all the way off the mat and into the second row of the bleachers on the black side. Wild Bill came over to pull us out.

The crowd was going nuts.

"Jesus, Malcom! What the hell you doing?" I said. "Coach said 'half speed,' you know?"

But Malcom had already run back to the center of the mat. He stood there waiting for me, staring down, feet shuffling and hands tapping the air nervously. I looked around at Kelly, who just shrugged his shoulders. I tried to find Coach Germano at the door, but didn't see him anywhere. As I strolled back to the center of the mat, I took my headgear off and played with the chin strap to catch my breath, and looked over at Danny Brown. He sat on a folding chair at their corner of the mat, his chrome walking stick in front of him, hands crossed over the top of it. He looked straight ahead, his face blank.

"So that's the way it's gonna be, eh, Malcom?" I said when I reached the middle of the mat. He didn't answer. Wild Bill stuck his hand between us again and blew his whistle.

And that's how the first period went. Malcom charged like a bull and I basically fought back in survival mode, riding him out of bounds most of the time, lying on my side other times. He tried to get behind me, but I had his ankle and wouldn't let him around enough to get his two points for the takedown. That just pissed him off. He wound up and threw a wicked cross-face on me that rattled my teeth. With eight seconds left in the first period, he finally got me with a good double-leg takedown, and I had to roll hard to keep from getting thrown on my back.

"Two. Two points!" Wild Bill yelled, as I hung my head and swore. Malcom was trying to rip my arm off when the buzzer sounded. He kept coming so I slammed my open hand into his face and grabbed the back of his tights as I slid off the mat onto the floor. The crowd booed and cheered, black and white, respectively.

"Easy there! EASY!" Wild Bill's eyes went wide. "Or I'll penalize you both for poor sportsmanship."

I walked over to the corner where Kelly sat and motioned for him to get out of the chair. I sat down and he fanned me with a towel. The crowd was still in a frenzy over that last little exchange. The white kids were chanting, "Give it to him! Give it to him!" with alligator-jaw arms. The black pom-pom girls were doing splits on the floor.

"About time you got mad," Kelly said, spraying water in my face.

"Shit. What happened to 'half speed,' you know?" I asked, gasping.

"This never was no half-speed match, Einstein." Kelly shook his head. "I've got ten on it myself. You're the last one to find out this is a real fight, eh?" He smiled.

I looked at Kelly, then I looked over at Danny Brown. And I knew it was true. A couple of girls in short skirts had come off the bleachers to fan Malcom and give him some water. He was lying on his back on the mat, breathing hard, his knees up.

"Well, you better pray hard for your ten bucks. We're behind here two-zip."

"Who said I put the ten on you, numbnuts?" Kelly shoved me off the folding chair.

Wild Bill was out on the mat, ready to go. "Miller, you're home wrestler. Call it." He flipped his red-and-black coin.

"Black," I said while the coin was in the air.

"Black it is. What's it gonna be, up or down?" I gave him a thumb's-down. "Okay, guys. Get to it."

I eased down to my knees, then leaned on my hands, dropping my butt on the heels of my shoes. I positioned my knees behind my hands in front of the two strips of tape across the Indian's face and bent my arms slightly at the elbows. Malcom eased himself down and then leaned on me, his chin on the center of my back and his left hand on my left elbow.

The whistle sounded and I exploded up out of my coiled crouch. I heard Malcom's teeth crunch together. I shot up and a little out, going for the two-point reversal. Malcom was stunned enough that I got my legs out freely and used his left arm as leverage to swing myself around him. I rode him from the top position, then swept his arm at the elbow and drove his shoulder into the mat.

"Two! Reversal!" yelled Wild Bill, holding up his hand in the universal "Victory" sign for the scorer.

I rode Malcom like that for much of the second period, lying across his back and taking away his arm every time he tried to get up. I grabbed an ankle when he got one of his legs free. As long as I kept taking away his balance points and kept my weight back, I could ride him all day like that.

He was getting frustrated and tired from struggling. I was resting while I rode him, and dug my chin deep into his back so he would know I was still here. He scooted off the mat a couple times, out of the circle, but I kept my "up" position at every restart, and was able to break him down each time he tried to get up or away.

Finally, with thirty seconds left in the second period, I

grabbed Malcom's left wrist, threw his arm up and shoved my hips hard into his armpit. I started walking around him then in an exaggerated circle on my toes, lifting and leveraging his arm and keeping my hips tight against his armpit. I ground the left side of his face into the mat, using it as the pivot point of my circle. Finally Malcom looked into my hips to relieve the pain. I kept walking, driving, faster now, and rolled him over. I kept my legs out for balance, drove my gut into his face and squeezed his chest for all I was worth.

Wild Bill was jumping back and forth like a rabbit, first one side, then the next, trying to see the points of Malcom's shoulder blades. I got up on my toes to put more weight on Malcom's chest, and squeezed harder. Wild Bill had his arm up, ready to slap the mat for the pin, when the buzzer sounded.

I rolled off Malcom and heard him groan. His cheek was raw where the skin was gone from the mat burn, but not bleeding – just shiny and kind of yellow, like new mat burns are. He lay on his back for a few seconds before he got up. I hung over him, pulling my knee pads up. "Should'a stayed down, sucker," I whispered. He shoved me as he went past to his corner.

"Three! Three black for near fall!" Wild Bill was on his knees in front of us, holding up three fingers. The scoreboard now read 5-2, my favor, with one more two-minute period to go.

This time Kelly was already out of the chair when I got there. I motioned for the water, and he gave me a generous squirt.

"Uh-oh," he said, fanning the towel quicker.

I wiped the water off my face and looked up to see Dave Jarrard, our blond fullback and unchallenged King of the Slicked-Back Greasers, walking over to us from the bleachers. Dave walked like he always walked: slow. The metal clips on his Cuban-boot heels scratched the gym floor. He looked across the mat at Danny Brown and Malcom, long enough to make sure both of them saw him sneer. Jarrard had tried wrestling once, but had been disqualified in the first thirty seconds of his first match. Somehow we forgot to tell him that high-school wrestling didn't allow street-fighting moves and that your body had to hit the mat *before* your opponent's.

"Hey." Dave stopped when he got next to me. Kelly stood back.

"Hey Dave. What's up?" I smiled, as tired as I was.

Jarrard took the towel from Kelly and leaned down to speak in my ear. "Take this sucker down."

"Huh?" I wasn't sure I'd heard him right.

Dave smiled, looked up at the crowd, and fanned the towel in front of me a couple times. Then he leaned down next to me again and pulled my headgear out on that side. "I said, 'Hurt this sucker.'" He let go of the stretched-out headgear and slapped my shoulder, hard. He backed away, his long blond ducktail bobbing on his collar. He pointed at me, then raised his arms and did an air pushup, to the delight of half the crowd.

"Nice of you to stick around for our little conversation," I told Kelly when he slinked back.

"No problem," he said. "Go get 'em, tiger."

Wild Bill was out on the mat again. I got there before Malcom and leaned down with my hands on my knees to catch a few deep breaths through my mouth.

Finally Malcom joined us, water still dripping from his chin. "Last period," Wild Bill said, as if we weren't keenly aware of that already. "Let's see some more movement this period, eh boys?" He was staring directly at me. I just stared back.

Third period started like most of the second period. Malcom jumped to his feet from the down position, but I broke him down and rode him again. I could see Dave Jarrard sitting smugly on the bleachers, a smile on his face. The duck-tailed kids around him were wild-eyed, slapping each other every time I pulled Malcom down.

I shifted my weight and looked the other way. On the other side of the gym the crowd looked more hostile than playful. Danny Brown sat stone-faced in his corner.

I dug my chin into Malcom's back and pulled his wrist back off the mat between his legs. He was ready to roll over and give up. Jarrard stood and pointed thumbs-down. The rest of the white crowd smelled blood too, and were jabbing their down-turned thumbs in the air. 'Stick him! Stick him! Stick him!" The cry surged from one side of the crowd to the other until virtually everyone, even Kelly, was saying it.

Even the guys in the pep band joined in.

Malcom tried one last desperation move, shooting himself out like a dolphin from under me. Normally I would have just sat down on his ankles. But this time I waved weakly at his right ankle as it went by and he stood up and pulled away from me.

"*Escape!* One point, Red!" Wild Bill yelled, pointing and raising a finger. Five-three. I was still ahead. I shook my head and looked at my hands, then looked over at Jarrard. I shrugged my shoulders and stood up. Jarrard frowned.

Now we were both up, just like the first period. The noise from the crowd died down. The "stick him" chant lost its momentum and petered out. Malcom put his hands on his knees and sucked a couple breaths in through his mouth. His mat burn shined bright red on his cheek.

There was just under a minute left in the match. We grabbed each other in headlocks and turned a small circle in the center of the mat.

"Shoot on me, Malcom, shoot," I whispered in his ear. I felt his hand tense around my neck. "Do it, dammit."

I felt him nod. He lifted my elbows and shot under my arms. It was a sloppy but effective two-leg takedown. I fought it as best I could, trying to crawl up onto his back, but he kept driving like he was supposed to, even steering me away from the out-of-bounds circle for once. He worked his way up to my thighs and waist until I fell back on my butt. Finally I had to roll over on my stomach or be pinned.

Wild Bill was right there. "*Two*! Two-point reversal, Red!"

Five-five.

The last forty seconds of the match Malcom and I finally did our wrestling demo. I tried everything I could think of to escape, only to be pulled back or swept out or rolled over by Malcom as he countered and attacked in turn. We did drills: sitouts, reversals, and arm rolls on each other in a smooth allegro rhythm, like exotic dancers. The crowd counted down the last ten seconds out loud while we each rolled in and out of a fireman's carry, then hung on the mat in a cradle at "five" that I kicked out of as the crowd reached "one."

Wild Bill was in a dance of his own beside us, a much choppier dance than ours as he ducked and bent, hopped over us and then moved suddenly to the other side. He was on the mat on his chest now, by our faces. He was ready to signal a near-fall for Malcom – three points. It was close but I thought we'd rolled out of it in time. He looked at me, then at Malcom. We stared back. We both held our breath. Then Wild Bill stood up, raised both his arms in the air and blew his whistle.

It was over.

Malcom and I untangled ourselves and lay there for a moment. He got up first and reached down to help me up. Then we each took our starting positions on either side of the warrior logo. We reached in and shook hands. Wild Bill grabbed the arms that we shook with and raised them both high. "Tie!" he said to the crowd on one side. He turned us so we would all three face the other side of the gym. "Tie!" he repeated.

Bill hung on to our arms for a few more seconds, didn't let us go. "Ain't gonna be no friggin' tie-breaker," he said so that only we could hear him.

Then he let go of us and Malcom and I man-hugged and grunted at each other. Kelly came out onto the mat and threw my arm over his shoulder and snaked his other arm around my waist, fake-stumbling under my weight and pinching his nose shut with his free hand. Danny Brown met Malcom in the middle of the mat and followed him off. People were already up out of their seats, heading in a semi-orderly wave for the gym exits, joshing around now, even laughing. There was only one double exit door on the main floor; people left in a single thick row, bobbing out into the hall to their next class. Coach Germano and Coach Dimitri stood at the exit on the third-floor landing of the balcony above the bleachers. Dimitri had his arm draped over Germano's shoulders. Their faces were close together.

As I panned the gym I saw Jarrard. He sat there quietly on the polished wooden bleachers with his chin on his hand, staring at me. Everyone around him had already filed out of the gym. Then Jarrard stood up, pointed at me again for what seemed forever, pointed at me all the way until he went through the door and left the gym himself, finally turning away and shuffling out slowly.

Malcom and I got a pass from practice that night from Coach Germano. I should have celebrated, maybe – but I just took a nap instead.

There weren't any more sports demonstration assemblies at West that year. Or any year since then, come to think about it.

WHY I'M HERE

"On an experimental basis." That's how they worded it. And they scheduled it for seven in the frigging morning – for graduating seniors only, honors students too, no less. When we heard Stokes had gotten permission from the school board to teach philosophy to us, we wondered what he had over them. How much it cost him. Rumor was that the school board thought that Plato was a planet, but they approved Stokes's request anyways. *Ideas of Man*, the class was called. Literature 352.

Stokes was a small man with a wiry build, five-foot-two, tops. If you saw him in the hall between classes, you might mistake him for a student, a freshman probably, a 98-pound wrestler or a long-distance runner, maybe. Except for the goatee.

I met Stokes that first day of the *Ideas of Man* class, in early January 1972. I was the fourth one of us to attend Rockford's West High. I'd already gone further in school than anyone else in my family. My sister got in trouble from (we think) Bobby Holland across the street and couldn't finish her senior year; she's never said who it was for sure because she was afraid me or my dad would go whip his ass. My dad got kicked out of West in 1950 for riding his big Indian motorcycle through the halls. It's not real clear whether he was ever actually enrolled as a student or not – they kicked him out anyways. My mom, in 10th grade at the time, quit school to marry my dad. Seventeen years later they'd had enough bickering and fighting. It was fun while it lasted, my mom always said, twisting her mouth tight in that way she had. It lasted while it was fun, my dad said, laughing and grinning broadly. Last time I saw him.

* * *

That first day of *Ideas of Man* Stokes sailed into class clutching a pile of books against his chest like a girl. He wore baggy khaki slacks, a loose tie, no suit coat, and rolled-up sleeves on his long-sleeve shirt – but they still came almost to his wrist. His clothes hung on his petite frame like rags on a scarecrow. His long black hair was combed straight back and hung over his shirt collar. Close up you could see specks of gray at his temples.

He heaved the books up on the teacher's desk because he wasn't tall enough to just let go of them. When he set down the books he dropped his lunch bag on the floor. He fussed loudly about his yogurt spilling and dove to get his dropped lunch bag. None of us even knew what yogurt was. I glanced at my practice partner, Kelly, the 175-pounder, and we just shook our heads.

Stokes ignored the large central desk and padded chair up by the blackboard, the traditional teacher's sanctuary, and came around to the first seat in the middle row (we'd all been warned ahead of time not to sit there). He flung the desk around and faced us: Still staring at us, he put his butt on the desktop, his feet in the seat, his elbow on his knee, and his chin on that fist. He let loose a big sigh.

We hushed each other and waited, hands clasped together on our desktops. But then he cocked his head back and forth like a chicken and squinted and scowled at us, shaking his long black hair. Finally someone snickered. Someone else laughed. Then we all laughed. Then Stokes smiled even more, too, his huge brown eyes dancing.

"This here's *Ideas of Man*," he said in an exaggerated TV-Western drawl. "You all in the right place?"

We must have looked like a flock of little birds in the nest begging for worms, our heads were bobbing so much.

"What'd you say?" he yelled, raising his voice and widening his eyes. He put his hand up to his ear. "What'd you say? Speak!"

If he hadn't acted so funny we would have been scared. We looked at each other, raised our eyebrows, shrugged our shoulders, shook our heads, stared down at our desks. One of the girls up front, Janey Thompson, the cheerleader and class president, raised her hand.

"Yes, Miss Thompson?"

The room was suddenly quiet. Magic had happened. We were

shocked he knew her name. Without using a seating chart. Most of the teachers at West could barely remember your name even with the seating chart held out in front of them.

Janey recovered quickly. "Sir?"

"I'm no 'sir,' I'm just Ernie, Ernie Stokes," he said, getting up off the desk. He started pacing back and forth across the front of the room. "Why was it you raised your hand just then, Miss Thompson?"

"Well, sir… Mr. Stokes. Sir. You asked us if we were in the right place, I think, and… you know, I'm pretty sure I'm like, in the right place. Here. Actually. Today. This hour. I think. Sir."

She clasped her hands in front of herself again, wiggled her ass deeper into her seat, smiled and showed her dimples proudly.

Stokes stopped pacing. He put his hand back on his chin, his finger up to his cheek. "Hmmm. You 'think,' do you?" She nodded her head quickly. "Hasn't anyone ever told you that it's dangerous to *think*, Miss Thompson? Especially in a place like *this*?"

Janey nodded back, her golden curls bouncing, shining.

"But you do it anyways. Good for you, Miss Thompson. How about you, Mr. Miller?" he said, turning his head from Janey to me, trying to look mean. "You in the right place, Mr. Miller?"

I was sitting sideways in my seat with my feet stuck out across the aisle. The snow from my work boots had made a little puddle there where it had melted from the treads and run down. "I'm where my schedule says I should be right now, anyways, Sir Ernie."

I caught Kelly's eye. He smirked.

"So according to that dark and murky alternate reality that is your second semester schedule, you *are* in the right place, Mr. Miller. Good for you.

"But is this the right *place* for you, Mr. Miller?" He straightened up, waved a hand. "Why are you *here*, Mr. Miller?" He pointed down at the floor. "In *this* time, in *this* space, at *this* moment?"

I looked around. Took a few seconds to answer. "Sounded a lot better to me than a 7:00 a.m. gym class."

We all laughed. And that's the way it started. Our little warm-up, our little ritual. Every day Stokes came in and asked in class, "Why are you here?" Sometimes, most times, he called on some-

Baffled

one, just to make sure everyone got a chance. Always people raised their hands. Kelly was here for comic relief, his own and everyone else's. Janey Thompson was here to make the world a better place to live, she said. Dave Leske, the greaser quarterback with his styled hair, paisley shirts, creased slacks and Cuban-heeled boots, said he was here to please all the lonely, disappointed women in Rockford.

For the longest time, Walker, the only black kid in our class, wouldn't answer when Stokes called on him. "Mr. Walker, it's your turn," Stokes tried again one day. "Why are you here?"

We waited for a few seconds, then a minute. Some of the class started getting antsy. Kelly blew his nose loudly into an oversized red-and-black farmer's hanky. He got the eye from Ernie. "Take your time, Jamal," Stokes said, quieting us and sitting on a desk nearby. "We care about what you have to say. We want to know what you think."

Another minute passed. Jamal muttered something. "What was that, Mr. Walker? I couldn't hear you," Stokes said, gently.

"I'm here to learn how to tell the truth to people that don't want to hear it."

Stokes blinked, swallowed. "Very good, Mr. Walker. Very good, indeed."

* * *

Stokes asked "Why are you here?" every day in class, first thing, until everyone in the class had had a chance to answer. Then we started over. The unwritten rule was that nobody gave the same answer twice. "Why are *you* here?" started every class, every day that spring with Stokes.

Our *Ideas of Man* class quickly settled into a comfortable but lively routine. First we read a few pages in the book about the great philosophers and what they'd thought: Plato. Epictetus. Immanuel Kant. Nietsche. The Uphanishads. St. Thomas Aquinas. Then we talked it over until we could make some sense out of what they said. Then we wrote a few words about what it meant to us, today – if anything, and handed it in for Stokes to grade. We'd get back comments in the margins like "Yeah!" "Yippee!" "You got it, man!" One time we all got ink stamps on our papers from one of those cereal box toys – one for "good," two for "great." Another time we got shiny gold stars from the VFW fund-raiser. Once we got Sierra Club stickers with pictures of endangered species on them – Kelly had to ask what an "endangered species" was.

* * *

That year I wrestled 167 varsity. It was a lot better than the year before, when I had to make 155 every week in case Van Kettel, the senior, didn't, just so the team wouldn't forfeit a weight class. If he made weight, he wrestled 155 and I wrestled 167, twelve pounds lighter than my opponent. I was strong from working so much – I'd worked for a landscaping company since I was thirteen. My boss got a winter contract shoveling clinkers out of the coal-burning schools' chimneys and boiler rooms to keep us busy, dirty nasty work that nobody else wanted. He welded iron strips to the bottoms of our scoop shovels so they wouldn't wear out as fast – but then they also weighed about twenty pounds empty. Toughen you up quick, he'd said. I could mop the mat with Kelly and probably anyone else at practice, except maybe Dempster, our heavyweight; but I got too nervous at the meets. I won about half my matches that year, good but not great. I was a hip-lock and arm-drag specialist, Coach Germano said – "my 'take 'em down and squeeze 'em' man."

One match I remember all too well was against a tall, skinny, long-legged guy from Jefferson. He had to be six-foot-five or more; I'm six foot and I had to reach up to lock up with him. He was so skinny I was surprised he weighed enough to be a 167-pounder. The first round I took him down and threw him around the mat for the whole two minutes. The second round I took top position, then tight-waisted him hard but couldn't stick him. Last round, I figured I'd stand up and escape from him and then throw him around some more; but he stuck his legs into me when I stood up, and I couldn't shake him off. He reached across my back and grabbed my arm while our legs were twisted together, then threw my arm behind his neck and arched his back – a guillotine hold. Coach and Kelly were screaming at me from the side of the mat – "Bridge, Miller! Bridge!" – as I rolled over and got stretched out across the guy's long skinny frame like I was on a Medieval rack. It was all I could do to arch my neck and pivot on my forehead or one shoulder to keep from getting pinned. The guy let me up a couple times to roll over after that, but then he just threw his legs into me again and rang up more points. In the end I didn't get pinned, but I lost 12-10 in a decision.

It was a long walk home that night, having to listen to Kelly go over both my early dominance and my late mistakes again and again and again. "What'd you learn tonight, Muscle Boy? Huh?" He laughed. "Why were you *there*, Mr. Miller?" he mimicked. "Why were you *there*?"

The next day I got to *Ideas of Man* class early. I couldn't sleep anyways – my neck was sore and I had a wicked mat burn about the size of a half-dollar on my right cheek and shoulder from having my face dragged under that guy. Stokes was already in the room. He came over to where I sat and eased into the desk in front of me, facing me.

"Tough night?" he said.

"You could say that."

I was afraid he was going to make me explain it all to him, but then he said, "I saw Coach Germano in the teacher's lounge this morning. He said you got out-smarted last night, but put up a hell of a fight anyway."

My head shot up when he said this and our eyes met, but then Janey and a few of the other girls came in. "Live and learn," he said, standing up, and started to walk away.

"That's what Kelly said." I laughed.

Stokes grinned back at me. "Ah yes, one more deep philosophical insight from our dear Mr. Kelly."

It hurt when I laughed. "Ouch," I said, touching the edge of my mat burn. And we laughed some more.

"What?" said Janey, looking down at her sweater, her skirt, her shoes, then at her arms. "What?"

* * *

The first time our comfortable class routine was interrupted in *Ideas of Man,* we were studying Thomas Hobbes. Stokes was trying hard, but he couldn't get anyone to disagree with Hobbes' basic premise.

"Really, people," he said, frustrated. He held the book at eye-level: " '…where every man is enemy to every man' – he flipped some pages – "where there's 'continual fear and danger of violent death'" – he flipped some more pages – " 'And the life of man: solitary, poor, nasty, brutish and short'? " He looked up, closed the book. "You all believe that the natural state of man is chaos – *war*?"

Yeah, sure, we mumbled.

"You believe that? In your heart of hearts you believe that?" His eyes were wide. He staggered. *"Why* do you believe that?"

We all assumed the position then and stared down at our desks. Finally Dave Leske raised his hand.

"Yes, Mr. Leske?"

"Take a gander," Leske said, sweeping his arm across his desk. "Right here in little ole Rockford, right here in little ole West High. Right here in this classroom." He stopped and flashed his best smile. "We all know what's what, what works around here. If you're strong enough to take it, you take it. If you're strong enough to keep it, you keep it. If you're not, you get it taken away." Our heads bobbed. "That's the way it is, that's the way it's always been, that's the way it'll always be." He crossed his arms. "Just ask Jarrard," he said, and shrugged his shoulders, and we laughed.

We all knew Jarrard. Dave Jarrard was the greaser fullback, Leske's best friend. Everyone here had had their lunch money stolen by big blond Jarrard at one time or other.

Janey blushed. Jarrard was her current boyfriend.

Stokes tished. "Thank you, Mr. Leske, for sharing your thoughts, thoughts that are obviously shared by everyone here. But people," he said, moving to the side, "There really is another way. Can't you see it?"

We all sat there in his gaze. The room was deathly still.

"What if I told you that living Hobbes' way is a life of fear, a life of scarcity, a life of little-ness?" He stepped away from the board. "What if I told you that man doesn't *need* material things, that our first mistake a long, long time ago was building our world around 'things' that we think we need, things to keep and to guard and to hoard – like Mr. Leske says?" Stokes pulled himself up as high as his five-foot frame would let him.

"I don't know, Ernie," I said after a bit, breaking the silence. "That sounds pretty good, but it's kind of *Fantasy Island* from where I'm sitting." We all laughed nervous laughs, then the bell rang, and we students hustled out. We left Stokes staring at the blackboard, shaking his head, looking sad.

* * *

The second time our classroom routine was interrupted, Stokes did it himself – he brought a new book to class not long after our "Thomas Hobbes" fiasco. This day he sat cross-legged on his desk and just looked out at us.

"Pay attention, people," he said after a minute, and it took us awhile to get quiet because we thought he was kidding; it was hard to tell with Stokes. "This book," he said, holding up a slim blue-and-white volume in one hand, "is written by a man named Richard Bach. It's called *Jonathan Livingston Seagull*."

"Yeah, so?" Kelly said, sprawled in his desk.

Stokes stared him down in the midst of a few giggles. "We're going to take the next few days off and read it. Out loud."

The room burst into snickers: "What – story time?" "Bedtime stories?" "I gotta go home and get my blankie." "I want my teddy bear – can I have a Hall Pass, Mr. Stokes?"

"It'll be my gift to you this week," Stokes said, unshaken. "Because you need to hear it. Not just read it. *Hear* it."

I looked over at Kelly. We rolled our eyes. But then we listened as Stokes read in his smooth, calm voice. We heard the story of a seagull who got tired of fighting for food every day and decided instead to be the best flier ever. All week Stokes read to us through first hour, and we sat as entranced as kindergarteners. Jonathan went away and found a great teacher and got better and better at flying and then came back to teach all the other seagulls how to fly better and be free.

And then too soon Ernie was done reading the book and when he finished, when he turned that last page and shut the book softly, we all just sat, still and silent, until the bell rang.

***

One Tuesday in March not long after Stokes read to us, Dave Leske made a pass at Danny Brown's girlfriend. Wasn't much of a pass, Dave said later, when he could talk again.

Danny Brown was black. Dave Leske was white. At West High in 1972, that meant war.

The chase started in the first-floor hallway. I was on my lunch hour when the fight spilled through the cafeteria. First came Leske, flinging chairs behind him as he ran like a wild man. Then Danny Brown and his friends came running close behind like a pack of wolves, hurdling chairs, dodging food, and pushing people out of their way. I tucked two folding chairs under my arm for defense or offense, to fend off flying chairs or throw some myself, I didn't know yet.

Leske ran from the hallway through the lunchroom through the lunch line over a counter and then outside. Danny and his buddies chased after him. One of the lunch ladies yelled at them to *slow the hell down*. The whole thing happened in seconds. I wanted to help Leske, but I froze like everyone else.

When I finally did jump up to help Leske, "Wild Bill" Stoglitis, the boy's P.E. teacher, stopped me at the door. "Back off, Shit-for-Brains," he said, stiff-arming my chest, staring me down. "Sit the hell down right now."

They caught up with Leske a minute later in the teachers' parking lot. In the end he was wheeled off on a gurney with a concussion, bruised ribs, and a broken jaw.

I should have been there.

The next day, Wednesday, Dave Jarrard got all us white guys

together for a march through the halls. We gathered at the parking lot entrance wearing our winter school jackets and wool watchcaps and leather gloves looking tough, and strutted through the first-floor hallways and cafeteria and out again. Thursday, policemen with side-arms and shotguns and dogs were in the school doing weapons checks on the lockers and on all of us. On Friday, by school board policy, the suspended boys came back to school. Not Leske, of course – he was still in the hospital, his jaw wired shut.

Over the loudspeaker that morning Mr. Dimitri the basketball coach announced a prayer meeting "open to everyone," immediately after school. Teachers stood close to their doors, arms crossed, hurrying people on their way. The women teachers looked scared. Coach Germano was assigned a spot in the first-floor hallway where the two corridors met; even he looked a little nervous.

Ten minutes into first hour someone yelled "Fight!" His voice echoed through the hallway. I ran out. Classrooms emptied into the hallway like they were spring-loaded.

The fight was in the southwest stairwell nearest my *Ideas of Man* room, so I was one of the first ones there. The fighters were struggling under the new Vietnam War display, the one that had started in the small shadowbox by the office but was moved to the stairwell last year because by then the memorial had too many wood-and-brass plaques bearing the names of graduates who'd died, and they'd spilled out of the little shadowbox container and spread over nearly three full walls.

Dave Jarrard gritted his teeth and grunted through his nose like a pig as he pounded on Danny Brown's back again and again. Spit and snot flew everywhere. A bright red arch of blood was already splattered across the pale green stairwell wall, but it was hard to tell whose it was.

Black and white students alike jammed the stairs. Teachers couldn't get through. Kelly and I held back what people we could to give the fighters room.

Danny Brown was a good athlete and all, but he was losing this street fight to the white boy. Janey Thompson, Jarrard's girl from our class, was in the opposite corner crying, begging for someone to *stop the fight, please, someone stop it.*

Unlike all the screaming people around them, neither fighter said a word. They just grunted like hogs and made short rasping sounds when they breathed.

I could smell the spit and the sweat and the blood from where I stood – rusty, coppery smelling – I could taste it on my tongue. A fast punch from Danny left a long red mark on Jarrard's chest. Jarrard barely flinched and landed a right upper-cut to Danny's gut that doubled him over and lifted him off the floor.

Small as he was, Stokes was the only teacher able to squeeze through all the bodies to get to the fighters. He passed behind me and clipped my knee going by; I almost fell. Jarrard had just driven Danny's head into the banister when Stokes grabbed his arm. Jarrard flung Stokes away without looking back. Stokes scrambled and grabbed Jarrard's arm again and caught his balance. Danny Brown turned and swung blindly. He missed Jarrard but hit Stokes squarely in the face.

The air left the stairwell. Jaws dropped. Eyes flared. Nobody spoke. Nobody moved.

Stokes lay stunned. When he finally stood up, blood had trickled down from his nose into his black goatee. He didn't wipe it off. Instead he went to Danny Brown, crumpled on the floor.

"Mr. Brown, you're hurt," he said, down on one knee, offering his hand. "Let me help you."

Jarrard stood over the two of them like a wolf, panting, feet spread shoulder-width apart, hands clenched tight in fists, still churning in small slow circles at his waist. His chest heaved with every breath. His shirt hung open.

Stokes caught his eye. "Mr. Jarrard. Your friend is crying. Help her." He pointed to Janey.

Jarrard just stood there, breathing heavily through his open cut mouth.

"Get out of my way, punks!" Above us on the third floor landing we heard Stoglitis bullying his way through the mob.

"David. Go to Janey. Help her," Stokes said calmly but firmly to Jarrard.

Then Stoglitis burst through the wall of students surrounding the fighters, wielding his rolled-up attendance book like a club, swatting anyone that didn't move out of his way fast enough. "What the hell's going on here?" he screamed. "Stop that shit right now, I say!"

But by then, of course, it *had* stopped. Jarrard spun and grabbed Janey by the hand. The crowd parted to make a path for them and they ducked down the stairs in the other direction. Stokes turned, ready to take Danny Brown to the nurse's office. He helped Danny to his feet and looked at me.

"Move it, Miller," he whispered to me. His hand was warm and gentle on my arm, soft and small.

I shifted to one side. Breathed. "You could have ducked that punch," I said.

Stokes just smiled, his hand still on my forearm. "Maybe. I'm no athlete, like you."

I stood there in the corner of the stairwell with my hands in my pockets and my head hanging down long after everybody else had left. A lady teacher appeared. Home Ec, I think. "It's all over now," she said, grabbing my arm and tugging me toward the stairs. Her voice was firm, but her eyes were wide and her hands shook on my arm. "C'mon, it's all over."

I looked down at her. "Ma'am," I muttered. "Is it *ever* over?"

* * *

We were in lock-down the remainder of that year. The draft lottery came and went in March; I got a high number, Kelly didn't. Leske got a high number too but joined the Air Force anyways, I heard. Jarrard joined the Rangers. Danny Brown ended up somewhere in Canada, they say, playing saxophone in a jazz band. Graduation, when it finally came in June, was a solemn affair, with fifty police lining the walls of the auditorium.

I returned to West High School as a Rockford College senior four years later for my student-teaching semester. "You can do better than me," Stokes said when I asked him to be my supervisor. He winked. "Besides, I've already taught you everything I know." Miss Nyman, the department chair whose spot I would eventually take, took me on and let me teach *Siddhartha* to her junior honors class.

Years after that, at our school district's annual party for the Rockford retirees, I pulled an old *Ideas of Man* book out of a plastic Ziploc bag, the book from what turned out to be the first and only philosophy class ever offered at West. "Property of District 205" was still stamped in bold black ink on the inside cover. I took the book out of the bag and held it out to Stokes.

"Stole it," I told him.

He took it from me and turned it over in his hands several times, slowly. "Good man."

His hair was all gray now, even his goatee. But his eyes were the same brilliant hazel brown, the same dancing eyes that I'd first seen back in 1972, almost fifteen years earlier. He wrote with a flourish on the inside cover and handed the book back to me. Then he smiled and moved away to greet some others. I waited until I got home that night to read it.

Mr. Miller, he wrote, *a guy who knows why he's here.*

My wife found me the next morning crunched into the bottom bunk with our son and daughter, our arms and legs tangled together like three dancers frozen in mid-leap of some exotic move. She took a picture of us that still sits on the shelf above my writing desk – next to my signed copy of *Ideas of Man*.

GARAGE SALE

"Now where we going?"

"Right here," Jeff said, slowing to turn the old pale-blue Chevy pickup truck at the next street. "There's a garage sale just down here."

"I didn't think you even knew what a garage sale was."

He looked over and smiled weakly. "Got somewhere better to go?"

Jenny shrugged. She blew air through her lips loudly. "Okay with me," she said. "I'm just along for the ride."

Jeff double-clutched to keep second gear from grinding on the downshift, a trick he'd learned plowing snow off driveways and parking lots last winter. He would've been working this weekend too, a side job, except he'd decided at the last minute that he better be with her instead of out at some farm laying shingles. There were groceries to buy and rent to pay and, since last fall, his student loans to pay off.

And now there was the baby.

Jenny settled back in her seat and folded her arms across her bulging stomach. She was eight and a half months pregnant. Her hair felt greasy all the time, she felt sick to her stomach constantly, and her boobs were swelled up and sore and hurt when they bounced too much in the truck.

Jeff took the turn fast and jammed the stick into second. This morning's round of yelling was about whether she'd go back to work after the baby was born, or stay home and raise him in what she thought was the "right" way. Again.

Jeff argued for the extra money: "We need your check to make ends meet, to save for the house."

She started out arguing for herself and the baby: "Do you really want someone else raising our baby?"

"We need your check to make ends meet," he said, slower and louder this time.

This made her quiet for a minute, then she said: "Do you really want my *mom* to raise our kid? Think about it."

This ticked him off. He pressed harder on the gas.

"I hate it when you drive like this," she said. He gunned the engine one last time, slowed down, thought maybe then it was over. But then she cleared her throat loudly and said: "It'll cost more to have me work because we'll need a babysitter and a second car, you know."

She said this casually, like everybody in the world knew this. But he hadn't thought of that. He drove even faster than before, reckless even, and slammed the gears even harder.

They were quiet for ten minutes, smoldering together in the dingy old cab of the pickup. When he turned one last corner, he caught a glance of her in the passenger seat. She was straightening her legs and stretching them out so she could look at her feet – ignoring him. She turned her feet from side to side. To Jeff, she seemed a little surprised to see that those fat little appendages were, indeed, her feet down there at the ends of her legs. Huh.

They found the house they were looking for at 502 Shaw, just like the cardboard garage sale sign tacked on the telephone pole said. Bright yellow-and-black streamers had been strung across the yard like so much police tape at a crime scene. Five-oh-two was a corner house with an alley in back. Jeff parked out front on Shaw Street. He got out of the pickup, walked a ways then put a foot on the bumper and leaned his chest into his raised knee, stretching his back and hamstring while studying the house. It took Jenny a minute or two to crawl out her side of the truck by herself. He let her.

She joined him in front of the truck and they stood there, silent. Jenny counted dandelions by the curb and shifted her weight back and forth on her swollen feet.

"Well?" he said, looking away from her at the house.

"Well what?"

"You see anybody?"

"I don't see anybody."

"*Someone* must have set up these balloons and hung that sign up."

Jenny sighed. "So are they open or not?"

"How should I know? I've never been to one of these things before."

"There's usually someone around to tell you."

"I don't see anybody."

"There's usually someone around to tell you."

"I *said* I don't see anybody around. Not yet." Jeff finally looked at her. "So I guess we might as well go in and find out?"

"In where?"

"In there."

"In there *where*?"

He rolled his eyes and stretched his neck before answering. "In there – *somewhere*."

"Somewhere *where*?"

"I don't know!" he said, throwing his arms in the air, standing straight and then moving away from the truck. "I just said I've never been to one of these things. I thought *you* were the expert on everything?" He walked away quickly, looked both ways when he got to the sidewalk that ran in front of the house, hesitated, then headed up the sidewalk that wrapped around the side of the house. He waved toward the house without glancing back at her. "This way, I guess!"

The homes on Shaw Street were old sprawling brick and stucco single-family houses built before the Depression, back when this was the ritzy side of town. No aluminum or vinyl siding to be found here. They walked down the sidewalk at the side of the house by a slew of daffodils and felt a coolness as they went between 502 and the house next to it. Jeff noted that wood-framed screens hung from their hooks on only half the windows on the side of the house they walked past. Two rectangular stacks of frames about eight deep each leaned up against the side of the house. One stack was screens, the other stack was storm windows. Owner must have been in the middle of changing them over this morning, Jeff thought. Off with the storms, on with the screens. Made sense. One of those jobs you did on a Saturday in spring if you owned a house.

He stopped and looked back, hesitating. "Shouldn't we have run into someone by now?" Jenny had her arms folded in front of her again, shivering slightly in the early morning air. She pulled her sweater tighter around her shoulders, knowing it was hopeless to try to button the front, even the top button. She didn't like roaming around in a stranger's yard and her face showed it.

"We probably should have seen someone by now," Jeff said again, louder. He kept walking. Jenny lagged several feet behind him. "There," he said. "I think I see someone. There, in back." He hurried down a set of cement steps, pushed through the back service door of the garage, and nearly fell over when he entered suddenly into the darkness. Jenny followed him slowly. If he had looked back he would have laughed at the way she clutched the lead pipe railing and waddled down the three steep steps one at a time.

But he didn't look back; he plunged instantly from the bright outdoor sunshine to the total darkness in the back corner of the garage and had to stop to orient himself. He froze where he was, afraid that if he kept going he would fall or run into something. The sweet smells of dirt, cut grass, rubber hoses and a trace of gasoline and something that made him think of mothballs filled his mouth and nostrils before his eyes could tell him anything. In the meantime, Jenny made it to the doorway and pushed past him, going slower than he did but seeing more, sooner, because of it.

First she saw another shorter set of cement steps with a small landing came off the service door inside the garage. Below them long tables were piled with dishes, pans, trinkets and clothes, lots of clothes. Racks the length of the garage held clocks and radios and tools and gadgets. Shelves on the walls overflowed with knickknacks. Neat, high stacks of folded clothes sat on many tables, so high that they had toppled over in several places. There closer to the front, closer to the tables, the smell of mothballs overpowered the smell of pounded dirt. It looked like someone was sorting things for moving, but hadn't put the stuff in boxes yet.

They'd been here five minutes, and still hadn't seen anybody else.

Jenny moved forward deeper into the garage, but Jeff remained where he was, in the back corner on the small cement landing by the service door where they had come in. His eyes finally adjusted to the dim light in back. The garage was huge. The big front doors were open wide, sunlight pouring in, but not reaching all the way to the back. His eyes slipped quickly over and past the tables and racks and piles of clothes. What he saw first was the way the garage was built. The large front doors of the garage, like the windows and screens on the house, were wooden, made up of solid two-by-eight planks, not plywood. His builder's eye also saw that a doubled-up two-by-twelve header spanned the opening for the two sliding doors, and was tied in to two round six-inch posts on either side set inside the doorframe. When closed the doors would have come together tightly in the center and shut out nearly all the light. His eyes moved up. The joists supporting the roof were two-by-fours on edge. The nailers on the roof and studs on the walls were on sixteen-inch centers, not weaker two-foot centers like most houses built today. This garage was built better than most houses you see nowadays, Jeff mused.

"Look at this, Jenny," he called out. "Do you see this?"

"Oh, I see it all right!" she squealed, moving quickly from one pile of clothes to another. A woman in her condition shouldn't have been able to move that fast, but there she was, Jeff thought. He stared at her for a second, thought about telling her that that's not what he meant, but then didn't.

"Look at this stuff, Jeff! Look. There're baby clothes galore here. Infant stuff, just what we need. Stuff you don't get at the hospital. Stuff you need just after, while the baby's growing so fast… And over here," as she lumbered across a small aisle, "here's toddler onesies and T-shirts and blankets and – and just *everything* we need! They're mostly old but they're clean, hardly worn, like new, even," she continued.

Jeff moved from where he had been admiring the garage to stand beside her. He nodded his head to let her know he'd heard her, but Jenny didn't notice. A couple of other women had pulled up in the driveway on the alley side of the garage and were getting out of their cars. Jeff heard them talk about a "Come on in!" sign hung on the side of the garage facing the alley. Jenny was too busy going through the piles of garments to notice, holding up shirts, then pants, then blankets, showing him, turning but not turning, moving from one table to another quickly, back and forth, draping things she wanted over her forearms and shoulders.

He stood watching her shop. Her face glowed, bright and soft. Her brown hair glimmered suddenly as it caught a beam of sunlight through the open doors and threw it back at him. His knees buckled beneath him. He caught himself. She looked so serious, going through those clothes, examining each item carefully, tossing it up and back like a human tumble dryer, throwing one piece over her shoulder and another one over arm or to some other pile on the table that only she knew the purpose for. He hadn't seen Jenny this happy in months. He hadn't realized he missed seeing her this way so much until just then.

"Jenny."

"What?" she said, not looking up.

He wanted to tell her what he was thinking, but said instead, "Where is everybody?"

She stopped in midair, gripping a rainbow-colored 18-month toddler top with black ponies sewn across the chest. "Right," she said, after a second, frowning. "I don't know. But you know what? I don't really care right now, either. Look at all this stuff, Jeff."

"Someone should be here. We need to find someone."

"Fine," she said. "Fine, Jeff. If you're so worried about it, why don't *you* go find someone, then? Just be back in time to pay!" She giggled, then surged forward to attack the next table of goodies.

Jeff left the garage and re-traced their steps all the way back to the pickup. Then he walked completely around the house twice. Still nobody. He found himself standing at the back door, on the opposite side of the house from the stacks of windows and screens they'd seen when they first came, the side furthest from the garage. He knocked softly on the outside door, politely at first, then louder. Finally he pounded on the door three times. Hard. No one answered.

Jeff took a deep breath, swallowed, and opened the outer screen door. A piece of construction paper sat between the doors, out of sight – it must have fallen there. He stooped to pick it up. It had a piece of blue painter's tape stuck across the top. Neat, thick cursive in a straight line which said, "Come on in!" That blue tape never does hold when you want it to, he thought. He reached down and despite the note he was slightly surprised when the handle to the large lead-glass entry door inside turned freely. Didn't these people know how dangerous it was to leave your doors unlocked? "Hello?" he yelled. "Hello! Is anybody here? Anybody home? Hel-lo-o!"

No choice, he thought. He took a last look around outside, sighed, set his shoulder against the door and walked into the house.

The inside of 502 Shaw was solid in a way the rough timber-and-stucco outside wasn't: Warm colors. Cut-glass and crystal. Smooth honey-colored polished hardwood. The house, unlike the garage, was spotless, uncluttered, and nearly shone with cleanliness and light, except for a skillet and spatula soaking in the sink. The lemony-tart smell of Murphy's Oil wood soap hung thick but sweet at the doorway. As Jeff walked further into the house he saw eggs and bacon for two set out on the kitchen table. Small portions were laid out on white china plates, one piece of bacon for one, three for the other. Crystal fruit cups sat next to silver forks and flowered plates with toast. There were even small white doilies under the salt-and-pepper shakers. He reached out and touched a slice of raisin toast. It was cold and hard.

The dining room was just off the kitchen. It sat majestic and dark in its presence, in contrast to the bright and colorful kitchen. Eight larger lace placemats and settings were laid out over the beige-cotton table cloth on an oak table that took up most of the spacious room, as if company was coming but hadn't arrived yet.

Jeff walked slowly through the dining room to the steps leading up the stairs.

"Hello?" He called out again, gripping the rounded banister, then went up a step. The walls were papered in white and purple lilacs with green swirling branches that went up the stairwell. Family photos hung from the walls all the way to the top of the stairs. The first picture he saw was of a young man in a letter sweater. Football player, it looked like from the shape of the pin stuck on the letter. Then a lady. A girl, really. She had a big bright smile full of teeth. There were several frames of her; she appeared mostly in outdoor settings, even some rugged-looking camping trips in the mountains. She became a mother young, a sideways shot of her in front of an old Ford four-door told him. There was the baby, first as an infant in her arms, held high to show off, here in a baseball uniform playing catch with his dad on the street outside, later, higher up the stairs as a football player in high school, then as a soldier, a Marine from the looks of the uniform. Jeff glanced at the pictures laid out in front of him one by one like he might glimpse scenes through a car window going down the highway, not really conscious of the stairs themselves as he glided upwards.

He stopped on the last step and looked back, feeling like he had missed something. He took a quick inventory. After the soldier pictures there weren't any more pictures of the son, or any other picture either, for that matter. Other pictures might have been missing, but then Jeff noticed there wasn't any fading on the wall where other frames might have been, so he figured that there simply weren't any more pictures to be hung here. The last picture hanging on the wall, a shadow-box, really, was a small blue star on a white cloth background in a red-bordered square, but he didn't know what that meant.

At the top of the stairs was another large wooden door, what must have been a bedroom. Jeff paused before going in; there was no welcome note hung with blue tape here. He thought about yelling again, thought better of it, took a deep breath, knocked once, then pushed the door open.

The morning's brilliant light poured into the room through a sheer-curtained window facing east. There, on top of the tight-knit sea-green comforter on the bed, lay the man and woman in the pictures. They were much older than they were in the pictures on the wall, but they were the same ones, Jeff was certain.

The two lay side-by-side with their heads close together. His bristly white mustache was trimmed neatly and stood out starkly against his tanned face. He wore pressed gray slacks, a checkered white and blue long-sleeve shirt with cuff links, suspenders, a tie, and shiny black wingtip shoes. The lady's short gray hair was done up in tight curls. Bright red lipstick stood out against her wrinkled skin, but her face glowed pale in the morning sunlight. Her hands had been folded neatly across her chest, fingers entwined over her heart. She wore an ankle-length, shiny silk nightgown and robe, all white, and black slippers with silver trim. A clear plastic mask and hose hung idly over the hook on the oxygen tank standing by her at her side of the bed. The attached respirator, like everything else in the room now, was silent. Jeff noticed that the bottoms of the lady's slippers were smooth, not a scratch on them, like they'd never been worn.

He moved, slow and quiet, across the room, easing himself the few feet toward them. The man lay slightly on his side, his right arm draped across her waist, his left hand under her shoulder next to him. A glass tumbler had dropped from his hand and lay next to her on her far side, propping up a couple of his fingers.

Jeff picked the glass up from the bed and sniffed. The sweet almond smell confirmed what he already knew. He stood over the bed and held his hand against the side of their throats, first him, then her, looking for a pulse like he'd seen them do on TV. Just to be sure, he held his hand in front of their noses, but he didn't feel any breath.

He went back to the stairs, and returned with the framed photograph of the young family with the old Ford and the new baby.

Jeff picked up the old man's arm. It was heavier than he thought it would be. He moved the arm so that the calloused right hand lay comfortably across the front of her hip and middle of her waist. It wasn't exactly the same way he'd found them, but it seemed right to him now. Better, even. He wedged the photograph carefully, facing up, between the old man's arm and the old woman's waist. He breathed deeply, then held his breath to settle his pounding heart. He watched the dust motes float in the sunlight in the silence. He took the glass off the bed, backed out the door softly, and pulled the door shut slowly until the cylinder clicked loudly in the lock plate.

Jeff returned to the garage, dizzy and weak. He took slow small deliberate steps all the way down the stairs and out the house and across the yard. He found Jenny going through yet another pile of clothes in the garage. More people had come, a dozen now, maybe. He watched quietly while one woman looked around, shrugged her shoulders, left a couple of dollars under an old coffee cup, got into her car with her two large piles of clothes, and left quickly without looking back.

"Look at this stuff, Jeff!" Jenny had seen him. She looked like some sort of fat shopping-mall scarecrow with five sets of baby clothes hanging from her arms and one shoulder. "How did these people know we were coming? How did they *know*? " She giggled again and put her hand to her mouth, happy.

Jeff stood still, silent, gripping the glass in his hand at his side, unable to speak.

THE SUM OF ALL FEARS

He sat on the front porch until the sun broke just over the treetops, then got up and climbed the stairs to their bedroom. It was deathly quiet there, and still dark. He slipped into his side of the bed, and watched and listened to make sure she was still breathing. His own breathing was louder than hers for a minute or two, until his heart settled.

Finally he brushed the side of her arm softly with his fingertips. She shivered, then pulled away.

"Don't touch me."

HER: I grew up on a little farm about ten miles west of Rockford, Illinois. On what they call "farmettes" nowadays. We moved out there from town when I was in grade school, when I only had five other brothers and sisters. Thanks to my devout Irish Catholic parents, I went from youngest to middle child in record time.

My dad worked ten hours a day at the Manning factory in town, then came home and worked until dark on the farm "just to feed all you damn kids," he always said. We always thought he worked so much just so he could avoid mom – but what did we know? They must have spent <u>some</u> time together in order to make us twelve kids. When he was done working for the day he sat in the garage in summer or in the basement in winter with his work shirt still on but unbuttoned, the one with "Karl" over the pocket, and drank beer and chewed his snuff until he fell asleep sitting up. But every morning like clockwork somehow he'd be up and out again by 6:00 a.m. to do it all again. He didn't say a lot, especially to my mom; he didn't have the patience for errors or the time for any feelings; I never even saw him cry, even when my little brother Jody and two little nephews Zane and Eddy got killed in the house fire that December. He just drank more. The boys did most of the outside chores, except when we raised a 4-H animal ourselves or when we all picked the caterpillars off the bean plants; so it was the boys that took the brunt of his anger most of the time. But he wasn't above *smacking one of us girls when we needed it, either, especially when we had boyfriends around.*

My mom was a good Irish Catholic girl who was great at having babies and being needed. She paid all her attention to the baby of the family, whoever that happened to be at the time; the rest of the mothering and household duties went to me and my sisters. When Mom ran out of her own babies, she took in foster infants so that she would always have a baby around. There were too many bodies to feed and clothe, too little time, too few hands to do everything that needed doing, even when all of us worked hard.

We rode the bus and went to school, did our homework and did our chores. We fiercely maintained the appearances of the model Catholic family at all times and at all costs. We went to church every Sunday, we had big Catholic weddings, and we had lots and lots of kids.

And we all left home the first day we possibly could, and never looked back.

HIM: I grew up on the wrong side of Rockford, and went to all the wrong schools; unless you actually lived on this side of town, then you liked it better because people weren't so stuck up.

I got in fights a lot when I was younger because I looked different. The doctors found out my leg wasn't growing when I was in first grade. Leg perthes, they called it, and I went through grade school in a wheelchair first and crutches next. Then one day in sixth grade they said hey, the x-rays say your leg is growing again. Just like that. No more crutches. No more "Class Cripple."

My leg growing again was like starting over. I buckled down in school, and even though I carried my tough-guy image with me through middle and high school, I got good enough grades and scored high enough on my ACTs to get into Northern Illinois down in DeKalb and got a degree in Accounting.

My parents divorced when I was five and my sister Katie was seven. I don't remember much about that. My mom never remarried; my dad got married a few more times – he said he'd ruined her for other men, and she said he was still trying to find a woman good enough. Mom always complained about money, called me on the carpet whenever Dad didn't pay his child support, which happened a lot, but she always seemed to have nice clothes and perfume and things she needed for her work.

I met Wendy Rittebauer through my neighbor Steve Anderson; he lived down the street from me a little, in between Lamanche's and Cassaro's. I worked for his brother-in-law the landscaper starting when I was thirteen years old for a dollar an hour. I thought I was rich. The trucks rolled down Lawndale, sometimes a red pickup truck, mostly one of the big dump trucks with a tilt-trailer and a Cat in tow, and picked us up for a sod or a tree job on sunny days or clinkers in the winter or a junk job to do on a rainy day. We jumped in the trucks when they went by; they only waited a couple minutes. If we missed them, we didn't work that day.

Dan, the landscaper, used to go pick up the Rittebauer girls for cheap whenever we had a big sod job to do in summer. "All that young pussy around keeps you boys hopping," he'd say to us often; and of course it was true. "I get more out of you boys in one hour when you're mooning all over those Rittebauer girls than I usually get in a whole day otherwise," he'd say, slouched in a bench seat, legs crossed, his dirty hand wrapped around a Gerry's cheeseburger or an orange drink.

The girls would lay the sod, roll it out and make sure it was bumped up tight against the previous roll, and make sure the roots were turned under. Us guys would carry the sod to them, lay it out in rows so that they didn't have to get up to get a roll when they needed it. We paired up pretty quickly, pretty naturally by age, although Wendy's big sisters bossed her around a lot and didn't trust me much, me being a big-city guy, I guess.

My best buddy Sam and I were the odd ones out in the bunch because we went to Rockford schools instead of the podunk farmer schools like Pec or Winnebago they all went to. Sam lived a few blocks down from me on Dresden. We were the big-city hoods on the sod crew, even though we didn't even know any real hoods, except maybe Jarrard. But we didn't say anything to make them think any different, either.

So when Wendy and I started dating, I sort of knew their dad Karl, and he sort of knew me, though we'd never met before then. He only knew whatever the girls had told him, if they talked.

Doug was my knight in shining armor. He was my first everything. He swept me off my feet, got me off that farmette. We met through Dan North and his landscaping business; Dan lived about a mile down Trask Bridge Road from me, where we would take turns babysitting his kids.

Dan would pick us up every once in a while to work, too. Doug worked for Dan, and my dad hired us out to lay sod to make a little money and make it easier on him – although he didn't seem to cut back his work hours much at all. It was like we were just slaves of his that he'd hire out to the neighbor for a job now and then. But it was always outdoors work, so it beat babysitting, and it sure as heck beat staying at home where all you got to do was work. If we wanted to work for Dan we have our own chores done and give Dad half of everything we made – for our savings accounts. Those were the terms. We thought that this was a good deal. Especially since we could use our savings to get away. Especially since he didn't let our brothers work for Dan, kept them to himself. "Can't spare 'em," he'd tell Dan whenever he asked. "Take the girls, they're strong and healthy. And smarter than the boys, to boot. You let me know if they don't work hard, I'll straighten 'em out."

I graduated from high school and didn't know what to do with myself – I'd never thought that far ahead. Dad got me a job at the factory doing piecework on the presses, a slimy, oily job. Mom was going to charge me $300 a month to stay there in my own room. Can you believe it? And I would've still had to do all my chores! But then Doug saved me by getting me out of the house; I moved in with him in our first little apartment down on Horseman. At the time Doug was going to college; he worked part-time for Dan when he could on weekends, and worked as a bouncer at a pool hall and pizza parlor at nights or winter weekends when Dan didn't have any work.

I wanted kids bad, maybe to prove to my mom I could do better than she ever did with kids, so we did. We had Belle first, then Joey a couple years later. Doug got a job right out of college with Sundstrom, the large aerospace engineering firm in Rockford. That's when we moved out of our rented farmhouse we'd moved into in Harrison, up by Sugar River Forest Preserve, and moved into town into our own place.

It was cheaper for me to stay home than to work, Doug said, when you figured in the extra gas and clothes and babysitting we'd need with me working. Besides, I didn't want anybody else raising my kids. Doug's job was great: he made good money, he had good benefits, and he kept getting promoted almost every year. We joined the Y; the kids and I went to classes or swam during the day, Doug came for a "spinning" class after work when he could. The kids had lots of friends and play dates; we celebrated all our birthdays at Chucky Cheese's; our house and yard were full of toys and games and neighbor kids, not kids cooped up on a farm doing chores all day with your brothers and sisters and with your mom or dad watching over you every second.

Life then was better than I ever imagined it could be.

Looking back, I think things started changing at Ruth's wedding that March.

Rittebauer family affairs were always worth going to, no matter how boring they sounded, because of the ever-present element of surprise: There was no telling how they would turn out. Ruth was Wendy's little sister, two behind her in line for the girls. Because Ruth lived in Atlanta and had come back to her home town to be married, there was an element of reunion to the wedding. All the siblings outdid themselves being extra nice to each other, for once.

The kids and I sat by ourselves at the reception while Wendy sat at the head table with the rest of the wedding party, which was just as well because someone had to help feed the kids. Despite the open keg and free bar the party was pretty stuffy until the disc jockey arrived and started playing old records. People began dancing little by little. Finally Wendy and the sisters had worn out all the men and boys around and began dancing with each other. They acted young and happy on the dance floor then, suddenly released from the years of chores and bickering and too many people living too close together in too small of a space that kept them cautious. They danced until they couldn't dance anymore, until they could hardly stand up. Then they collapsed, sprawled over chairs and across a couple tables, and caught their breath.

Tony Parrello and Tim Rittebauer wandered over with drinks in their hands and sat down among the sisters. Tony and Tim, Wendy's oldest brother by ten years, had been best friends since childhood.

That's when the stories started.

Tony was literally in the midst of it all, sat next to Tim in the center of this family circle, relished his part like an emcee. He and Tim were main characters in many of the stories, so many that an outsider listening in would have thought Tony really *was* Tim's brother. First was the time they took their dates into the "haunted" barn, where they had set up a shotgun to go off and shoot a scarecrow when the closet door opened—and Tim's date fainted. Then the time they lined all the kids up, made them spit on their palms and hold hands, and then made Wendy grab the electric fence so they all got shocked. After that, the time they stole Tim's dad's old Ford and got stopped by the cops heading down to Byron.

The girls hung on their every word, drinking in the stories like a potion; but Wendy especially savored the story-telling. She sat at Tony's elbow, stared up at him and Tim, caught the smiles, rejoiced in the shocked looks of her sisters and the quick asides from Tim or Tony. The men went on and on into the night, story after story. I sat with Tony's wife Marie at a side table, while Joey slept on my shoulder and Belle slumped across my lap. Tony's two boys and three little girls sprawled on or around Marie in various stages of sleep and boredom. Marie herself looked like either a young fifty-five-year-old grandmother or a withering thirty-year-old mother—it was hard for even me to tell. Karl, Wendy's dad, sat over there by us, too, away from the siblings' circle, drinking beer after beer. He'd kicked his shoes off and sat with one foot under him and the other leg up on the chair, so that he rested his drinking arm on his knee. He just shook his full head of gray hair over and over, and with his big hooked nose high, squawked like a parrot on his roost. "Big talkers," he mumbled, smiling. "Big talkers." Then to me he squawked: "Watch your back, boy. Watch your back." And he just smiled and chewed his snuff and drank more beer.

I tried to catch Wendy's eye whenever I could. Pointed to my watch a few times when it got to be after eleven. By then both of our kids were asleep. We finally got out of there around midnight. Karl was still at his perch cawing at whoever passed by.

The next day Wendy was a far cry from the glowing little girl at the center of the circle she had been the night before. She'd suddenly transformed into a fretting, depressed old woman.

Yeah, I think if I had to name one spot, one time things started to change, it was at Ruth's wedding.

My life was suddenly an empty shell, aching to be filled. I felt cheated, scorned, and I didn't even know why. Overnight, everything and everyone around me seemed ordinary, old, boring. The kids. The house. The cars. Doug. Our life together. My life. I couldn't get myself out of bed until two the next afternoon. Doug tried to keep the kids quiet, but they're a man, a five-year old boy and a seven-year old girl. The TV was too loud, they slammed cupboard doors and dishes around trying to be quiet, and it seemed like they went in and out of the house every two minutes. I knew they were trying to be quiet for my sake, but that just made it all worse.

"It's not you," I told Doug when I tried to explain how I felt. "I hate me and everything in my life right now." The feeling stayed with me all that day and then the next. We missed the kids' Guppie and Dolphin swimming lessons at the Y Monday morning and I didn't even care. I could hardly get myself up to fix breakfast by noon, let alone be at some stupid swimming lesson on time.

It finally came to me sometime Thursday: "I missed out on so much growing up. It's not fair!" I said that to Doug during a take-out supper of pepperoni pizza for him and cheese pizza for me and the kids. "I never had a real family, you know, never had any real friends like everybody else does."

"What are you talking about?" Doug said. "You've got us. Me and the kids."

"That's sweet, Doug. But you're my husband and they're my kids. That doesn't count. I need more."

"More? More than this?" He stood up, spread his arms out at the messy kitchen with dishes in the sink and pizza crust and empty pop cans all around and smiled.

"I know what it sounds like. It sounds bad, especially at my age. But is it really so much to want? Is it so much to want the best friend I never had?"

I stood up, I was so excited. "I never had one, never had a best friend or even a good friend growing up. Mom and Dad never let us be in sports or be in a school play, never took us anywhere, never took a turn driving us around like all the other parents did, never let us have anyone over at the house to play, never let us off of that stupid farm of theirs." I paced the room. "I want it all. I deserve it all." I stopped and stood with my hands on my hips, I remember. "Why should I settle for anything less? I want to have my family and I want to have a friend, a real friend I can talk to and do things with." I started crying. "I was always the odd one out. Heck, my family drove away and left me at Great America once. Drove away without me!" I sat down on a stool at the kitchen counter then. "Around here I can't be the friend, I can only be the mom or the wife: the one that fixes supper, does the dishes, takes everybody else places; the wife that washes your underwear, irons your shirts, shares your bed."

I looked Doug in the eye. "Do you know what that means to me? Do you know what I'd give to have a friend I can talk to and be with and do crazy things with?"

Doug said he knew.

He said he knew.

She kept saying it wasn't me, but you had to see her face when she said that. I couldn't help feeling that somehow it *was* me, that it was all my fault, and that she wouldn't be all right. At least not anytime soon.

I couldn't call anyone in her family. They didn't do things like that. There was nobody in my family to call, either; because *we* didn't do things like that. So I called Tim's friend Tony. I explained a little about how Wendy had been so depressed since the wedding, and was so depressed now, and asked him if he thought he could come over and cheer her up. He said he'd be glad to talk to her.

So Tony showed up at the house Sunday afternoon, a week after the wedding. He had little trinkets for the kids: candy, gum, gumball toys. He raved about how great it was for them all to be together again at Ruth's wedding.

I was glad to see him but felt a little odd. "Where's Marie and the kids?" I asked.

"Oh, they had some project due for school tomorrow, had to stay home and finish it," Tony said, waving me off.

Tony stayed for dinner that night. Wendy seemed to regain some of the energy she'd lost the last few days. She ran around cleaning the house while she talked, got coffee, whipped up a salad and even set the table with the glass dishes and good silverware. She perked up when Tony told more of his old stories. I watched as Wendy made Tony tell story after story, acting like a toddler who'd found someone to read a book to her. I felt good seeing her happy, and the kids could tell she was feeling better, too. I thanked Tony and said goodbye.

But then Tony kept coming over. At first he only came over when I was home. Once in a while he brought one of his kids, but he never brought Marie. And then he started to come by more often. He had a seemingly endless supply of balloons, Ace magic tricks, Black Cats, and Bazooka bubble gum for the kids. He would just "drop by" to talk about the good old days with Wendy. In the evening or during the day, when I was at work – it didn't seem to matter. Each time he came over when I wasn't home, Wendy would call me at work and tell me Tony was there. Sometimes she'd ask my permission to go somewhere or do something with Tony for his work as a self-proclaimed repairman: "Tony has a microwave delivery in Rockton and wonders if I want to ride along." Or she'd say, "Tony wants to go flying and give the kids a plane ride. He knows a guy at Cottonwood but they can only get the plane for an hour today at two…"

At first I was glad that Tony helped lift Wendy out of her depression, so I always said "yes." Later, though, I felt torn. I wanted her to be happy, but now I felt afraid to say "no" and being accused of ruining her "only chance ever" at friendship. I could hear her saying that: "You ruined my only chance ever to have a friend." Every time Wendy and Tony went on some excursion of theirs, Wendy told me how wonderful it was to be with Tony, and then showed me the little gifts that he had brought her and the kids that day.

I kept my mouth shut.

We fell into that routine slowly, almost without knowing it.

Life that summer wrapped itself around us like a cocoon, secure and snug. I went to work as usual every day, and Wendy and the kids enjoyed their summer between home, the parks, and the Y. At nights and on weekends we all went to the park together, went on walks, went for ice cream, went shopping, went to my softball games, did everything we usually did, except ever so slowly and all so surely our lives began to include *him* as well.

Tony? To me Tony is sunshine and air and goofiness all mixed up together. When I'm around him it's like I'm twelve again. When I was twelve Tony always took a moment to listen to my thoughts. Tony noticed the new way I put up my hair. Tony included me in his conversations – in his plans, in his dreams to be an inventor – he had so many big ideas. Tony paid attention to me, gave me attention I didn't get anywhere else growing up.

When Tim and Tony decided to volunteer for the Army under the buddy system and go fight in Vietnam, everyone thought it was just another one of their pranks. But they followed through this time. Tim flunked the physical with his asthma, Tony passed, and in he went. We got letters from Tony for the family, and I wrote back. Pretty soon, Tony would write the letters just to me, and tell me all about the war and his patrols and the jungle and his Army friends and how much he missed all of us back here on the farm.

In a few years, Tony came home. He and Tim picked up right where they left off. Tony used his Army training and worked as a microwave repairman to keep food on the table for his wife and kids. He worked part-time inventing electronic gadgets too. Tim followed our dad into the tool and die trade at the factory.

Tim didn't purposely ignore me. It just never occurred to him that he should pay any attention to me, his little sister. If I couldn't have Tim as a big brother, then at least I'd have Tony as a big brother.

Tony was better than a brother.

She got there late again the other night. Not until the last inning, bottom of the seventh. She'd said she'd be home an hour before the game to watch the kids. By the time she got to the park the kids had hung out around the bleachers and all the other guys' wives and girlfriends and kids like a couple of orphans.

We were down by two runs. I came up with two out in the seventh, with the tying run at the plate. The pitcher had given me two inside pitches so far, so I figured that he'd put this next one outside, hoping I'd screw up and try to pull it like some newbie amateur and pop out. Instead I put all my weight on my back foot and held my hands back for what seemed forever. Then I swung hard and away.

The ball exploded off the barrel of the bat and screamed down the first-base line.

With two outs, the runner ahead of me got a jump and was already past second. I stretched for extra bases, ran head down. When I rounded second I looked at the third-base coach. I could tell from the way he hesitated that the outfielder had already picked up the ball, but I didn't really care. I was going.

I rounded the third-base bag short, leaning in. The catcher straddled the plate and braced himself. In front of me I saw the throw arc in from right field, and saw the ball slap into the webbing of the catcher's glove. I knew I was out, but I barreled into the catcher anyways, just for the hell of it.

"Jesus, man," the catcher moaned, crumpled and rolling on the ground, holding himself. The pitcher came up to see if he was okay. "Shit, man," he said to me. "This is supposed to be a friendly game."

"Tell your little buddy to quit blocking the plate then, asshole," I said, picking myself up off the ground. The pitcher got in my face. I was ready to take him out too. The umpire stepped between us. "Go sit down, Doug. Cool off." He followed me a step: "That was a cheap shot, Doug. I don't expect that – especially from you."

I threw my hands up. "Yeah…Hell, I know. I'm sorry, Owen. It's not like me." I squatted down by the catcher, still moaning on the ground: "Sorry, man. Bad day. Didn't mean to take it all out on you." I patted him on the shoulder and walked away without shaking anybody's hand, feeling good, only smiling a little.

I went over and plopped on the bleachers outside the dugout. Our game was done. The next two teams took our places in the field. Wendy stood close as I brushed sand off my leg and dumped it out of my shoe, not touching me but close, so that I knew she was there without looking up.

"Mad?" she said sweetly.

"Mad? Yeah. You could say that."

She held my bat bag and glove, and gathered up the kids and the toys they'd left lying around.

"Are you going to go have a beer with the guys?" she asked.

"No."

"Why not?"

"Not in the mood."

"Do you want to go home then?"

I inspected her closely for the first time that day, for the first time in many days. Her hair was glistening in the setting sun, a reddish tint in the brown that only came out in summer. She looked especially beautiful standing there in her sandals and tight white shorts. Her blouse was open just a little at the top so you could see some breastbone and where the collarbone came together at the bottom tip of her throat. A tiny pearl of sweat hung at that spot on her tanned skin.

"I don't want to hang around here...but I don't want to go home right now either," I said. My hip and shoulder throbbed. Joey was making a mudpie with someone's left-over Mountain Dew ice. "Let's go get an ice cream cone, okay?" I popped a handful of Ibuprofen into my mouth, swallowed them dry, and swung Belle over my shoulder until she whooped and giggled. "I'll meet you at the usual place, okay?" She nodded. "C'mon Joe," I said, "wipe that shit off your hands and let's get going."

Dairy Queen was the only place in town we could get ice cream cones with flavored paraffin candy melted over the top: red, orange, or green. It was nice because Wendy and I sat at the picnic tables outside and talked without worrying about who or what the kids spilled on.

"So you really are pissed about today?"

I sighed. "Yeah. Afraid so."

"I'm sorry. It's just that we were having such a great time... I, I just forgot. I completely lost track of time."

"Seems like that's been happening a lot lately." I stared down at my spikes. "It really bothers me when you're with him, you know."

She took my hand. "I know it does, but I keep telling you: I love you. You're my *husband*. He's my friend. A *friend*. Nothing more!"

I cleared my throat. "Why can't you just have a fat girlfriend like everyone else?"

She locked her eyes on mine. Her face went hard. "Don't be mad at me for wanting a friend." All the white showed in her eyes. "You know what this means to me."

"Then don't be mad at me either," I said, shaking my head. "This is new for me, you having a *guy* friend. It's hard for me to handle." If I ever *do* handle it, I thought. "I'm trying."

"And I love you all the more for trying," she said, and took my hand and held it tight while we watched the kids smear their cones all over their hands and the cement table.

In the evenings, Doug and I walked. We walked as much to get rid of the tension as to talk about anything. We talked and talked while we walked, but it was always about the same things, the same feelings, over and over.

"I'm not handling this well," Doug'd say.

"You're doing great," I'd say back. "I love you even more because of it."

And so we'd walk some more, and I'd hook my arm in his and say, "None of my sisters have a husband half as good as you."

And Doug would listen, and then he'd say something like, "That's not much of a compliment." And then he'd smile. God, I love his smile!

We'd walk a little more, though, and then his smile would fade and he'd say it again: "I'm just not handling this well," and we'd start the whole thing all over.

And when we got home after our walk, after we gave the kids their baths and they were asleep, we'd talk with the lights out for hours, and he'd say something like, "I don't know if I can stand to be this much better of a husband than all the rest," and I'd laugh. Then we'd go upstairs and make love.

I wanted to show him how desperately much I truly loved him. Only him.

I usually fell asleep okay but then after just a few hours I'd wake up. Sometimes I had to get out of bed so I wouldn't wake Wendy up. My mind would churn at first, then race.

What kind of man are you to let this go on, anyways? I'd think.

It's just an innocent friendship, that other voice would say.

Bullshit, the first voice would say back. *You're her husband, for Christ's sake! Say something. Do something. Shit!*

But then I'd get cold, start sweating. Afraid. Afraid of where a confrontation might lead. Afraid of turning out too much like my old man. Doomed like my parents, doomed to repeat their history. They too had gotten married young. They too had two kids quickly. They too had a boy and a girl just like Belle and Joe. Then they ended up getting divorced, when I was Joey's age, when my sister was Belle's age.

I know what that was like. I felt it in my bones still, a pain like a toothache that won't go away. Is that what I wanted for my family? Could I risk that? *Would* I risk having my kids grow up like that?

No way.

Then the alarm would go off and I'd take a shower, get dressed, kiss her goodbye and drag myself back to work again.

And back to the same sad routine.

Belle asked me the other day, when we were at the mall looking at dresses, of all places. Our little girl!

"Mommy, are you and Daddy mad at each other?"

"Why no honey, of course not," I said, stroking her hair, "Why would you ask that?"

"I don't know. You just act mad at him all the time, I guess. And Ginny Parks at camp said her mom and dad got mad then they got divors-sid and now she has to go stay at two different places every week and they're still mad at each other anyways even after that and she said she didn't like it one bit." Her eyes were wide by the time she finished.

"Daddy and I have our troubles once in a while, darling, but that's nothing you need to worry about." I held her face in my hand. She nodded but still looked like she might cry.

"I'm afraid Daddy might leave us someday like Ginny Parks's dad left Ginny and her mom," she finally sobbed.

I tished her thoughts away. "Your Daddy would never leave us, honey! He loves you and Joey and me too much to leave us!"

And besides, I thought, hugging her, if we ever did split up, why, he'd live just down the street from us, close, and he'd always be there for us, and he'd see us all the time, every day.

One night at the house, while Wendy was giving the kids a bath after a cook-out dinner, I tried talking to Tony. He was the only one I *could* talk to about this. Nobody else would believe it.

"Tony, what's going on here?" I cornered him alone, on the front porch.

Tony looked startled, like deer-in-the-headlights startled, like he had never thought about it. "What do you mean, Doug?"

"You know what I mean. First you weasel your way into the Rittebauer family, acting like you're their own son and a brother. Isn't that right? And now you're trying to weasel your way into our life somehow too, acting like—like what? What would you call it?"

"Whoa now, Doug. That's not what's happening here."

"Then why don't you tell me what's happening here, Tony, because that's what I'm seeing is happening here." I tried to keep my voice from breaking.

"Wendy missed out on a lot, growing up out there on that farm. I'm giving her back some of her life by telling her a few stories, is all." He smiled. "She wants me to be her friend, Doug. What's wrong with that?"

"It just isn't right, Tony. It's just not done like that." I hung my head and sighed. "It's something married people don't do." I looked up at Tony. "It's something one guy isn't supposed to do to another guy, either, man. You know. Put him in this spot, put him in a spot like this." Put like that, it sounded like a whine, even to me.

Tony stared at me for a moment, then looked away. "What 'spot,' Doug? There's no 'spot' here." And then he laughed. "You called me to come over that day, remember?"

I remembered that call, all right. I regretted it every day lately – I'd never forget, I was the one that called him. "Do you know anybody else that has a relationship like this, like the three of us?" I paused, then threw down my trump card. "What's Marie think of all this?"

Tony turned to face me. "Doug. Wendy wants me around. I want to be around. I'm going to be around as long as she wants me around."

I stared back at him. "And what about 'us,' Tony? Wendy and me? What about that? Huh? What about Belle and Joey? What about them? And what about what I want, Tony? Don't I get a say about anything here?"

"You're doing good, Doug, you're doing good." Tony put his hand on my shoulder, the prick. "It's not everybody that could let their wife have as good a friend as me. It's not everyone that can sacrifice a little bit of their own selfishness for the greater good like you're doing."

I snorted. "Yeah, well, this just feels wrong to me, is all I know. The whole damn thing feels wrong to me."

"You gotta have faith, Doug. Have faith. You love her, I love her, she loves both of us, she loves her kids. You just gotta have faith that it's all gonna work out fine."

Tony drew himself up. "If she ever says she doesn't want me around, then I'm gone, you know? Like that." He snapped his fingers in my face. "But until then, I'm gonna try to make up for all those years she didn't have any friends. *Capiche*?" Tony looked at me sadly with his big brown eyes and clay face.

The next day Tony left a cheap Catholic prayer pamphlet titled *Virtue* on the table with my name on it. I waited until the next time Wendy wasn't around and burned it.

I enjoyed watching the pages wrinkle and shrink in the flames.

I called my oldest sister Pam once, just to have someone else to talk to about what I was going through.

"Greg banned Tony from our house a year ago," she said after I explained the situation. "I don't know what it was, exactly. Tony was hanging around here a lot one day, then the next day he was gone, and I haven't seen him since. Never asked. Greg won't talk about it. And you know Dad doesn't have much use for Tony either…"

"We're not talking about Tony. We're talking about me."

"Okay. So why can't <u>Doug</u> be your friend? You're still married, right?"

"Yes, of course we're still married."

"So how come <u>he</u> can't be your friend? Explain that part to me again?"

"Because, silly. That's exactly why. We're married. He's my husband first, my friend second. He'll never be my best friend."

"Okay, yeah, well I guess so, I don't know. Don't they have any moms around there that you get together with? What is it you called it? Play groups?"

"Yeah, there's a few of them, but we're all so busy with the kids, there's just not time enough to make any serious friendships with any of them."

"What about other couples? Do you guys get with other couples to play cards and stuff, or games at least?"

"We get with other couples, sometimes. Usually for a potluck or a cookout. But we don't have time to get to know anybody real well, either. It's just not the same, you know, not the same as real friends…like the friends Doug has at work."

Pam paused, maybe stirred her coffee. "What makes you think Doug has any friends at work?"

"Well, he's there all day, and he plays softball twice a week with a lot of the guys in his department…"

"But isn't he a supervisor now?" she snorted. "You ever have a supervisor that was a friend of yours?"

"Well no…I didn't have many supervisors… but that's different too. Doug's different that way. People like him."

"So then what's wrong with you? Why don't you like him?" She laughed. "Or hey, put the shoe on the other foot – what if Doug had a 'girl' friend at work, how'd that make you feel? Huh? Huh?"

I hung up on her right then.

Pam was useless.

I tried to explain my feelings to Wendy again one night. She listened while she walked, glanced up occasionally.

"I finally realized just how deep we're in this thing. It looks innocent, it sounds logical. You want a friend, I *want* you to have a friend, I know he's *just* a friend. But there's something wrong with it. It's like that experiment with the frogs, you know? Ever heard of it? How they sit in water that's slowly heating up, and how they'll just sit there until they get so hot they explode? It's like I'm the one sitting in the water. Hell, we're *all* just sitting in the water, getting hotter and hotter, waiting for someone to make the first move, waiting to explode…"

I stopped. "And another thing that's like a frog: There's something slimy about it, something wrong with it."

She pulled away from me. I chased after her and nearly ran her over when she stopped suddenly.

"What's wrong with it?" she said. "Tell me."

I went on. "If this is so right, why don't you tell someone else about it? Let's use that as a test. Who have you told about this?"

She didn't say anything.

"*Anybody?*"

She glared at me.

"I mean it's so frigging weird…No one would believe us!"

She smiled. "It's not *that* weird," she said.

We laughed.

"It's good to laugh about it," I said. "I guess?"

"I guess so," she said, but then her face went pale.

"What?"

"I suppose you have to find out sometime." She walked away from me again.

My heart sank. I caught up to her, and she went on.

"There's something else." Her steps slowed. "Tony's moved away from home. They've separated, him and Marie. He's living down at his shop. Sleeping on a cot." She stopped walking and looked up at me. "He's going through a rough time right now. He needs me. He needs a good friend to talk to right now. To help him sort out his life, *this* part of his life." She took my hand in hers. "He wants me to have dinner with him Friday night."

I stood there with my mouth hanging open. "On a date? He wants you to go with him on a *frigging* date?" My breathing came hard. My heart pounded.

She stared at me. "It's not a *date*," she scoffed.

"Whatever you want to call it, don't kid yourself. It's a goddamn *date*. And *you* want to go with him, don't you?" I stared back at her for a second. "I don't frigging believe it!" I screamed, turning away. "I don't *frigg*ing be*lieve* this!" I walked tight little circles around her, fighting my urge to run.

She threw her hands in the air then, and jabbed her finger at me. "Tony told me you were going to act like this. Just like this." She blew air out across her lip. "We knew it." She turned and stomped off.

"How do you *expect* me to act?!" I yelled at her back. "I'm sure you'll tell him how I acted tomorrow, too, when he comes over and he sits his ass in *my* chair and he drinks *my* coffee in *my* house. Won't you?" I felt the veins pop out on my neck. "Doug blew a gasket again, Tony," I mimicked. "Don't know what's *wrong* with him."

By then I was pacing back and forth. I squeezed my fists until they hurt. Wendy was a football field away. "I'll probably get another goddamn Prayer Book from him for this one too, huh? On *Patience* or some other such shit? Eh? *Eh*?" My voice was so high it pinched. "Tell him to take his goddamn prayer books and shove 'em up his ass!"

I shook my fist at her bouncing back. "Or I'll do it for him!"

It was dark by the time Doug got home. He said he'd just wandered through the neighborhood. He looked spent, ragged, like a beat dog.

But at least he came home.

I was curled up in a corner of the couch in my housecoat. The living room was dark. "There's hot water on the stove if you want some tea," *I said. He went out and poured himself a cup without saying anything. He came back and stood at the other end of the couch.*

I had to start. "I know it's hard for you," *I began.* "But it's hard for me, too. I've finally got a friend. A real friend!" *My throat tightened. My eyes welled up.* "And this is my chance to be a friend back. Maybe I'll never have any friends in my own family. I don't know about them. But maybe it can work with Tony and me. I've got a chance to make it work." *I looked up into his eyes.* "I've got to do it, I want to do it." *I took a deep breath.* "But if you don't want me to, I won't. You're my husband. I want you to say it's ok. I need you to say it's ok for me to help my friend." I had to grab a tissue. "There's nothing wrong with it. We're just two friends, going to dinner, talking, trying to be there for each other as friends."

Doug stood there staring at his hands around his cup. They were shaking.

Finally he sighed. His hands settled down. "There's got to be rules," he muttered. "Rules. Boundaries. Something. Limits. Check-ins." He shook his head. "I just can't handle it any other way."

I flew across the couch. Grabbed him tight. Stared into his face. "We can have rules. Rules are good. Good. No problem. You won't be sorry." He must have been surprised because he dropped his cup of tea. He swiped to catch it but missed. I heard the cup hit, bounce, and roll on the floor while I squeezed him tight.

"Strong cup," he said, finally hugging me back.

I couldn't wait to tell Tony Doug said I could go.

I felt like a man sending his daughter off to Senior Prom – except my seven-year-old daughter was at my side and wouldn't be going to Prom for ten more years. No – I was sending my *wife*, instead. Kind of a practice run, I thought. Wendy even *looks* like a teenager going to Prom. It wasn't her clothes – even though they were new, kindof hippy looking, if you asked me – it was her face, glowing in the low evening sun, eyes shining bright, lips straining to hold together so they wouldn't burst out in a smile that made me think of her as a teenager.

"You do look beautiful," I said, clutching Belle next to me. "Doesn't Mommy look nice?" Belle raised her arms high and spread her legs out in a cheer. "Yeah, Mommy!"

Wendy smiled, almost wiggling with excitement herself.

"Tony's here!" Joe called from out on the porch. "Tony's here!" Belle ran out the door. Wendy turned and started to get her purse.

"He can come up to the door," I yelled out at Joe. My stomach was an instant knot. I turned to Wendy, took her head in my hands. "Remember, ten o'clock, like we agreed? I'll come get you anytime you need me to. Just call me. I'll be there in a second."

"Ok, ok, *Dad!*" Wendy said. "You won't be sorry you did this," she whispered. She kissed me a quick goodbye on the chin.

Tony was at the door coming in. I noticed he had brought some small balsa-wood toy airplanes that the kids had already unwrapped and were putting together in the yard.

"Hi ya, Doug!" Tony said, stepping in and reaching out his hand. I could smell his aftershave from across the room, that cheap fruity shit you buy at Wal-Mart.

I didn't take his hand. "Tony."

Tony looked over at Wendy. She looked more radiant to me than I'd ever seen her. "I just got a couple little things for the kids," he said. "It was nothing." Got that right, I thought. We were all standing in the living room, Wendy nearest the door, Tony in the center of the room and me in the corner farthest from the door. I caught myself with arms crossed, rocking back and forth, wanting to be someplace else. The kids came in, nearly knocking Tony down as they ran by him to show me their airplanes, and then ran out again.

"Neat!" I called after them. "Pretty neat!"

"Sooo – guess we'll be going, eh?" Tony clapped his hands together, and reached out to open the door for Wendy. Asshole doesn't even have the good sense to be nervous, I thought. My hands were twitching.

"Bye!" cried Wendy. She was already out the door and didn't look back. "Kids! Kids! Come kiss Mommy goodbye!" I forced myself out onto the porch. I watched Tony take Wendy's arm and walk her down the sidewalk and steps, run around and open the door for her, then run back around the front of the car. As was usual for him, he'd parked on the wrong side of the street, in the oncoming traffic lane, so that the passenger door was in the middle of the street.

Don't you dare wave, you asshole.

Tony waved.

Being with Tony is so easy. I laugh when I'm with him, and I laugh a lot. He is so funny. He's such a gentleman. Even at a time like this, even when he's down. Marie's insisting on divorce court, he says, demanding alimony, full custody and child support. "Well there's not much on the books that will get her anything," Tony said. I didn't know exactly what that meant, but it made Tony's friends laugh.

Oh yeah – this turned into a real party, not just dinner. We went over to the Olympic, on the west side, just the two of us. Thought we'd have a better chance to talk there, he said. Tony picked a table in the corner, something apart and quiet. But then in walked Bill Armano and his girlfriend Jill, then a couple of Tony's old Army buddies, Fred and Phil, I think their names were, and their girlfriends. It was just a bunch of people hanging out, all come together to take care of Tony.

At first he seemed uneasy about so many people paying so much attention to him. I asked him about it.

"I feel bad that it's not just the two of us," he said, "Like I'd hoped." He took my hand. "I have some things I want to say to you. In private." He's so open, so able to express his feelings.

"I know you have a lot you want to talk about," I said. "I'm so sorry about you and Marie splitting up, the way she's acting...."

"No, no, that's ok – that's not it," he said. "My buddies are here. It's not like we can just get up and leave and go somewhere else now that they're all here?" It was hard to tell whether he was asking me a question or stating a fact.

"Well, I'm having fun...but if you want to go somewhere else...?"

"That wouldn't be right now, would it?" And he smiled a little, but I could tell he was hurting inside.

Those next four hours were hell. I tried to keep busy with the kids. First we had a Pizza Party. Then we had some ice cream. I crushed the toy airplanes Tony had brought in my hands and threw them in the trash while the kids were finishing their pizza. We played Frisbee in the front yard until dark. I cursed myself for looking at the clock so often, and cursed the time for going so slow. I tried to watch *Mary Poppins* for the ump-teenth time with the kids after their baths, but couldn't sit still for it. So I got up and sat on the porch step. I got up to pace every few minutes, then sat back down and rocked forward until my chest touched my knees, took some deep breaths, then got up and paced some more.

Finally, after the kids fell asleep in front of the movie, it was ten o'clock. Wendy and Tony would be home any minute now. I didn't think I was going to make it, but I did. Doug, you bastard – you made it, I thought.

Then the phone rang. "Hello?"

"Doug, hi. It's me."

"Where are you at? You're supposed to be home."

"Yeah well, we're having a real good time, just sitting around talking. Some old friends of Tony's are here too…old Army buddies…"

I squeezed the receiver until my fingers turned white. "You're supposed to be home."

"I know, I know… but…"

"But nothing. You're supposed to be home. Now."

"But I told Tony it would be okay. I told him I'd call you and tell you and that you'd say it was ok. Just a little longer, Doug, ok? We're having a great time talking here…"

I pronounced each word slowly, evenly. "You were supposed to be home at ten. That was the rule. We agreed. Home at ten."

Neither one of us said anything for ten long, cold seconds.

"Well, I gotta go. I've got to get back to the table. They'll miss me. I'll call you later." Click.

I stood staring at the phone in my hand, my heart pounding. I couldn't believe what I'd just heard. She was supposed to be home by ten.

She was supposed to be home.

People hung around the restaurant for hours, they felt so sorry for Tony, you know, all he was going through. They cared. That's what friends do. I tried calling Doug five more times in the next couple hours, but he wasn't answering the phone.

I was getting pissed.

He was sitting on the porch with the lights out when we pulled up. I got out of the car and yelled at him before Tony got out to open my door. "Thanks for ruining my night, Doug!" I screamed. "I kept calling you and calling you and you wouldn't even answer." I stormed around to the front of the car, wagged my finger at him over there across the yard on the porch. "I know everyone at the table was wondering where I was going all those times. You can only go the bathroom so much, you know!

"What was I supposed to say? Huh, Doug? What was I supposed to say?" I was spitting I was so mad at him.

"*Thanks for ruining it. Thanks for ruining the only night I ever had with a friend!*" I had to fight back the tears, I was so hurt. "*I know lots of other people that have a family and a husband and a friend – why can't I have that?*" I slammed my fist on the hood of Tony's car. "*Is that too much to ask from you?*" I pointed at him. "*Apparently it is. Apparently it's too much for you to handle, Doug. Thanks a lot!*"

In the dark on the street they didn't even notice I had my bat in my hands. I just got up and walked toward the car slowly, listening to her rant and rave out there like some spoiled little brat. Good thing the kids were in bed sleeping.

"You done yet?" I asked her as sweetly as I could.

"You asshole Doug. You're such an asshole."

By now Tony was out of the car and standing next to it on the curb. He went to move closer to Wendy, to get her out of the street, probably, when he saw the bat in my hand.

He stopped in his tracks. "Whoa – what's the bat for, Doug?"

I looked down at my bat, rolled it slightly in the streetlight. The light bounced off the dull aluminum barrel. Wendy gasped.

"You know, Tony, I'm not quite sure." I said. "Yet."

"C'mon Doug," Tony said, smiling his big smile. "Why don't you just give me the bat? We'll all feel a lot better, ok?" He stepped forward and reached toward me.

"You know, no, I don't think so. Tony." By then I was close. I held the bat like a pool cue, shoved the bigger end of it hard into his chest. "Why don't you just get back in your car. Why don't you get just in your car and get the hell out of here forever, eh?"

Tony blinked. Looked at his shoes. Backed into the fender. "I just want us all to be friends here, Doug."

I imagined slamming his head into the car with my right hand, breaking his knee with a quick swing of the bat in my left. I could see the sickly angle of his knee bent the wrong way in my head. Instead I just sighed. "Not gonna happen, Tony. Not tonight. Not this night." I patted the bat in my free hand once more. "So why aren't you leaving?"

Wendy looked over at Tony. She stared at him a couple seconds then moved toward the house. She gave me a wide berth on her way up the curb, up the steps, and up to the house, sputtering all the time. "God you're such an asshole. You're such an asshole, Doug."

She stopped in the doorway. "Why are you doing this to me?"

Tony hung by the hood of the car for a second, to see what Wendy would do, I guess. Then he walked around to his driver door, next to the sidewalk I was on. He went as far away from me as he could get, but he had to get close to me, the way he'd parked. He had his hand on the door handle. I took a step closer to him. I leaned into him, put my face next to his ear. "You pathetic piece of shit," I said to him softly. Then I turned quickly, smashed my bat hard across the top of the concrete retaining wall by the street. Sparks flew as the old gravel crumbled under the metal bat.

I didn't even have to point the bat at him again – he finally got it. "Get the hell out of here. Don't ever let me see your face again. Understand?"

For a second then, I wondered if he had a gun in the glove box or under the seat. It was just the sort of crazy shit he would pull. If he did have a gun I was dead, plain and simple. I wouldn't go down easy though, not now. I imagined myself leaping forward, one last swing of the bat at his head as he pointed the gun at me and pulled the trigger.

But Tony just shrugged his shoulders, shook his head, gave me his sad-eyed look, got into his Olds Cruiser station wagon and drove away, squealing the tires as he left.

I stood there for a while to see if any neighbors had heard anything, if any came out. They didn't.

I sat on the curb for a while longer to see if Tony circled back. He didn't.

Doug spent a sleepless night on the porch, half-expecting Tony to come back with some of his Army buddies. He watched the sun come up. It was early fall, and there was a hint of frost in the morning air. The leaves stood out as if in relief against the morning sky, orange and red and yellow against black then purple then blue sky, the colors sharpening as the early sunlight slowly overpowered the porch and street lights.

Dampness hung heavy in the air. A few birds sang, but in the cold morning their songs were shrill and short.

It had been a long time since he'd watched a sunrise, and he found himself enjoying this one. The light was so different in the early morning that it was easy to pretend that last night didn't really happen. But he knew from the ache still in his chest that that was a lie. The only thing dreamlike about this day was the way that time moved even slower now than before.

As the first light of dawn flowed in and a cold wind swirled the autumn leaves, Doug's mind raced back to another time and place. He closed his eyes. He was at the softball diamond, and the lights were bright globes painted against the early dusk. He was laying in the sand at home plate, stretched out, looking up at the sky and the light like he was now. The breeze was hot, like a breath. The gravel of the diamond was warm against his back. He'd lost track, didn't know whether the catcher had held onto the ball this time or not. He felt the point of the plate pressed hard against his hip, the catcher's weight pressed across his chest. He felt the muscles in his legs twitch, tasted the dust in his mouth. He also felt the tingle in his hands from the bat smashing the ball, the grip around the knob of the bat at contact lingering still. He saw again how big the catcher's eyes got, saw him take the relay and brace himself for the collision, felt his body absorb the impact of the crash, smiled as the silence immediately after impact settled calmly in his mind, listened for the umpire to make the call.

But the call never came.

He sat on the front porch for a while longer. When the sun broke over the treetops, he got up and climbed the stairs to their bedroom. It was deathly quiet there, and still dark. He slipped into his side of the bed and watched and listened to make sure Wendy was still breathing. His own breathing was louder than hers for a couple of minutes, until his heart settled.

Finally he brushed the side of her arm softly with his fingertips. She shivered, then pulled away.

"Don't touch me."

WORKING CLASS

Jeff woke with a start, one minute before the alarm sounded. Four a.m. came quickly in the dark bedroom. He noted it had snowed a little overnight and grunted as he rolled out of bed. It was always tougher to get Rob out of bed when it was cold. Sam would be dropping off the newspapers any minute – you could set your watch to Sam. Jeff pulled on his cold crumpled socks and jeans and stumbled to the bathroom, closed the door behind him before turning on the light. He threw on a T-shirt frayed around the throat, added a turtle neck and pulled a ragged old Rockford College hoodie over that. He yanked his White Sox cap over his uncombed hair, then shut off the bathroom light before he opened the door.

"Pongo, Perdita. C'mon," Jeff hissed, waving his arm. Ten seconds passed. "Dammit, you two: Get a move on!" The two Dalmatians lay still on the bed for several more seconds. Then they rolled lazily from their backs to their sides to stretch and yawn. Pongo looked at Perdita out of the corner of his eye and leaped off the bed, and then she was after him, and they ran noisily down the stairs, pushing and shoving, jumping back and forth over each other like two dolphins playing in the wake of a speedboat.

Jeff heard Jenny moan and froze. He watched her shift herself to reclaim the now-vacant warm center of their bed. Then she rolled onto her stomach, pulled the blankets over her head, and lay still. He waited a few more seconds, then headed downstairs.

At the door, Jeff slipped on his worn insulated coveralls, tugged on his half-laced boots and let the dogs out into the fenced pen against the garage. Wearing his brown and red coveralls made him think of his days building pole barns years earlier: Would be a good day to work *inside*, he thought as he rubbed his hands together and watched clouds of his breath freeze while the two dogs did their business; but more likely the pole barn crew would've been framing or roofing on a day like today. Their three-man crew could build a good-sized pole barn in a week. Nothing like having ice cold wind blow up your bare back a time or two to get the ole juices flowing, he remembered fondly. How many times had that happened to him before he finally broke down and bought a pair of insulated coveralls like the farmer's wore?

By 4:15 the dogs were in the house. He waited at the curb, stomped his still-untied boots on the thin layer of new snow. When the *Register Star's* panel truck turned the corner and pulled close, he stepped to the back of the van. Sam the newspaper guy popped his head through briefly when he opened the van doors.

"So what's the news today, Sam?"

"Same ole same ole," Sam said, sliding one bundle of papers to Jeff and flopping the second bundle to the curb. "Rape. Murder. Kidnappings....Usual shit and mayhem." He hopped back into the driver's seat and drove off without saying any more or looking back. Jeff carried his bundle into the living room and walked down the hall to Rob's son's room.

Rob was crammed on one side of his Tom Slick racecar bed, covers and sheets thrown all about, one pillow at the foot of the bed and the other on the floor. Pongo and Perdita didn't budge from their sprawled position in the middle of his mattress, but their bright brown eyes followed Jeff as he picked his way through the piles of dirty clothes and boy-debris on the floor. The bed had big broad stylized numbers and oil and towing company decals along both siderails, a windshield headboard and a silver-painted grill across the footboard. It had been a small indulgence to a little boy enamored with NASCAR several years ago. Now Rob's bare feet hung far out over the end.

Jeff shook him once, then walked away. Four dog eyes and a groan followed him out the door. "Time to get up," he said as he flipped on the light. He pulled pliers from his coveralls to snip the straps on the first bundle and was at the living room couch folding and rubber-banding papers when Rob came stumbling in, his hair sticking straight up except in the middle, where his cowlick twisted every which way.

"Not too bad today. Not many ads, no inserts," Jeff said.

Rob squinted in the light.

"Looks like we missed old Tareyton down on Washington Street yesterday." Jeff shook a green-and-while lined printout at Rob. "These misses count against us, you know." Rob grudgingly took the printout Jeff held out and yawned loudly. "Go get the sacks. And the second bundle out on the sidewalk."

"Geez!" Rob crumpled the error report and tossed it on the floor before he spun away toward the front porch. "I'm *going* already. I'm going!"

"And be quiet so you don't wake up your mom! Or your sisters!"

* * *

The paper route had been Jeff's idea. A few weeks ago, around Rob's thirteenth birthday, the paperboy came to the door doing his monthly collection. He told Jeff that this was his last week on the job. When Jeff asked him who they should call if they were interested in taking over the route, the boy gave him the dispatcher's name and number. Jeff called the next day and set it up. "I worked when I was his age," he told Jenny that first evening. She just rolled her eyes. "Rob needs to learn the real meaning of work," he'd said to her again after supper the next night while they were washing dishes.

"He's just a kid," Jenny said.

"Yeah? Well, he's thirteen now. High time he learns what it's like to work." Jeff set a glass on the counter.

Jenny clicked her tongue. "He's got plenty of time to learn about work. Just let him be a kid." She rinsed a dish and shoved it into the plastic rack on the counter. "It's not like we need the money."

Jeff paused. "That's one way to think of it, I guess," he said, drying a dish. His manager's job at the aerospace plant let Jenny be a stay-at-home mom. "But if half the guys I work with had worked anywhere else but Sundstrom's their entire lives, my world would be a much better place." He snorted. "Those preppy college boys wouldn't know real work if it jumped up and bit 'em in the ass."

"You're just mad because you had to take out loans for college and they didn't."

"No I'm not! But I know none of them had to work forty hours a week after classes. None of them missed any football practices or games because of work. None of them missed a date with some stupid cheerleader because of work."

"Besides," Jenny said, ignoring his rant. "The kids already have jobs. They have to finish their chores every week or they don't get to do any extra activities."

"Yeah, right," Jeff snorted. "When's the last time either of us told Rob he couldn't play soccer because he didn't do his chores? Or told one of the girls that they couldn't go to their swimming lessons this week because they forgot to water the plants?"

Jenny smiled.

"They do chores because they live here," Jeff said sternly. "Chores are an obligation."

Jenny frowned. "The kids will be stuck working for the rest of their lives whenever they start. So let's not rush it, huh?" She smiled and flicked a little soapy water his way. "I can't help it that you had to work since you were old enough to walk. Just let him be a kid, OK, Jeff?" She put her wet hands on her hips. "If you want him to be a paperboy so bad, go ahead. But leave me out of it." She started to walk away but stopped to wag her finger at him one final time. "And if this dumb job affects his schoolwork, it's gone. Agreed?"

Now Jeff stood alone in front of his living room couch at four-thirty in the morning, getting black ink all over his hands wrapping rubber-bands and plastic bags around "Rob's" papers, wondering if he'd made the right choice. He remembered when his dad took him in the truck down to the Piggly Wiggly yard to switch trailers sometimes, how good that made him feel. The cab always smelled clean and dirty at the same time, an oddly-soothing mixture of sweat, leather, Windex and his dad's Old Spice. His favorite part was when his dad lifted him down from the cab when they were finished; he laughed and jumped into his dad's wet, hairy arms, and his dad's forearms bulged like Popeye's while he hung there.

Jenny had the girls, their hair appointments, nails to be done, exercise classes, her weekly massages and the WomanSpace Reading Circle – she had her time with the girls. Jeff thought he'd get a little of that from Rob with this newspaper route. But Rob was somewhere else now, not even here with him. "What's wrong with *this* picture?" he grumbled outloud to no one.

"Time's a-wastin'," he called. "Better get moving, buddy!" Rob came back to the living room. He had his jacket on and the yellowed, dirty canvas carrier slung over his shoulder. "And get a hat on!"

"Alright already!" Rob turned on his heels. "I don't see Carol or Annie up working this early…" he mumbled as he walked away.

"Girls are different, you know that. They need all the beauty sleep they can get, right?" Jeff said in his best *compadre* fashion. "Now quit your whining and get a move on."

They didn't have a big route – about fifty papers on weekdays, a few more on weekends. Three north and south streets, three east and west streets, nine square blocks total. Good little starter job for a boy, Jeff reassured himself.

Rob trudged along with the rolled papers stuffed in front and behind his head in the canvas sacks. He already held one wrapped newspaper in his hand, ready for the next house. Jeff followed him, walking in the middle of the street, slower, his flashlight on the large crinkled route map he usually carried folded up in his coverall pouch. "You remember which house is next?"

The air was crisp. The new snow sat on the ground and still hung from bushes, muffling what few street sounds there were that early in the morning.

"Rob – Which house is *next*? You remember?" Jeff yelled again, stopping.

Rob pointed to a house two down on the left with the rolled-up newspaper.

"That's right…I think," said Jeff, checking his list. "Make sure you get that paper all the the way under that overhang for the old gal, all right? What's the number?"

Rob walked close by him as he zigged across the street to the next house on the route. "Can't see a number," he mumbled as he passed. Jeff could tell Rob wasn't breathing hard, even though the bags were pretty full and this part of the route was going uphill. There's another good point I can use with Jenny, he thought. This job keeps Rob in good shape for soccer.

"I could probably figure out the number from the last one we did if I could remember that one," Jeff said aloud, the hood of his sweatshirt getting in his face. "Three down, same side of the street…?"

Jeff jumped as a car behind him honked lightly; he moved over so it could pass. He thought he saw Rob glance at him and shake his head.

"Twenty-five fifteen."

"What?" The car must have disoriented Jeff.

"Twenty-five fifteen!" Rob repeated, louder.

"Yeah. Yeah, that's it." Jeff fumbled with the map and flashlight. "Hold on. Which one's next?"

Rob blew air through his nose loudly. He pointed. "I'm heading to it, I already said!" Then he stopped and blurted, "Geez. Don't you have anything better to do?"

"What? What do you mean? Anything to do? When?"

"Right now," Rob said, his shoulders hunched. "I've got all the papers right here. We've been doing this a couple of weeks now. I know the route. So why don't you just let me do it *myself*? By. My. Self!" He ticked each point off with a gloved finger.

"Well, that's a hell of a note!" Jeff sputtered. "How can you say that? I've been breaking my ass with you every morning. I *got* you this job."

"Oh yeah. Thanks a lot for *that*. I love getting up at four in the frigging morning." Rob waved his arm. "You didn't even ask me, you just up and did it. The girls don't have jobs, none of my friends have a job, but me, oh yeah, I have a job…a job with my *daddy*."

Jeff stood looking at Rob for a long time, considering whether he was going to squash this little act of defiance or let it slide. He decided. He waited another thirty seconds just to make Rob squirm.

"Fine, smart guy," Jeff said. He set the list and the flashlight down slowly in the middle of the street. "Fine. Have it your way. I'll see you at the Sweden House when you're done." He stopped and wagged his finger at Rob: "And you had better be quick about it, too, mister." With that Jeff walked away and didn't look back.

* * *

The more he walked, the more angry he became. He'd hoped Rob would see this route as a chance for them to do something special together, like he did. Some great frigging opportunity *this* turned out to be, eh?

Jeff shivered. He remembered another time with his dad, years after the Piggly Wiggly times, when he was more Rob's age. His dad was gone weekdays then, driving trucks cross-country instead of in-town; but one Saturday afternoon Jeff talked him into a game of catch. Jeff was so excited he could hardly stand it. He ran to get the ball and their gloves. His dad had a black Wilson with Ted Williams's autograph in silver letters; he had a tan Rawlings Trapp-Eze. But even though he could pitch back and forth for hours with his friends, he couldn't throw the ball straight to his dad to save his life.

"The object is for you to get the ball to me, remember?" his dad said, pointing into the pocket of his Wilson. "Like I'm doing to you, see? Not four feet to my left. Not five feet to my right. Not way over my head." He waved his arms as he talked. "Straight and hard, like I throw to you. Got it?"

Jeff concentrated and told himself to throw the ball straight, straight, straight, but the next one he threw bounced on the sidewalk, skittered three feet to the right of his dad, and rolled out into the street.

"And not at my goddamn feet, either," his dad said. He shrugged his shoulders and took his glove off. "Jesus Christ. Go get the ball before it goes down the goddamn gutter." And then his dad threw up his hands, dropped his glove, and walked away.

And that was the end of their ever playing catch.

Jeff walked faster to get out of the cold.

* * *

Big band music from the forties played softly in the Sweden House. Uli filled his coffee cup for the third time. She was a fifty-something, stout dirty-dishwater blonde in an apron with a pen stuck behind her ear. She'd waited on them every morning since they'd started the paper route.

"Where's that boy of yours today?" Uli turned to look out the big plate-glass window at the front of the restaurant.

"Wanted to do his route all by himself today. Knows everything. Doesn't need my help," Jeff snorted, squirming against the red vinyl cushion back of the bench seat. "Kids."

"Want me to dump that hot chocolate and get him a new one?"

"No, not yet, thanks. He'll be here." Jeff smiled and cleared his throat.

"Okey-dokey. Not a problem." Uli moved on down to Norm, another early-morning regular two booths down.

The sun was rising now, a crack of pink, white, and purple light on the horizon. Jeff could just make out the tallest of the maple and pine trees that crowded their neighborhood. Rob should have finished ten minutes ago, tops. Jeff put his paper down and walked over to the front window, cupped his hands up around his eyes and leaned into the glass to see out better. He thought about going back outside, walking a block or two up the sidewalk. Maybe he should call the house; maybe Rob'd gone there instead.

No, he wouldn't go home. The food was here.

Jeff walked back to his booth. He heard Norm behind him rattle his paper and say, "Looks like they're gonna parole that slug that killed the Matthews kid after all. Jesus, the guy shot him in the back of the head, point blank. Tied his hands up behind him, even." Norm slurped his coffee. "Sons'a'bitches. They ought'a all be hung up by their nuts. All of 'em, the prisoners *and* their freakin' lawyers!"

Jeff's heart flopped to his gut like a cold fish. He threw a ten on the table and bolted.

"Hot chocolate'll be here when you get back," Uli called after him. He gave a little wave in her direction as he hurried out the door.

Once outside he ran fast. He swung his arms back and forth to gain speed. He retraced his steps to where he'd left Rob. Not there. He followed the route he thought Rob would take to deliver the rest of the papers. He could see Rob's footsteps in the snow. That was something anyway. Early enough, no one else had been this way yet. What was Rob wearing? He thought. Tennis shoes. How'd he let him out of the house without his boots on?

Jeff scurried down the hill on Shaw, going parallel now to Washington, scanning the street up and down. He let gravity take him over for a few seconds to gain speed but then held himself back because he was afraid he was going so fast he'd miss something. He pictured Rob crumpled in the street, run over by some early-morning drunk trying to get home before getting caught. Imagined him twisted and bent in the snow, all alone and dead like that poor little Matthews kid.

A sudden squeal of snow from his boots made him hear Jenny's voice in his head. "Just let him be a kid, Jeff." And then she blurred and he saw his dad standing on the summer sidewalk in front of their Lawndale house with his black Ted Williams glove at his side: "Get the ball to *me*, remember?"

Snap out of it, Jeff told himself. Focus. Don't get carried away. Not yet.

The tennis-shoe tracks stopped him. He saw them veer off between two houses on St. Louis, three blocks from where he'd last seen Rob, now at the far western edge of the route – mostly rentals and cheap Section 8 housing here. Footprints went up the hill on the sidewalk and across the yard to the back. He took a chance and followed the ones going between the houses. He slipped as he climbed a small dirt mound, crawled on his hands and knees as he cleared a retaining wall.

"Dad! Over here!" Rob's voice was high, on the verge of cracking like teenage boys' voices sometimes do. Jeff stumbled toward him. Rob sat under a small group of evergreens, in a dark pile of clothes and undelivered papers and yellow carrier sack and something else brown. Jeff put his hand to his mouth and bit down on his fist, swallowing his impulse to yell.

"I don't know how long he's been out here," Rob said, pointing at the dirty heap of a dog next to him. Jeff ran his hands over his son quickly to make sure he was okay. He wiped a small smear of blood off Rob's cheek – clean, wasn't his. "He got caught up in this chicken wire somehow," Rob said, holding up the big Lab's feet to show Jeff. The dog's back legs and one front leg were tangled in the wire in a three-leg tie like a rodeo steer. The wire was the kind people on the block used to keep rabbits out of their gardens in summer. It was mostly rusty now, tossed aside months ago as someone's junk. The twisted strands had wrapped tighter and tighter around the dog's feet as he tried to kick the wire off, and cut his legs in a couple places.

Rob spit words out fast. "I pulled and pulled but couldn't get it off and I didn't want to leave him here alone not like this I couldn't leave him. Not alone. Not like this. Couldn't..."

The words trailed off. Rob looked up at him, blinking. The dog looked up at him, too, brown eyes wide and hopeful, his big tail thumping the ground. Probably weighs more than I do, Jeff thought, moving his hands from his boy to the dog. For a moment he thought about the strength in that thick neck, teeth, and jaws, but shook those thoughts away. The dog looked calm enough with Rob holding him. Hard telling how long he'd been tangled up, how he'd managed to drag himself here under these pine trees.

"Let's see what's going on," Jeff finally said. He noticed the dog wasn't wearing a collar. He moved his hands to the wire around the dog's feet, and the dog pressed his head down and pinned Jeff's hands hard against the dirt. Jeff shivered slightly. "Hold his head back."

"I named him Beau," Rob said. He coaxed the dog's head to the side. "Easy, Beau. Easy, boy."

Jeff wiggled the wire up and down. "I can't break it," he said. "Let me try to untwist it." He moved the wire from side to side. "That's not cutting it either."

"That's what we need!" Rob said. "Something to cut it with!"

Jeff snapped his fingers. Beau jumped. Jeff felt in the legs pocket of his coveralls for the pliers he'd used to cut the straps off the paper bundles earlier. That seemed like days ago now.

"These should do the trick. Good call, Rob." By cutting through a few of the outer links, Jeff was able to work the dog's back foot free from the front. Rob talked to the dog faster now, stroked his head and rubbed him behind his ear, laid his body across the dog's like they were wrestling. Jeff reached in with the pliers and untwisted some more wire, enough to separate the dog's back legs from each other. Beau jerked each time he heard the pliers click.

"Almost there, not quite done yet," Jeff said, and leaned his shoulder harder into the dog. The dog sighed loudly then and held still, conceding. Jeff gained slack each time he cut though more wire.

"Got it!" Beau shook his head and surged to his feet, tossing first Rob then Jeff aside like rags as he heaved himself up. He danced back and forth in the small space under the trees, barked loudly, wagged his wide tail. He stopped suddenly to bend and lick his cut leg. He bowed low in front and stuck his butt high in the air. Then Beau was running at them, into them, over them, licking everything, wagging his tail hard and climbing up onto their chests and shoulders with his front legs.

Jeff and Rob both put their arms up across their faces in self-defense. "Let's get out of here before he *thanks* us to death," Jeff shouted. He rolled away from under the pine trees to the snowy grass outside. Rob did the same, even with a handful of papers still in his carrier bag.

They lay together in the snow and watched Beau enjoy his new found freedom. The dog bounded at Rob and stopped an inch from his face. Then he barked deeply. "Eww. Dog spit," Rob said. He rubbed the spray out of his eyes with his dirty hands, and for the first time in a long time, laughed.

The sunlight came over the tops of the houses to the east. The big Lab lifted his leg beside the closest maple tree, marked it, then nose to the ground made his way to the next one.

"You know I'm going to have to put you over my knee and spank your ass for scaring the shit out of me this morning, right?" They were still lying on the snow.

"Oh yeah?" Rob said, smirking. "Try it."

Jeff grabbed for him, but Rob spun away, ducked and dodged, then ran a little circle around Jeff like the dog had just run. The canvas paper carrier spun around his neck, making him fall to one knee and hand like a football lineman. Beau came running between them, barking, and knocked Rob over.

Rob got up on one elbow. His face clouded over. "What do you think Mom will say about the dog?"

Jeff turned toward Rob and shrugged. "Damned if I know. That's *your* problem."

Rob flashed a broad smile.

"Not telling you what to do here," Jeff said, winking. He got up and brushed the snow off his chest. "But if I were you I'd take Beau on home, give him a bowl of food and water, and put him in the garage." Jeff gestured with his arms. "Use your belt as a leash if you have to. Put the belt through the buckle to make a loop and stick it over his head, you know?" Rob made a makeshift leash out of his belt and put it on Beau, who was already dragging Rob up the street. "We'll have to look for his owners later this morning." Jeff turned. "Then hurry up with the rest of those papers and meet me at the Sweden House," he called as he walked away. "Your hot chocolate's getting cold. Worse, so's my coffee."

I'll call the office and tell them I'll be late today, Jeff thought. "I'm having breakfast with my son." With that, he broke into a run. After a few yards he spread his legs and arms and slid down the middle of the snowy street like a surfer. Then his boot caught on a patch of dry pavement that threw him to the ground. He rolled twice, then jumped to the curb and scooped up a handful of snow and packed it quickly. He picked out a tree 50 feet in front of him and threw as hard as he could.

The snowball splattered against the cold black bark in the crisp morning air with a resounding slap.

TURNABOUT

Jack looked at his fifty-four-year-old body in the steamy bathroom mirror. In his younger days he'd wrestled in high school, been a brown belt in Tae Kwon-Do, and played Class A softball three nights a week. Being fit came naturally back then. But then those twelve-hour days on the construction crew gave way to long days sitting in the office, frequent-flyer Gold cards, and way too many expense-account appetizers. The receding hairline and gray hair were bad enough. Getting reading glasses last year just about killed him.

Even *he* had to admit that he was "past almost gone" now, as his wife Karen liked to put it. What's a guy gonna do? Might have to think about doing something about all that one of these days, he mused in the mirror. Getting old ain't for sissies.

On The Waterfront music festival was a Labor Day tradition to almost all Rockford natives. To make *OTW* even more special this year, Cheap Trick, Rockford's boy-band-made-good, was playing downtown at the Great Lawn tonight. Karen bragged to Jack and the kids all summer about how she had been in high school Madrigals with Robin Zander, Cheap Trick's lead singer. Sally and her husband Dave came home from Bloomington for the big event. The two older kids and their three grandkids lived out of state. Chad, Karen's son, had a girlfriend again – so they hadn't seen *him* for a few days.

"We've got to get there early to get a good spot," Jack said for the fifth time that morning.

"We know!" Karen and Sally said in unison, laughing and rolling their eyes together.

"Geez – hold your horses, Jack," Karen said. "We'll get down there when we're ready."

"That's what I was afraid of," Jack said under his breath.

They got downtown mid-afternoon, well ahead of the main crowd. Jack, Karen, and Sally'n'Dave took the shuttle bus from the Target parking lot to save having to get a parking spot downtown. Jack called the couple "Sally'n'Dave" because they were never more than ten feet apart – and Sally was usually leading. The crowd in the shuttle bus line was in good spirits despite the heat and stifling humidity. Volunteers walked up and down the parking lot line giving frequent drinks and squirts from an *On the Waterfront* sports bottle.

Rockford's central streets were blocked off for the festival when they got downtown. This meant you could walk down the middle of Main Street without getting run over by anything bigger than a golf cart. They made their way through the security gates to the food and souvenir stands and finally to the Great Lawn down by the riverfront. Only a few small groups of people were here.

"Early enough for you, Jack?" Karen couldn't resist. "Good thing we hurried to get here, huh?" She made eyes at Sally, and they laughed again at Jack's expense.

Jack leaned one sling chair against his leg as he slowly uncovered and unfolded the other one he carried, trying to be casual about observing the few other people in the field. His eyes wandered to the young family at his left. They all sat on a large blanket. Three children had books and pens and paper in front of them. "Dad" lay on his back with his legs crossed. Mom sprawled leisurely on one hip, keeping order and being the task-master.

"Hey," Karen said, kicking the bottom of the sling chair hard. "You gonna set that thing up, or what? Don't just stand there gawking."

Jack grunted, embarrassed. "Over here," he said, pulling the cover up and off his folded sling chair with a flourish. "Front and center, but not so close to the fence that we'll get squished when all the people get here tonight."

"You exaggerate," Karen said. "Again." She looked at Sally. "Still."

"You think there isn't going to be a mob here tonight for Cheap Trick?" Jack caught Sally's eye. "All here to see *Robin Zander*?" they said together.

"Get off it, you two," Karen scoffed.

Smiling broadly, Jack set up his sling chair about eight feet from the orange plastic-link fence. Sally'n'Dave followed suit. In front of them, on the other side of the orange plastic-link divider fence, was the "real" Great Lawn, twenty or thirty rows of white plastic lawn chairs people had to pay a premium to sit in. No one was there yet – but that was reserve seating, not free. The sound stage and light tower were in front of them about a hundred feet. The stage itself was at least two hundred feet away.

"Make sure we sit where I can see them," Karen said.

"Oh yeah," Jack said. "I forgot." He looked over at her. "It's going to be wild in here once the show starts. Can't you just look at the jumbo-trons like everybody else?"

"I came here to see Cheap Trick, and I want to *see* Cheap Trick." Karen puffed a little through her nose. "I would've stayed home and watched MTV if I wanted to see them on a little screen." She moved her chair roughly to the left so her line of sight to the stage wasn't blocked by the light tower.

"Yeah right," Jack mumbled. "On the *History Channel*, maybe." Dave grinned quickly.

Moving left meant moving closer to the neighboring family. Jack walked over to them. "Excuse me," he said. "Do you mind if we set up camp right over here?"

The mom looked at Jack blankly for a moment. Then she shook her husband's shoulder. "Samuel," she said softly, not taking her eyes off Jack. "Samuel?"

"I'm sorry," Jack said. "I just wanted to make sure we wouldn't be intruding on you if we set our chairs up right over here. Out from behind the towers." He pointed.

The dad, Samuel, looked around at the empty field slowly, then at his wife, then finally at Jack. "No problem," he said, with a flip of his hand. "Just so the kids can see, and don't get crowded out from the fence later. OK?" He looked at Jack. "They've been talking nonstop about this concert for the last three weeks, so it's bound to be swamped!"

"Yeah!" said the teenage boy, jumping to his feet. "Dad used to work for Cheap Trick. He drove their bus and everything!"

"Yes!" the little girl piped in. "And he was friends with Bunny too," the other boy cried.

"Now now, children!" Mom said. "Father asked that we not make a scene today. Jeremiah, please sit back down."

"Yes ma'am." The teenager sat. The other two kids went silent too, and hung their heads.

Jack smiled at the kids. He hadn't been around young kids enough lately, he thought. Samuel the dad shrugged, shook his head back and forth at the kids.

"Oh, hey, been there, done that," Jack said. "Best thing I ever did, being a dad." Karen came to stand next to him. He put his arm over her shoulders. "We had five by the merger, two hers and three mine," Jack offered. "We've made it through so far, but not without a few little rough spots." He smiled and held up his crossed fingers. "Fingers crossed, though." Karen smiled. "Yep, never ends." She held up her crossed fingers too.

"Well," Samuel said from the blanket, clearing his throat. "That's something. Mariah." The mom stared at them a moment then turned away, her face pale and her jaw set. Samuel turned his back to Jack and Karen then too and lay back down, covering his head up with his straw hat.

Karen and Jack looked at each other, mouths open, then brought their crossed fingers down together as if on cue. "Alrighty then," Jack said softly as they turned back to their chairs.

After a few minutes they took turns "grazing" the food booths with Sally'n'Dave. One couple would walk around the festival and get food while the other couple saved their places by the fence. Karen and Jack went first, because Sally was busy grading her freshman English papers.

"Well, I guess WE just got dissed," Jack said when they were out of hearing distance.

"Home school," Karen said.

"What?"

"Home-schooled. As in, 'my kids don't need to be exposed to that den of corruption that passes for public schools in this town' home-schooled."

Jack stopped. "Really?"

"Oh yeah. Did you see the lesson plans in her lap?" Karen had been a school psychologist in the public schools for almost thirty years, and knew school lingo. "I've seen her type before. My guess is that she never finished high school, and got the curriculum from her church."

"Oh boy," Jack said. "And they can do that – without any certification or anything?"

"Yep. It's their constitutional right," Karen said. They laughed all the way to the roasted cinnamon almonds.

Once Sally'n'Dave got some food too, they all spent some quality time making fun of Sally's students' papers.

"C'mon. You've got plenty. Divvy them up. Pass them out. It'll go faster."

"I'll get in trouble," Sally whined.

"Only if you get caught," Jack said, smiling.

"We'll just circle the obvious stuff...in pencil," Karen offered. "You can erase the ones you don't like, and then write the actual comments."

Sally frowned. She had four sections of twenty-five students this semester, lots of grading. "Ok, ok... but don't tell anyone."

She handed each of them ten or more freshman English papers. Soon it became a contest to see who could find the stupidest mistakes.

"Look at this one," Karen crowed. "This kid used 'actually' eight times on the first page! What d'ya call that?"

"Pretty stupid?" asked Jack.

"Bland repetition," Sally said smugly, trying not to smile.

The minutes passed quickly. By the time Jack and Karen had had their third bag of cinnamon roasted almonds, soft drinks and a gyro, several hundred people were jammed into the free space in front of the stage, behind the paid seating. The sun set, and it began to get dark.

"Guess you were right," Karen said, looking around. "The place *is* filling up fast."

Jack just nodded, pleased with himself, pleased that Karen would admit he was right for once.

"Got any more papers to grade, Sally?" Jack called from his chair.

She looked up. "It's too dark. You wouldn't be able to see them."

"It probably wouldn't make that much difference!" Jack said, laughing.

"Quit it. You're being mean," Sally said, her face tight. "Besides, I shouldn't have let you see them in the first place. It's against the rules." She sat straight in her chair, her lips drooping. "I could get in trouble."

Jack smiled. Sally certainly was her mother's daughter. He looked at Karen to make sure she'd heard her, but she was being distracted by something else in front of them.

"Look at that guy," Karen said, pointing. She didn't usually point.

"What guy?"

"The short blond guy. Right here in front of us. He just moved up next to the fence."

Jack turned forward and immediately saw who Karen was talking about. Sure enough, one couple stood nonchalantly just in front of them, leaning against the orange plastic fence.

"Huh," he said softly.

"Maybe they don't *really* plan on staying there," Karen said. But even as she said this, the couple in front of them settled in. The man, short, blond, his Hawaiian shirt hanging open to show his bare hairless chest, was joking with the woman. He hung his arm over her shoulders and leaned into her heavily. He was shorter than she was; he had to reach over her at a weird angle. She had on a white tube top and tight short shorts that were both too small for her. Her hair was dyed black and was too long for a woman her age. She had some sort of braided feathers, leather strings, and knots hanging out of her hair and down the side of her face, things a teenager might wear. The blond man had a beer in his hand.

"Some nerve, huh?" Karen said.

Jack got out of his chair, stepped closer to the blond man and waited to be noticed. After a minute standing there he tapped the blond man on the shoulder. "Excuse me," he said, the smile set hard on his face. "You two are standing in front of us. We can't see over you if you're standing here. We're sitting right back there."

He motioned with his hands. Waited. "Could you just move on, please?" Jack showed the man their seats just behind them once more. "We can't see over you if you're standing here," he repeated.

The blond man looked back at Jack and studied him up and down for a moment. Jack outweighed him by a hundred pounds, and was at least a foot taller than he was. "I don't know," the blond man said, rubbing his chin. "What time did you say you were here today?"

Jack's throat pinched tighter. His face was getting red, he knew. "We've been here since about three this afternoon. That family over there was here even earlier than we were," he said, motioning behind him again to the man, woman, and three children on the blanket.

"Well, we picked this spot out this morning," said the shorter man. "So we were here first."

Jack blinked. He couldn't speak. He noticed the woman was staring at him. "Who the hell is *this*?" she said sloppily.

"I'm sorry," Jack talked directly to the blond man as if the woman wasn't there. "You couldn't have been here this morning. If you were we would have seen you here and sat someplace else."

The man exploded with laughter. His hot breath poured out on Jack's chest. "We were here, all right – you just didn't see us." The man stepped closer until he was four or five inches from Jack's face. "We ain't moving," the blond man said.

"Yeah, we ain't movin'," said the lady, moving closer still. "We was here first."

Jack looked down at them both and blinked three more times.

He tried reasoning again. He breathed fast and shallow now. Instinctively he spread his feet apart for better balance. "Look, I don't want any trouble here." Jack held his hand up and counted his arguments out on his fingers as he spoke. "We've been in our spot since three this afternoon. You weren't here then. That man and his family over there" – he turned and pointed, turned back – "they were here when we got here. You weren't."

Jack dropped his hands and stepped closer himself, almost touching the shorter blond man, and stared down at him. "Look. You're in our way. You need to move. Now."

The fat lady wedged herself between them and jabbed her finger in Jack's chest. She apparently didn't care that her heavy breasts smushed against Jack's stomach. "Hey asshole, he just said we was here first and we ain't movin'." She slurred the word *asshole*. "Sit back down. Give us a freakin' break." With that she turned to her husband. They grabbed each other's shoulders and laughed loudly into each other's faces.

Quick as a snake Jack grabbed the little man just under his jaw and lifted him off the ground. The man's beer spilled down the woman's front. His eyes opened wide. "Listen, *ass-hole*," Jack mimicked. "You came in here just now. You got in front of *my* family and *that* family, like I said. Who in the *hell* do you think you are? Huh? What makes you think *you're* any better than any of *us*? Huh?" Jack took a glaring look around, daring anybody in the now-gathering crowd to argue with him, and tightened his grip on the man's throat. "We were here first. That family over there was here before us. You need to move. Right now. I'm tired of screwing with you." And with that he threw the man hard against the plastic fence.

The fat lady screamed. "Ha-lp! Ha-lp! Police! He's hurting my man!" The blond man bounced off the fence and fell to his knees on the grass at Jack's feet. In a second, though, he was up. He pushed his wife out of the way and got his face back into Jack's again. "Who are *you* to tell ME what to do?" He grabbed Jack's shirt. "Huh, asshole?"

Jack couldn't believe this twerp wanted to fight. But if that was what this prick wanted, he'd give it to him. He drew his hand back like an archer. He pictured himself hitting him hard with a straight arm and tight knuckles, right between the upper lip and nose, and drive the punk's nose back into his brain.

Karen grabbed Jack's fist on the backswing with both hands, threw all her weight against his arm, and hung on. Still, he came close to making contact.

"Jack, don't." Karen was talking softly, quietly in his ear even though her breathing was as strained and forced as Jack's. "Don't."

Jack expected to see the man's head explode like a melon dropped from a moving truck, like the 2-by-12's did in his karate exhibitions. But the little man's face was still there. Sweaty. Intact. Smirking.

"Who are YOU to tell ME what to do, huh?" the little man croaked. "Sucker!"

"Jack." Karen was pleading, but still spoke in a quiet voice. She was in his ear. "Jack," she said. "Jack, you're scaring the kids."

Jack looked down at Karen. The fat lady screamed when she could gather enough breath. The crowd around them had formed a semi-circle by now, but kept their distance. People had their mouths open and were screaming too, he thought – he couldn't hear them just then.

Jack turned to look at Sally and Dave. They shrunk down in their lawn chairs hoping nobody would notice them. He looked down at Karen. Her eyes were small, calm, normal. "Not those kids, Jack. *Those* kids." Karen motioned with her hand. "The kids on the blanket."

He turned and looked. The older boy was standing next to his father. The younger boy clutched his mother's skirt and was crying. The little girl had her head buried in the other side of her mother's skirt and just barely peeked out. They weren't screaming their heads off. They weren't jumping up and down. They weren't even moving.

The mother stared at Jack, her face frighteningly blank.

The strength drained out of Jack's raised arm. He dropped it to his side. He began to hear the band again, see the crowd again, smell the beer breath of the man again and hear the wife's shrill stupid cries again. "Halp! Halp! Somebody hallllllllllll-p."

"He's not worth it Jack," Karen muttered. "He's not worth it." Jack's legs trembled as he stood there, the adrenaline rushing through him. He hung his head and threw a sheepish look at the family next to them.

A man who looked to be a security guard made his way to the screaming woman.

"What happened here?"

"That man grabbed me and shoved me down into the ground," whined the blond man. He rubbed his throat and pointed at Jack. Then he pointed down at his grass-stained pants.

"Yeah. That big guy there," added the woman, pointing too.

"Officer," Jack started. "I can explain. You see, we've been here since early this afternoon..."

"Never mind all that. Did you assault this man?"

"It *looks* a little like that," Jack tried. "But it didn't happen quite that way..."

Karen moved in front of Jack, between him and the security guard. "Jack asked this couple politely to move." She waved her arm to include the family on the blanket next to them. "They cut in front of all of us just now, us and that nice family there. Isn't that right?" Karen asked, looking directly at the mother on the blanket with her children. The security guard followed Karen's eyes.

"Is that so?" the guard asked the mother.

"I don't know anything about that," the mother said, gathering herself. The father said nothing. The children were silent too. "This one acted like a heathen and grabbed that other man," she said, practically spitting. "In front of me and my children."

"My children are terrified and this man is to blame." She took her hand off of her daughter's head to wave a finger at Jack. "Jesus said violence is never the answer. Never a solution."

"But..." Jack and Karen said at the same time.

"Yeah," said the blond man and his wife, looking at each other. "Violence is never a solution." He rubbed his hands together and grinned.

Jack looked to others in the crowd for support. The men and women who had cheered him on a minute earlier in the fight ignored him now. The opening band had just finished, and they knew the time for Cheap Trick was close.

"Will you be filing charges, sir?" The security man had to talk loudly to be heard over the cheering.

"I *am* pretty sore." His hand slipped again to his throat, rubbing where Jack had held him tight. He looked at his wife, but by now all her attention was on what was about to happen on stage.

Jack looked at the man coldly. He hated that his own face was flushed, that his legs still trembled, that his breathing was shallow. A criminal record would be unheard of in his company, at his level, but he refused to beg this man.

You gotta draw the line somewhere, he thought.

"Sir?" The security guard asked the blond man again. Already the crowd was crushing in on them, jostling them forward into the orange plastic-link fence. "I need your answer."

The little man was enjoying the moment, making Jack sweat it out. A wicked smile twisted his face.

He put his finger to his lips and closed his eyes. "Nah," he said finally. "Let it go." He waved his hand in dismissal. Then he looked directly at Karen. "He's not worth it."

Karen gasped and jumped for the man. Jack caught her. Then he shifted his gaze from the blond man to the security guard. "Now what?" he asked.

"Now you're gonna have to come with me," the guard said.

Jack nodded. He moved forward. Karen reached around to gather up their chairs.

"No. No. You stay," Jack looked at Karen and put a hand on her shoulder. "I'll go with the security guy. You stay here." Karen froze. "You've wanted to see this concert for a long time. I don't want to ruin it for you." He said it even though he knew he'd already ruined it for her.

Karen paused. "You're sure?" she said.

"Sure I'm sure," Jack said, trying to be nonchalant.

"You don't need me to go with you?"

"I don't think so." He glanced at the guard. The guard nodded. "You can stay here."

"I guess you should go, then, if that's what you need to do." Karen crossed her arms on her chest.

"Yeah," Jack said. "That's what I need to do. You stay here with Sally'n'Dave, okay?" Jack glanced over at them and smiled. They stood clinging to each other. "You guys wave to Robin for me, okay?"

A weak smile crept across Karen's face, despite herself.

She tried one last time. "You're sure about this?"

"Sure I'm sure." He smiled as best he could.

"Okay then…" Her voice trailed off and was smothered by Cheap Trick's opening chords.

The security guard touched Jack's arm. "Let's go," he said, pointing ahead. The two men made their way back to the exit, pushing hard against the crush of the crowd leaning toward the stage. Behind them Cheap Trick's "Dream Police" rang out.

They'd gone about fifty yards when the guard smiled, then chuckled a little. He stepped closer and yelled in Jack's ear.

"Should have slugged that little shit when you had a chance," he said. "Put him down."

Jack stopped in his tracks. He had to concentrate to shut his mouth.

"No blood, no foul, right?" The man turned to look at him squarely. "I saw what you were trying to do. Lucky for you he didn't press charges. Then I would have had to book you," the guard said, laughing a little more. "And don't think I wouldn't have done it, either," he said, wiggling a finger in Jack's face.

"Now get out of here. Go for a walk. Cool off, cool down, whatever." He waved his free hand. "I've got bigger fish than you to fry tonight. All the idiots and perverts come out after dark." The man paused, sighed. "And if *your* wife's anything at all like *my* wife, you'll have hell enough to pay when you get home anyways." With that he gave Jack a little smile and a shove and left him.

Jack tried to stammer "thanks," at least, but he couldn't say anything. He just stood there. People bobbed and pushed around him, trying to get closer to the stage. He forced his legs to move. "I'll go get the car," he said aloud to no one. But finally his brain kicked in. "I'll go catch the bus back and get the car," he thought. He lurched forward, patted the keys in his pocket. "I'll get the car, and park down here close so I can pick Karen and Sally'n'Dave up after the concert. So they won't have to walk so far."

It wasn't much of a plan, he knew. But in his dazed state it was enough to get him moving again, to get his legs going in the same general direction. "I'll call them," he thought, adding details to his plan as he walked. "I'll park down by the library. No, the Ice-house." He nodded his head, swung his arms to keep the circulation going, walked toward the bus stop faster now. "They'll get home earlier. Get to bed sooner."

This talking to himself worked for a while, but by the time Jack got to the bus stop to the off-site parking lot his mood had shifted. Now he was pissed. What the hell happened back there? His heart pounded harder and his pulse surged again. *I was right. I was in the right*, dammit! He smirked. *I should have pressed charges myself.*

The streets were nearly empty; most of the crowd was at the Cheap Trick concert. *Where I should still be,* Jack thought, getting angry all over again.

"Shit!" he yelled, drawing stares and a wide berth from a young couple that walked down his side of the street. He sat on a brick ledge near the bus stop. There were just a few people around him, an old couple with plaid sashes and bright silver medallions from some sort of ethnic group performance, a few teenage boys with iPods, and a young woman and her three small children.

Jack's attention was drawn to the woman with the kids. Twenty, twenty-five at most. And three kids already. She was a petite woman with short black hair. She wore shorts and a beige cotton top. Practical. A mom's outfit. One of the kids, the oldest, a curly-haired girl of four at most, was asleep on her mom's right shoulder. Another baby, a boy, a toddler perhaps, was cradled in her left arm. The third, definitely an infant, lay in the stroller, but squirmed and fussed and kicked her blanket off.

The bus to the Target parking lot rounded the corner. The old man and women closest to the bus stop were nearly run over by the teenage boys jumping and dodging, trying to be first on the bus as soon as it emptied.

Jack watched the women and her children struggle to hold her spot and then try to move toward the bus. He took a deep breath and stepped forward.

"Here, let me help you."

She looked up at him, startled at first, then smiled slightly. "I'm okay. I can get it, thanks."

"No problem." Jack reached to keep the stroller from rolling off the curb into the bus. "Let me help. Tell me what to do."

She stared at him for a moment. Did a thorough take up and down. "You're not a serial killer or a rapist, are you?" She smiled again, a little broader this time. Then she said, "I can do this, but my arm's about to fall off. Can you take Christie?" She nodded as best she could toward the child sleeping on her shoulder. "She's my biggest load."

"You bet." Jack reached out, pried the sleeping girl from her mother's body, and hoisted Jackie into his arms. He moved her head against his own shoulder, his big hand covering her whole head. Christie woke up for a moment, barely opened her eyes, then smacked her lips loudly and buried her cheek into Jack's shoulder.

Then he and the woman got the other two children and the stroller into the bus. They went all the way to the back and sat together across the long bench seat over the engine. The young woman turned and looked at him and blushed.

"I don't know what I was thinking," she said. "Taking three kids down here was a little risky, but I had it under control. When they were all awake and Christie and Aiden could walk alongside, we were just fine." She looked down at her lap.

She continued, quieter. "I lost track of time, that's all. And Christie held out as long as she could," the mom said, nodding toward her daughter on Jack's chest.

Mom was quiet, looked down. Jack felt the weight of the little girl cuddled into him.

He reached out and touched her arm. "I know what it's like. I'm a dad. I have a few of my own, you know." He smiled broadly. "You did fine."

"My husband Mark. He's deployed. Army." She swallowed hard. "Iraq. Calvary." Her eyes glistened and she looked away.

Jack's throat tightened for the second time that night. "You were just trying to give your kids a little fun." She turned to him. He looked right at her, his eyes steady. "You're doing the best you can." He shifted the girl on his shoulder. "It isn't easy. And it sure as hell ain't easy going it alone like you're doing."

The woman had wedged her toddler son Aiden between her own hip and Jack's leg. The boy leaned against Jack's side, his little body rocking with the starting and stopping of the bus as he struggled not to fall asleep. Jack laid his free hand and forearm over the boy's shoulder to make sure he didn't fall. The boy soon leaned against him and closed his eyes.

The baby in the stroller fussed some more. The mom took a hand-knitted nursing shawl out of the diaper bag and slung it over her shoulder on her free side. She picked the baby up with practiced ease. She opened up her blouse discreetly under the blue-and-white shawl, adjusted the baby, opened up her bra and guided the baby to her nipple. Jack found himself staring and looked away hotly, remembering that warm amber time in his own life when *his* children were nursing.

A few of the teenage boys sat on the side seats. They sat like teenage boys sit, legs far apart, shoulders slumped low, chins nearly to their chests. A couple of them stared at the nursing mom.

Jack cleared his throat loudly.

"Gentlemen," he said, looking squarely at the two boys that were staring the most. They both jumped and averted their eyes, their cheeks rosy. The mom threw Jack a quick, appreciative look, then turned slightly and looked out the side window as her baby sucked and cooed noisily.

Jack settled into his seat. A cool evening breeze from the open windows danced across his hot face. The gears and driveshaft engaged loudly and spun under him as the bus moved up and down the streets and hills of his home town. The street lights glared bright, fell dark, then came back bright through the windows, over and over again like the refrain of an old folk song as the bus rolled through that melody of light. The young girl on his chest burrowed closer to him in her deep child's sleep, and smacked her lips. Drool puddled on his shoulder, wet and warm through his shirt. Soon his heartbeat matched hers. His breathing matched her breathing. Her baby brother slept peacefully in the crook of Jack's elbow, under his thick forearm, head burrowed into the soft little paunch that Jack had noticed that morning in the bathroom mirror.

Jack took a deep breath and let it out slowly. He settled himself deeper into his seat, careful not to disturb his two charges. Finally he closed his eyes, let his head lie back on the seat's top, softly, and let himself sway, loose and silent, in time with the bus.

COMING HOME

Jim hadn't been back to the farm for three years since his fight with Ike, his dad. Took off the day his mom died. Didn't even stay for the funeral, whatever that was like, what with Ike in charge.

The only reason he was going home now was because Dutch called him and told him that Jimmer had had a seizure. Dutch had grown up on the farm next to theirs, gone to school with Jim's mother, had been his 4-H leader and wrestling coach through high school. Dutch was more than just a neighbor. But Jim needed to see for himself that the old hound was okay. Needed to get Jimmer out of there, make sure his old man Ike didn't do something stupid.

Like put his dog down.

He didn't put it past him.

"Seizures like that're fairly common in an old boy like Jimmer," Dutch said when he called Jim on Thursday. "Scary, yeah," he was saying, "But common in a big dog like that."

Jim wasn't so sure. "Well then," said Dutch. "You come on down and see for yourself. Be here Saturday so's you can join us for the coon hunt, too."

"Should be fun," Jim quipped.

Right, he thought now as he drove. Should be.

It took him less than two hours to drive down to the farm from his south-side Chicago apartment, even though the two places were worlds apart in his mind. He rounded the bend in the gravel driveway and saw the rusty old windmill tower first, still standing although a few of the thick brown blades were missing from the fan. Then he passed the milk house with its scratched galvanized tank full of cool water and capped hot milk cans from the evening milking by now. Finally he got in front of the square two-story farmhouse he'd grown up in. He remembered waking up mornings to the sounds of Ike pulling the milk cans from the barn to the milk house, shuffling along at the yoke of his old wooden-planked cart. Someone that didn't know Ike, like Jim's big-town friends, would look at Ike's short, cover-alled frame and wonder how such a small guy could pull such a load as that.

But then they didn't know farmers. And they didn't know Ike.

Those early days, the deep rich aroma of coffee brewing, bacon frying, and biscuits browning would rise and reach him from the kitchen where his mother bustled about. He'd lay there in his bed purposely until she called up to him, sometimes listening to the south-bound train coming through Byron before he got up and hustled downstairs.

From what he could see now from his seat in the car in the driveway, little had changed in the three years he'd been gone. Those missing blades on the windmill – the old man wouldn't haul his ass up there to fix those, and he sure as hell wasn't going to pay anyone else to do it. The door on the milk house sagged a little now. A few more chunks of stiff green siding were gone from the house. Scraps of clear plastic sheeting hung from fir strips around the window frames, flimsy insulators flapping uselessly in the autumn breeze. Several bales of straw sat crookedly against a basement window, gray from many months of rain, sun and snow.

A number of pickups were parked around the yard and the driveway. Farmers' trucks, working trucks, with dirt and weeds and straw and dust and cow shit crusted thick on every one of them. Full gun racks hung in the cabs. Wire kennels and hounds sat in the back of most of the pickups. A few of the hounds were whining, but most were settled in, quiet. A handful of men milled around between the house and gravel driveway, clustered in small groups of two or three, standing easy, waiting for something important to happen, patient men used to waiting, farmers waiting now for the hunt to start.

Jim parked in the driveway next to a faded blue Chevy pickup closest to the house.

Dutch turned to the group of men he was standing with, said something and pointed to Jim. Then he strode all the way across the yard with an outstretched hand as Jim got out of his car. Dutch was a tall man, six-and-a-half feet at least, pushing 275 pounds, short-haired and deeply tanned. It occurred to Jim that he'd never seen Dutch without a tan.

"Hey, Dutch," Jim said, as he grabbed Dutch's hand. "What you been up to?"

"Up to no good. Nothin' good," Dutch replied, grinning and taking his hand. "You guys all know Ike's boy Jim," Dutch yelled to the yard full of farmers. They all stopped talking for a second. A few nodded slightly in his direction. Jim nodded back. He felt good about recognizing so many of the men he'd grown up around, but he felt a little embarrassed to be the center of attention now. He put his hand to his blond head self-consciously, tipped his baseball cap. His face went red as he realized he'd done this small formality without a thought, something he wouldn't dream of doing in Chicago, and the little-boy dimples that his mom liked so much burned into his cheeks as he looked down at his boots. The men's voices quickly surged and fell over the lawn again, though, like the ebb and flow of the wind, or a dinner bell sounding over the grass.

Jim pulled his cap tight on his head.

"Your old man's in the house," Dutch said with a grin and a nod. He paused. "What's a twenty-year-old boy like you do up there in Shy-ka-go for fun these days?"

He'd put a lot of emphasis on *boy*. "Not a lot," said Jim. "Got into playing paintball with some of the guys. You know, big-time? Obstacle courses and all? Teams?" He looked into Dutch's blank stare. "It's what city folk do instead of hunt, Dutch," he said smugly. "We've been champs of our league two years running now."

"Sheee-it," Dutch said. He spat on the ground. "Full-grown men playing with popguns and water balloons. What's next, huh? I ask you," he said to the crowd, doing a little circle in place. "What's next?"

Then Dutch reached over and knocked Jim's cap off. He tried to ruffle Jim's blond hair, laughing, but Jim ducked away. Dutch tried to catch him in a half-nelson, but Jim spun away from it, smiling. Quickly Jim whipped off his jacket and threw it to the ground. He set his feet and raised his arms to a fighting stance and tried to look tough. "So Dutch, you gonna tell me where the hell my dog is, or what?"

Dutch smiled back and pointed behind him. "If you aren't careful with all your stupid dancing around, you just might step on 'im."

Jim flinched and turned like a snake bit him. He saw Jimmer. He'd just crawled out from under the porch. Jim dropped to his knees.

"Hey Jimmer boy – how ya doin'?" The old coonhound struggled to his feet, his hind parts stiff from lying down. Jim ran his hands quickly over the hound's body, then caught his head between his hands, and roughed his ears back and forth. Jimmer's tail swung back and forth in quick rhythm. Then Jim tugged on each ear and pulled them both back together with his thumbs around the dog's head, just like he used to do.

He stared deep into Jimmer's big brown eyes, and Jimmer stared back.

Once he was satisfied that his dog was all right, Jim buried his nose into the nape of Jimmer's warm neck to suck in his strong musty smell. He felt the dog's breath on his skin, warm, knew Jimmer had his mouth open, had his tongue hanging out. "Scared me, you old bastard." He leaned back and ruffled the top of the dog's head again.

"Get away from that dog before you ruin him." The screen door slammed against the jamb. Ike burst through the door and came down the stoop – he might have been there watching all along or he might have just come to the door. Jim jerked at the noise and landed hard on the grass on his butt.

"Oh yeah," Ike said, tossing his words behind him, never slowing down. "Too late. You already ruined him."

Jim bit down on his lip. His cheeks burned for the second time in five minutes. The men in the yard didn't show any signs that they'd seen or heard anything unusual. But all the hounds in the pickups were on their feet. They knew it was time. They knew something was going to happen soon. They flooded the yard with their excited yips.

Ike stopped by the blue Chevy. "Alright," he said. "It'll be pitch dark by the time we get down to the river. You boys ready?"

"Yeah, Ike, yeah, we're ready," Dutch said, stepping closer. "We're all set."

"OK then," Ike said. He turned back to Jim and pointed. "You'll be going with me." And with that he walked around the nose of his truck and pulled open the driver's door.

Jim leaned to his feet and turned for Jimmer. He threw on his jacket then scooped the dog up in his arms and carried him to the back of Ike's truck.

"Jimmer don't hunt anymore. Can't keep up," Ike said, crossing his arms across his chest.

"Yeah? Well tough shit, old man." Those were his first words to his father in three years. "I'm not going without him," Jim said. He set Jimmer in the truck bed and stood there.

Ike smiled a tight smile and shook his head. "Wasting your time, bringing him." Then he grabbed the steering wheel and struggled to pull himself into the driver's seat.

"Whatever."

Jim slammed the tailgate shut and walked slowly to the passenger door. Across the cab he saw Ike drag his left leg up from the ground to the floorboard with his arms. Ike had caught his pant leg in a power-take-off last summer getting off the tractor while raking hay. He'd gone up and down that tractor with the hay rack hitched with the PTO whining thousands of times before, but that didn't matter that one time. Laid there most of the day before anyone found him, Dutch said when he called Jim to tell him. Now Ike strained to push down the clutch and put the truck in gear. He insisted on a hard spring-loaded clutch to keep the wear down. He gunned the gas, popped the clutch, and the truck lurched forward.

Jim just smiled to himself. No automatics for ole Ike. No way. First a stick shift, always a stick shift. Gotta be a stick shift.

They drove down to the river in silence, the headlights catching bits of the now-harvested fields and scattered scrawny underbrush along the road, the dash lights highlighting Ike's two-day stubble and the deep creases in his face. His face was tanned like

Dutch's, but showed more cracks around the eyes and mouth. Tufts of gray shot out around his temples and behind his ears. Something new since Jim had left.

There in the truck Jim wondered again what his mother had ever seen in Ike. She was a good-looking woman. She'd been to college, had a career in the city, had an apartment of her own. She could have done anything she wanted to do in the world. But instead of going out on a career of her own, she came back to the farm when her dad died and settled for marrying Ike.

"So did you miss me, too?" Ike startled Jim by speaking, yelling over the strained sound of the engine, wound-out in second gear. "As much as you missed that damn ole dog of yours?"

Jim didn't know if he was expected to answer or not. He decided not.

Ike finally shifted from second to fourth, and the truck rattled and sputtered, then groaned forward. "What's it been – three years?" Ike looked over at Jim, then turned his head and spit out his open window.

On his side of the cab Jim let his arm rise and sink in the strong airstream outside his rolled-down window as the pickup lurched down to the river through the cool night air. He cupped his hand in the current, feeling the difference between an open and closed hand. He breathed deep before answering. "Somethin' like that, I guess."

"You guess." Ike grunted and blew air through his nose. Jim stared out at the flat fields they were passing, thinking Ike was going to say something else. But that was all he said.

Jim thought now about the first time he and Ike went hunting together. Jim was fifteen at the time, ancient for a first hunt by farm standards. He'd been begging Ike to take him hunting for what seemed ages.

"Every other kid's already been hunting for years!" Jim whined.

"Hunting's a dangerous affair, too dangerous for a boy like you," Ike said, every time Jim asked. "We'll go when I say you're ready to go. Not before."

"I'm ready!" Jim always said. "How would *you* know if I'm ready or not?"

Ike always shook his head and walked away. Jim finally had to beg his mom to get Ike to take him hunting. He knew she had her ways of convincing Ike, and he couldn't turn her down forever. Of course, Jim had been hunting with his friends a lot by then, but he never had much fun because he worried about getting hurt somehow and then having to confess to Ike. And he'd been to every coon hunt since he was eleven, except for the last few years while he was in Chicago, but Ike had never let him carry a gun in a single coon hunt.

The day he turned fifteen, a Saturday, he remembered, Ike handed him the old single-shot .22 rifle that hung in the screened-in front porch. He gave him one brass long-rifle shell which Jim put in the breech, and then silently led him out the west road to the upper cow pasture where some old farm machinery sat rusting away.

Jim wanted to hunt with a real gun, not the old .22. He'd shot plenty of cans and bottles at the garbage pit already with Tommy Gordon's .22, though nobody else but Tommy knew that. A .22 wasn't nearly as good as a shotgun, in his mind. But he took it. If this is what it takes to prove to Ike I'm ready, I'll do it, he thought. Besides, Jimmer got to come along. He ran from one side of the pounded-down dirt farm path to the other, tail wagging, mouth hanging open, excited as a little kid.

They saw the rabbit sitting in the pasture as they opened the four-planked wooden gate between the yard and the pasture. It stopped nibbling grass and stared up at them. When Jim closed the gate, the rabbit bounded under the old manure spreader with the high iron seat. They walked closer.

The rabbit had Jimmer's full attention from the start. He'd squeezed under the gate ahead of the man and boy but held point, barely breathing, shivering all down his back and sides.

"Well?"

"Well what?" Jim said, looking up at his father.

"Well—there's your rabbit. Go shoot it."

Jim blinked. This wasn't at all like what he'd imagined. He'd pictured Jimmer flushing the rabbit from some high grass and him leading the brown bounding rabbit just right, picking him off with a perfect shot from at least fifty yards away, impressing Ike, saying when Ike patted him on the back, "It was nothing. Had him all the way," like he shot rabbits all the time just for sport.

But here now in the field it was different. Ike knelt in the dirt pasture, bent down and looked under the old manure spreader, so Jim did too. There was the rabbit, hunched up tight, his chin over his white-fluffed belly and long narrow feet, his ears flat against his round brown body, his eyes opened wide like a statue's.

"Shoot him."

Jim didn't shoot, sat frozen. Ike stood up.

"Shoot him," he said louder. When Jim didn't shoot, again, Ike waved his arm toward the old shit spreader and blew air loudly through his nose. "Shoot him, dammit."

Still on the ground on his belly, Jim lined up the bead on the .22's barrel with the rabbit's narrow head and stared at him. The wide eyes stared back at him. The dry grass pricked his cheeks. The dirt hung thick and rusty in his nose. Finally he laid the gun down and looked up.

"I can't."

Ike frowned at him. Jim tried to hold his gaze but couldn't. He looked away. Jimmer lay next to Jim, glancing from the man to the boy and back to the man. Ike finally snorted, stooped to the ground again, grabbed the gun roughly by the stock and pulled the trigger.

The rifle puffed and jerked, hardly making a sound.

Ike reached under the spreader frame and dragged the rabbit out by its hind legs. He put his boot over what was left of the rabbit's head and yanked up hard. The rabbit's skull and face stayed under Ike's boot while the rest of him tore off at the neck easily, a brutal but clean field dressing.

Jim stared. He couldn't turn away.

Ike spun on his heels then and started walking home, still holding the rabbit by the feet. The headless rabbit swung from his side like a pendulum as he walked. Its blood left red splatters in the dry winter dirt and grass.

Jimmer came to the boy's side and leaned against his leg. Boy and dog sat this way for a moment, then ran to catch up. Ike was already through the gate, left it standing open behind him. Jim went through, closed the gate, caught up and reached for the gun.

Ike jerked it away.

"Guess you aren't ready yet after all, huh?"

Jim never told anyone about that day, not the details, at least – not even his mother. But because of that day he'd dedicated the next two years to proving Ike wrong in everything he did. All that time he'd felt Ike's eyes on him – through the injuries, the detentions, the warnings from the local cops for driving too fast on the country blacktops.

Jim got suspended from school three times, nearly got expelled once for fighting Bruce Lewis over a brownie at lunch. He quit going to church, even though he knew it hurt his mother. He'd hear the bells ring down at the Stillman First Presbyterian church on Sunday morning, sit there at the table with his coffee while his mom passed through the kitchen in her Sunday best, stop, wait, not say anything, then, finally, after two or three minutes of silence, sigh and go on out to Ike waiting in the truck. Jim didn't go to church because it made Ike look stupid. He felt bad about hurting his mom's feelings, but he couldn't see a way around it, and he felt like he couldn't give in.

Other than her silent Sunday ritual, Jim's mom stood gently, vocally at his side through these bad times. Why did he do such crazy, risky, stupid things? She begged him to stop, pleaded with him to stop. And every time she pleaded, he just shrugged. Every night he and Ike ate dinner at his mother's table without talking to each other, while she sat between them and told them about her day, related her news of the town, tried to be cheerful. Eventually, though, she didn't say anything at supper, either.

They all got used to living that way, thought that was just the way it was for them now.

Then Jim's mom got sick. It was like he sprang awake from a deep sleep. He snapped out of his funk with a new mission in life: If he could be better, maybe he could make her better. Overnight he became the model student, model friend, model son – to her, anyway, even as he got madder and madder at Ike. He even started back to church, just to please her: He got ready and out to the truck Sunday morning's before they did, before the church bells rang, even, sat on his side of the cab with her, again, between him and Ike. He blamed *Ike* for making her sick, for neglecting her, for treating her worse than one of his old pieces of farm equipment, worse than that old shit spreader out in the west pasture where Ike'd murdered the rabbit. But for her sake he swallowed his anger and tried to be there.

Now in the truck heading to the river on a cool autumn evening nearly four years after his mom first got sick, that old familiar silence wedged itself between him and Ike again easily. Jim slumped down in his seat and stared out the window. By the growing number of trees he saw in the headlights, he knew they were getting closer to the river at the far west edge of their property.

The late-October days here were sunny and still mostly warm, but the nights were cold, and the coons were fat now in their new winter coats – their thick hides would bring a good price down at the Field and Game. A clear sky and a full white moon hung in the sky tonight. They pulled off the blacktop highway and followed the other trucks down a rough dirt road to the river. The coons liked to come to the river at night and eat.

Over the years, sportsmen from town had built ponds and blinds in these woods to attract flocks of ducks and geese so they could shoot them easier. These blinds became a nuisance to the farmers this time of year, something you had to walk around and keep the dogs out of while you were trying to run down a coon.

Ike pulled in line with the other trucks at the clearing. Jim got out first, quickly, walked around and opened the tailgate. He could smell the black water of the river more than see it through the Illinois pines and maples and oaks. The woods crowded the water here, and Jim could feel the weight of the trees on his shoulders, on his back – a presence not a burden, like smoke from a fire, familiar, natural, just there.

Jimmer came up to him slowly in the bed of the truck, tail wagging. Jim ruffled his ears and then lifted him to the ground.

At his side of the truck Ike had his .22 pistol and holster on already. He pulled a double-barreled 12-gauge shotgun out from behind the seat, and slipped two brass-and-red-plastic shells in the breech. The gun's blue barrels, older than even Ike himself, were now almost white from wear and age. The stock was badly scratched and pitted. But even six feet away, Jim could smell the gun oil. That sweet sharp smell rushed right up his nose and slammed his sinuses. He could almost taste it.

"You take this." Ike held out the still-breeched 12-gauge. "Probably nothing you can do to it that hasn't already been done a couple times." Ike blew air through his nose again. "Just don't shoot at anything smaller 'en a bear, eh? They don't call'em scatter guns for nothing." He sneered. "Think you can shoot it?" The gun hung between them.

Jim took the shotgun, snapped the breech shut and checked the safety. "I can shoot it." He cradled the gun in the crook of his arm like he might hold a baby.

Ike shook his head, then reached out and pushed the gun barrel down until it pointed at the ground. "Kids," he snorted. He turned away and headed toward the fire pit where the other men already were. He yelled at Herbie Olemeier, and together they walked out to look for tracks.

Dutch was already sitting in the large circle of men surrounding the fire in what was basically a large meadow. He was at the north end of the ring. Three or four guys had started the fire, thirty feet from Herbie and Ike and Dutch. Someone had obviously set it up sometime earlier that day, because it caught quickly and lit up the clearing fast. Jim could feel the heat pouring off the fire as he walked past it to where Dutch sat.

Dutch grinned. "Long ride over here, Jimmy?" He laughed, tried to look serious. "You guys bond much on the way over?"

Jim punched Dutch in the arm. Dutch wasn't fazed. They leaned their guns against their log and breathed easy. Dutch folded his arms behind his head, leaned back and shut his eyes. After staring at the fire several minutes, Jim broke the quiet. "Believe it or not, we did talk a little," he said, eyes closed.

"Good," said Dutch. "Good for you."

"Yeah, right. But not about anything important. Not about anything good."

Dutch grinned as he resettled himself on the log. "What's the good stuff?"

"You know. Him. Me. The fight." Jim cleared his throat. "Mom." Jim sat up.

"Oh, *that* good stuff," Dutch said, smiling.

"Why'd she have to marry *him,* for Christ's sake, Dutch? What did she ever see in that old man?"

Dutch stared right at Jim, answered quick, not blinking. "She loved him."

"Oh, right." He laughed. "You're so full of shit."

"And Ike loved her back."

"Now I *know* you're full of shit, Dutch." Jim crossed his arms. "Been hitting the applejack a little hard, have we?"

"Seriously. He'd do anything for her. Anything." He paused. Jim thought he saw the corner of Dutch's eye twitch. "Trust me."

"Who told you that big fat lie?" Jim scoffed. "Who in their right mind told you that Ike loved my mom?"

Dutch took his time answering. He turned his head and spit, then looked directly at Jim. "She did."

"What?" Jim's eyes went wide. "*What?*"

"Your mom," Dutch repeated, slowly. "She told me. We did grow up next to each other, you know. Known each other forever." He swallowed hard. "*Knew* each other, anyways." Dutch looked away, looked up in the sky at the moon. "She asked *me* to do it – you know, asked me first and all –" the fire sucked in the air around them "– but I couldn't do it. I just couldn't."

Jim felt a little dizzy, a little sick. "What do you mean she asked you to *do it* – asked you to do *what?*"

Dutch looked away, toward the river this time. "Your mom, she was a proud woman, Jimmy. Smart. Full of life." He paused. "But she was sick, in a lot of pain in the end. A lot of pain. You didn't see it, you weren't there enough – you were at school."

Jim kicked the dirt. He remembered that spring, half of him not wanting to go to school, wanting to stay with his mom, but the other half relieved to get out of the house and have someplace else to go.

"I only went to school 'cause he *made* me go to school!"

"Yeah, I know – he *made* you go to high school so you'd graduate with your class. What a bastard." Dutch took a breath. "She told him to make you go. Didn't want you to have to listen to her moan all day." Dutch looked down at his boots, was quiet for a few seconds more, then spoke. "She wanted it over, I'm telling you. She wanted out. Wanted it done with."

Dutch looked up at Jim again. Dutch's wet eyes shined bright in his tanned face. "You know what I'm talking about?"

They sat silent for several moments, not looking at each other. Jim's stomach flipped in his gut, and his chest tightened. He knew. He'd suspected, at least on some level, for a long time, maybe since it happened. That was why he came back now: He was afraid Ike was going to put Jimmer down. He knew Ike was capable…

Jim cleared his throat. "Why didn't you tell me this before?"

"She asked me not to."

"So you just did what she said?" he snorted. "Ok. Why you telling me this *now*?"

"I've watched you and your dad ignore each other for way too many years. Seems high time someone said something. This seemed as good a time as any. Better than most, even."

Then: "Can't hold it in any longer."

Jim didn't know what to think. But it was true, he knew. One look at Dutch and he knew. Dutch looked like a hundred-pound weight had just been lifted off him, like he'd just confessed a crime of his own.

But now what?

Jim stood up and brushed off his pants. He took a deep breath, then let it out slowly, loudly. "I gotta go talk to the old man about this." He searched the small groups of men, made his way around the fire and over to where Ike was now sitting on a log with Herbie Olemeier. "Hey old man," Jim yelled. "Dutch just told me you killed my mom, put 'er down like some dumb animal."

Ike stopped talking in mid-sentence. He turned his head toward Jim slowly. Herbie looked down, then gathered up his gun and gear and left. Jim stood his ground.

Ike put his hands together in front of him. "Dutch talks too much."

"Yeah – he's a real blabbermouth, all right, that Dutch." Jim stared at his father. "So'd you do it? Is it true? Did you put 'er down like some animal?" Jim's lips curled.

Ike looked from his hands to Jim, back again to his hands. "So what if I did?"

"So what!?! So you'd be a damn murderer, is so what!" he yelled. Jim stood dangerously close.

"Watch your tone with me, boy." Ike turned and stared down a couple of the other men that had looked their way. "Sit the hell down and listen. For once."

Jim paced back and forth, his breaths shallow, his clenched fists white at his side. Finally he sat down a few feet away from Ike, on a separate log. "You make my skin crawl. You make me want to puke."

Ike stared at Jim until the boy looked away. Then he went on. "Those were bad days – long, bad days toward the end. Your mom knew what was coming. Knew it wasn't going to be pretty. But she stuck it out til you graduated." Ike filled his pipe from the tobacco bag in his pocket, pushed the tobacco down, lit it, took a long draw. "She asked me to do it." He took another draw on the pipe, blew that smoke out his nose. "And I did what she asked me to do."

Jim swallowed hard. He hoped his stomach would settle soon and that he wouldn't really puke in front of Ike. He heard his pulse pounding in his head, felt like a little kid in the dark, scared of the monsters he heard shuffling and scraping their way toward him.

He didn't know what to say. What came out was, "Why didn't you tell me any of this before?"

"She made me swear not to tell you, that's why. Afraid you'd think she wasn't tough enough to stick it out or some other goddamn stupid thing like that." He snorted again.

Jim was dizzy. He could barely breathe. "That day. At the end. Why didn't you let me see her?"

Ike took his time smoking his pipe. "You ever seen a vet put down a dog or a horse or anything? No," said Ike, answering for him. "No, you haven't." He paused. "Sometimes they just drop off and flop over, go to sleep easy. And sometimes they don't."

Jim sat still. Tears smarted his eyes. He was pissed when his voice came out high and thin. "You should have let me see her."

Ike cleaned mud out of the cleats in his boot with a twig. "Maybe," he grunted. "Maybe not."

Jim waited for more, his thoughts spinning. But it was like it was in the truck – there wasn't anything else coming. Not from Ike. At least not now. He rocked forward on the log, grabbed his knees. "So who else knows?"

"Milly, of course. She came over and pronounced your mom – hospice nurses can do that, you know." He tossed the twig away. "Apparently she told Dutch."

"Apparently." Jim smiled weakly and looked down at his hands, wet from tears he hadn't felt roll down his cheeks. Then he stood, shaking, breathless. "I gotta go think some about this."

"Yeah," said Ike. "You do. You go do that."

Jim stumbled back to where Jimmer and Dutch still sat in the log ring around the fire. He sat down next to Jimmer and buried his head in his crossed arms to think. He wondered now when it was that Ike actually did it. Wondered if his mother had heard him come home from school that day, or whether she was already gone by then? Wondered more about what happened in that room between her and Ike: "Sometimes they just flop over easy, sometimes they don't," he'd said.

Thursday, June 10, 1972. Milly'd propped his mom up in her bed so she could see him in his graduation gown. Did her hair up special even though she knew she wasn't going with – she chose not to take chemo so she could keep her hair and live these last few weeks or months alive the best she could. She sat there in her clean blue housecoat with white ruffles on the sleeves and ruffles down the middle where it was buttoned shut. "Let me see you," she'd said to him when he came into her room. Milly smiled and stepped out.

"What a handsome man you are, all dressed up. Too big to give your ole Ma a kiss?" He balked. "How 'bout a hug?" He hugged her lightly so he wouldn't hurt her. By then she couldn't lift her arms to hug him back. Jim couldn't remember now if he said goodbye to her or not. Probably, he thought.

Then the blur of graduation, rushing home to show her his diploma. But when he got home the house was locked, bolted shut. He pounded and yelled at Ike, screamed at him, pleaded with him, beat his fists on the door, swore at Ike for not letting him in.

Ike finally came to the door. Finally showed his face.

"She's gone," he said, looking down at his feet. "Your mama's gone."

"No." Jim stepped back. Then: "Let me see her, Ike."

"No," he said. Ike opened the screen door, leaned his head out to spit.

Jim grabbed him then and yanked him out. They struggled out on the porch, down the porch stairs, and into the yard, but Ike just pushed him hard and held him tight to the ground at the end. It wasn't much of a fight. Jim twisted and turned and struggled but he couldn't get away.

"Stay down, boy."

"Screw you, Ike!"

Ike held Jim like that until he quit moving, then finally let him up. Jim threw his new diploma against the wall of the house, swore a few more times at Ike, stomped off, jumped in his car, peeled out in the gravel, and never looked back.

Now by the fire in the woods on a cold October night three years later, only five minutes passed while he remembered, while he relived it all yet again. A man's yell made him look up. The dogs were out of the trucks and on long leather leashes now. He saw Ike glance at his watch then wave a hand over his head.

"Hang on to Jimmer," Dutch said, pointing at the dog and standing. "*Jim.* You with me? Hang on to him. Hook up that leash." Jim shook his head, reoriented himself to where he was. He watched his own hand sliding slowly toward Jimmer's neck with the hook of the leash. The dog whined and squirmed against him, excited.

Then Ike pumped his arm and pointed toward the woods. Herbie Olemeier gave a shout, and the men turned their dogs loose. Jim had a hand on Jimmer's collar, but Jimmer shot out of Jim's grip and lurched forward with the other dogs – the leash still in Jim's hand. Ike tried to grab Jimmer as he rushed past, but he was too slow. He disappeared into the dark woods with the other dogs.

"Dammit Jimmer – get back here!" Jim called weakly. He stood. Ike gave him a cool look, then turned away.

"He'll be back once he gets tired," Dutch said, putting his hand on Jim's shoulder. "He'll tire out quick and be back in a few minutes, you watch."

A hush settled in around the men then, broken by the occasional yip from one or two of the dogs in the distance. After a few more minutes with nothing happening, they all sat in their places on the logs around the fire again.

"They haven't hit a trail yet," Dutch said after another five minutes. "We'd of heard. Nothing yet."

As if on cue they heard some of the dogs yelp. Shouts went up. "Now they're on to one! Now they got one!"

"No – listen close!" someone said. The men strained their ears. "They got *two*."

"Shut up!" cried Herbie, even though by then nobody was talking. They listened some more. Ten dogs raised their voices together in harmony. But then another dog's howl rose above the others'.

"That one's Jimmer," Ike said. They listened harder. "There he is again. They're split. Going different directions. That's Jimmer, I'm telling you. " He started off in a rolling gait toward the river, his injured left leg stiff beneath him. "I gotta go get him. You all go after those others."

Ike came hobbling right at Jim, where Jim could see his strained face clearly in the light from the fire. He saw something deep and dangerous in the stubble and creases this time that he'd never seen before. Ike pushed past him, using Jim's shoulder as leverage to spring himself forward.

"Let's go!" Dutch cried. "Let's go to those dogs!" He flicked on his flashlight, grabbed his gun, and ran toward the other men.

Jim stood there stupidly for a moment. He looked both ways. It was suddenly, harshly quiet with everybody gone. As he stood still he heard the pine sap pop in the dying fire, heard the dry leaves rustle in the slight breeze. He ran in the direction Dutch and the other men had gone. Then he stopped, his heart beating wildly in his chest. He stood for another second, shifting from leg to leg, unsure. "Shit," he finally said out loud to the fire. And then he turned and ran the direction Ike had gone.

He'd lost precious time deciding which way to go, he knew. Ike was almost a minute ahead of him. As he ran through the needle-littered path in the woods he realized that with the moon where it was he could make out most of the trail without his flashlight, so he turned it off and tossed it aside to free his hand. He fell quickly into a smooth running rhythm once he could pump his arms freely. The shotgun was heavy in his hand but balanced. He felt his heartbeat settle. A trickle of sweat rolled down from his armpits to his ribs. Another slid down the middle of his back. Even in the path, small tree branches slapped him in the face and he had to be wary of roots. The dog's howls were getting louder, which meant he was getting closer, all right – but also that Jimmer was getting closer to the coon, too.

Jim pushed himself faster.

He burst into a clearing and would have fallen headfirst into a duck blind if Ike hadn't caught him. He felt Ike's strong hands wrap around his arm, felt Ike's warm coffee breath against his face, smelled a weak wisp of this morning's Old Spice. "Heard you coming," Ike said, breathing heavy. "Goddamn coon is taking Jimmer into the water." Jim looked up into Ike's wide eyes. "You didn't pick my pistol up someplace, did you? " Ike let go of him and held the empty holster flap up at his hip. "Dropped it." Jim shook his head no, catching his breath, his heart pounding hard again, his face flushed.

Ike put his hands on his knees. Sighed. "She's here, you know."

Jim started. "She who?"

"Your mom. She's here. Close by here, anyways."

Jim looked into the dark duck-blind pit with horror, scrambled back.

"Not like that." Ike snorted. "Here somewhere. Around." He moved his hand over his head in a circle, like an umpire signaling a home run. "I spread her out here. Her ashes. Here and by the river. She's still part of the farm. Like she always wanted."

Another long howl jerked his head up. "Gotta get Jimmer." Ike pushed off Jim's shoulder again and shuffled away in his rolling, awkward gait.

"Frigging leg."

Jim bent over the edge of the pit, stared into the deep blue of the hole. He felt sick again. His chest heaved. He breathed hard through his mouth. His body shook with fatigue. He grabbed a leg with both hands and forced himself forward with a groan. Gained momentum again, swayed forward. Jimmer's howls were loud and close now, with hardly any time at all between howls.

Sure doesn't sound old, Jim thought, and smiled to himself. That Jimmer.

The coon was leading Jimmer straight to the river, no denying it now. No weaving. No backtracking. No circling. No, this old coon knew right where he was going and he wasn't wasting any time getting there. Maybe that's what Ike heard. Maybe that's what that look on his face was.

No dog's a match for a raccoon in the water.

Then suddenly the howling stopped. Jim heard Ike's voice calling, ahead of him, still moving. "Don't you go in that water, Jimmer. Don't you go in there, dammit."

First Jim heard a light splash. Then he heard two more splashes close together, one light and one bigger, rougher splash. He ran wildly, broke through the tree line, lurched forward and fell and slid on his chest to a stop at the water's edge. The ground smelled rotten from the wet and the clay and the dying leaves on the shore. Mud greased his hands and chest.

In the moonlight Jim could see his father standing in the river, fighting to keep his balance in the current, thirty feet away. The water there was up to his waist. Ike stood between the coon and Jimmer. He held the dog by the scruff of the neck with his left arm, straight out. Jimmer hung there, twisting and snarling back at the coon. Ike grabbed at his empty holster with his right hand and swore. The coon snarled and growled. Ike slapped at the water to keep the coon away. But then the coon grabbed his slapping arm and started clawing his way up Ike's arm to get to the dog.

Jim stood then and whipped the shotgun forward. His hands were slippery from the clay and water. He raised the gun and buried his cheek into the stock.

Ike saw Jim and yelled. "Shoot, shoot goddammit!" He tried to shake the coon off his forearm and elbow. The coon hung on. Moved up higher.

Jim took a deep breath. Tried to focus. Swallowed hard. Finally lowered the gun. 'I can't!" he cried. "I *can't!*"

The coon was at Ike's shoulder now, intent on getting to the pesky dog that had chased him here, even if it meant going right through the man. "Jimmy!" Ike was hanging on to one of the coon's dark brown ears as best he could, grasping wet skin and fur.

The black-masked coon snarled and lunged, teeth snapping, claws digging into Ike's face and neck, still driving toward the dog. "Shoot, goddammit, *shoot!*" Ike cried.

Jim took a step closer and was in the water. Scatter gun, he thought. He raised the shotgun. Sighted as best he could in the moonlight. He leaned in, stretched his arms out and held the shotgun as close to Ike and Jimmer as he could with one hand. Jim saw the white of Ike's one uncovered eye, held off. He teetered a little on one foot in the current as he stretched forward. When the coon covered Ike's face completely and reached for Jimmer, Jim leaned in a hair further and squeezed one trigger. Bright yellow flames gushed out as the plastic shell exploded in the right-most chamber and sent shot flying forward. The shotgun jumped out of his hand, slammed into his cheek and shoulder and knocked him down into the shallow water.

Jim grabbed his ears. The bitter smell of cordite burned his throat and nostrils. His head hurt from the noise. He noticed his cheek was bleeding. When his eyes adjusted back to the moonlight, he saw the shotgun lying behind him on the shoreline, white barrel tip in the water.

He heard his own shaky breathing first, then farther away he heard the soft jerky paddling of the old dog's front feet in the black water. In the moonlight he saw a flash of Ike's bare skin against the black water. He scrambled to his hands and knees, then dove face-first into the river. Fish-tasting water went up his nose and down his throat as he grabbed at where he thought Ike's leg was most likely to be. The current tugged against him hard as he dragged Ike back toward the shore. He felt through Ike's wet clothes for a pulse, stopped and listened for breathing as he pulled.

The old coon – what was left of him – was still wrapped around Ike's throat. Jim plucked the coon off Ike with both hands, quickly, throwing pieces of him out into the river, gagging deep in his throat as he dug.

By then Jimmer stood next to them in the shallow water. Long, twin steam funnels shot out of the dog's nose as he breathed. His tail wagged. Jim sat and propped Ike against his leg. He ran his hands over the dog's body. He found only a few pellets in his rump and side. He took the dog's head in his hands and tugged hard at his ears, then laid them back flat with his thumbs. Then he stuck his nose deep into the dog's wet neck and sucked in his thick musky smell through the wetness – and the hint of Old Spice there now.

Jim crawled and tugged Ike some more until they sat at the edge of the water. He pulled Ike's head into his lap. Ike's left shoulder was shredded, and he'd taken some heavy shot in the arm and chest – but the old coon had taken the brunt of the shot and saved him.

Jim wiggled out of his coat and threw it over Ike. Jimmer squirmed and circled and scratched until he was lying curled up on the coat in a spot where he could touch both men. Ike moaned. Jim bent down and whispered in his ear. "C'mon old man. Don't you wimp out on me now."

Behind and above them, on the other side of the woods, the other men and their dogs returned to the fire. Jim heard shouts, thought he heard people yelling their names. He pulled the gun around, set the stock in the mud of the bank, and fired the second barrel into the air. Then he just let the gun fall. Dutch and a couple men ran forward, arguing about where the shots had come from. The hounds at the fire milled around in small circles and quickly joined together in an urgent howling. Their high anxious cries rang in the sky and rose in the night, then fell down upon the boy and the man and the dog and the river and the forest around them like the fervent clanging of so many church bells.

GARY'S "EXTRAS"

How to Get More Out of Any Short Story

Often, in literature as in life, the answer to understanding is to question. Use this abbreviated list for quick reference. A more detailed discussion on each question follows for you to use on your first few times through the process.

READY
- Define: who, what, when, where (save "why" and "how" for later)
- Which character changed most? Explain.
- Who tells the story? Why?

SET
- What words or images are repeated?
- What ideas are suggested in the opening? Repeated in the close? In both?
- Is the story told in chronological order? If so, why? If not, why not?
- Describe the writing style, and cite specific examples. Does the style add or detract from the story, in your opinion?

GO
- What sticks with you most about this story? How does it make you feel?
- How does this story compare to other stories you have read? What is similar, and what is different?
- What other stories that you've read made you feel or have a vivid reaction like this story?

How to Get More Out of Any Short Story (Expanded)

As is so often true in literature as well as life, the answer to better understanding is to question. Ask the ten questions below (expanded version) for any story, to enhance your understanding, discussion, and enjoyment. This section can be used by readers and writers alike:

Readers: Learn to "Read like a writer." In English composition class, they call this the "rhetorical situation/analysis." This section will enhance your experience of short stories by adding to your understanding. How a story makes you *feel* counts a lot, too.

Writers: Learn to "Write like a reader." Become acutely aware of what you're doing to your reader – through characters, actions, word choice, length, writing style, writing techniques, other tools in your craft toolbox. Reverse-engineer every story you read to identify and apply techniques you like/that work for that story to your own writing. Become more intentional in your writing to get (more of) the reactions and intent you want.

READY

Q1: Ask: Who, what, when, where (we'll leave "why" and "how" for later).
  a. Who are the main characters in this story? Identify them. Describe them. What do you know about them?
  b. What happens (action, plot)? Map it out. What *really* happens? What *doesn't* happen? Explain.
  c. When is the story taking place – today, yesterday, a time in history – or is it any time?
  d. Where is the story taking place (setting)?
  e. Which of these – who, what, when, where – strikes you as most important to the story? Which strikes you as least important to the story? Why?

Q2. Which character changed the *most* during the story? How did they change (from, to)? Or just as important: Which character should have changed, had an opportunity to change, but did not?

Q3: Who is telling the story? (first person = "I," second person = "you," third person = detached, omniscient). Is the point of view (POV) appropriate for the story? How would the story be different if it was told from a different POV?

SET

Q4: What word/phrase/image is repeated in the story? Where? How many times? When in the story? Why – what does the word/phrase/symbol mean to you? What does this repetition do for the story?

Q5: Now that you've read the story, go back and re-read the first sentence. What aspects of the story do you discover there? Now go to the end and re-read the last sentence and/or paragraph. What aspects of the story do you discover there? Compare the two discoveries. What (if anything) do the beginning and end do for the story? Explain.

Q6: Take a look at how the writer presents "time" in the story. Is the story in chronological order? Is it out of chronological order? For those stories *out* of chronological order: Make a chart (two columns) that compares events (action) first in chronological order, then in "story time" (i.e., as presented by the author in the story). How are they different? *Why* are they different? What does the author accomplish by putting a story "out of chronological order?"

Q7: Look at the writing style of the author – sentence length, number of sentences/paragraphs, language, tone, dialogue (or none), description or not. How would you describe this writing style? Does it add to the story or distract from the story? How? Explain and justify your answer with examples/quotes from the story.

GO

Q8: What struck you or sticks with you *most* about this story? Find one or two lines in the story that capture that meaning for you. Explore/explain them, ask yourself why these lines affected you so. What does your selected line(s) say about the story? What do they say about you?

Q9: How did this story make you *feel*? Find one or two lines in the story that capture that feeling for you. Explore/explain them, ask why they affected you so. What does your selected line(s) say about the story? What do they say about you?

Q10. What other stories that you've read made you feel or have a vivid reaction like this story? What is that story? How is *this* story different from *that* story? How is this story *the same* as that story? What does it mean to you, that you would compare these two stories, that they would both capture your attention and emotions? You might want to read more by the two authors whose work engages you this way.

Now apply your learning to a short story you know to see if this works for you. Of course, you could use the stories in this collection or any other story of your choosing. A few of my favorites are, because they are so different: Hemingway vignette VII (*In Our Time*). Joyce Carol Oates: "August Evening" (flash fiction). Rod Kessler: "How To Touch A Bleeding Dog" (flash fiction).

INTERVIEW WITH THE AUTHOR
Or, Everything A Writer Ever Wanted Someone To Ask Him

Gary's Write Stuff: Who are you, Gary?

I've been many people in my lifetime, and I think I am a composite of all that, every minute: my past, my future expectations, all crushed into the present moment and changing every moment. It's not something you choose, it's someone that you are. Stray from it too long or try to be someone other than who you are, and trouble starts.

GWS: Sounds like there's a story there.

I strayed from who I was in my own life, but I'm finding my way back, I'd say. I got a degree in English and got a teaching certificate for high school teaching, and then worked as a technical writer for an aerospace company instead – for about thirty years. I had a falling out and a bit of soul searching after the local company was bought out by a big East-coast multinational. I retired early before the corporate world killed my soul completely. I knew I wanted to be a college English teacher, but I needed a master's degree to teach. I went to Vermont College of Fine Arts' low-residency MFA program, got that job teaching college English (composition classes, as an adjunct in Glendale AZ), and here I am.

GWS: Did you learn anything from that journey?

I'm a little more impatient now, as hard as that is to believe for those of you who knew me when. But I *am* more impatient with myself – I just don't make as big a scene as I once did, hopefully. If I'm doing something I don't like or that doesn't feel right, I simply don't do it anymore. I showed myself that people don't have to live unhappily – especially me. And another good lesson learned? I am not responsible for everyone around me being happy – that's their job. My wife Linda, a school psychologist-turned- Unitarian Universalist minister, uses a saying I like a lot: "You are what your parents made you. But it's your fault if you stay that way."

Another answer to your question is that I'm just a guy who grew up in Rockford IL with what I thought were middle-class parents: my dad was an over-the-road truck driver, my mom was an executive secretary. I have two sisters, one older and one younger. My parents got divorced when I was 12. Coincidentally (?) I started working when I was 12 for a local landscaper (the brother-in-law of the guy across the street I used to play with) who would do practically anything for money: lay sod, cut trees, haul junk, shovel clinkers out of the school furnace rooms in the winter – whatever. I wrestled in high school, went to Rockford College, quit college once after breaking up with a girl, worked construction until I almost sliced my hand off at a work site, got married, had three kids, went back to school, got a job with an aerospace company, got divorced, got remarried, picked up two more good kids in the merger, retired, went back to school again, got a teaching job…Same ole stuff. Just like everybody else – right?

GWS: What was your childhood like?

Flannery O'Connor said that anyone that has survived to the age of ten has enough to write about for a lifetime. I had enough to write about by the time I was five, I think. Everything after that was icing.

GWS: What's the most significant thing that happened to you as an adult?

Getting divorced. Not so much the divorce itself – in many ways I think that was the best thing for all involved. What I couldn't shake, for the longest time, were the parallels between my parents' lives and my life: married young, three kids (two girls and a boy, like my parents), divorced about the same age…I think I did okay with a lot of help from a few of my friends. For the most part.

GWS: What's the best thing you've done with your life?

Besides this book? You mean so far? The best thing I ever did by far was to be a dad. Not just a biological sperm donor – a dad.

And with my second marriage, I got a chance to be a dad of a slightly different sort. I love my kids because they are my kids – but I also like the people they turned out to be. I can't take all or much of the credit for that – but I like to think I played a small part in forming who they are, and set a decent example for them.

A far second? I get to teach. One of these days soon, I'll get to teach creative writing and literature, hopefully.

GWS: Why do you write short stories?

The short answer is I love short stories. It's wrong to sell short stories short, as some "way to the means," as some precursory "practice exercise" that writers go through in order to write a novel. The skills needed to write a novel and a short story are both similar and significantly different. Short stories are a legitimate and underappreciated literary form all their own. It ticks me off when critics or writers or teachers can't do any better defining a short story than to talk about length: a short story as something "longer than a poem," "shorter than a novella or novel," "prose fiction under 30,000 words."

I like what Ben Percy said recently in *Esquire*: "A short story can be perfect. A novel cannot." (See the February 2013 issue for the whole quote – it's great.) Percy gets to the essence of a short story, a writing form capable of portraying any theme, character, or plot successfully, perhaps more successfully than a novel – in a smidgen of the space. Short stories work because of the time constraints – you can't screw around getting to the point in a short story like you can in a novel.

Wallace Stegner tells aspiring writers to think of their short stories as a boulder rolling downhill: Start the story as far down the hill as you can, while the rock is rolling hard, and still tell the whole story. He was also, unfortunately, warned by an agent to quit writing short stories so that he wouldn't use up all the "beginnings and endings" he needed for his novels… which goes to show most, perhaps, how misunderstood the short story form is, even by people in the business who should know better.

Yet, sadly, novels sell and short stories don't. To me our reading values need better alignment.

GWS: How do you come up with your stories?

The way it works for me is that an idea gets stuck in my head: Usually an incident or event, often from my history somehow. The scene sticks with me, like a song in your head that won't shut off when you're trying to fall asleep. This may go on for days or weeks. I can try ignoring it, but it won't leave. I try to make connections, figure out why this scene or event keeps coming to me. When I say "pay attention," I mean subconsciously – If I try to consciously analyze what is going on, I will lose the scene – or perhaps I am afraid of losing the scene, like waking up from a dream and telling yourself you'll remember in the morning, you know?

Often, not always, a second, seemingly unrelated scene or event will creep in as well. Sometimes, most often, I'll put it together in my head; sometimes not as often, I'll start freewriting and let it flow, and things will come together – organic writing, I think that is called.

At any rate, for me the process is an unexpected gift, grace, serendipity: When the universe speaks to you, listen. When the universe yells at you, write it down and work it til you figure it out.

GWS: How would you describe your stories?

A friend of mine once said all my stories are "daddy stories." That was years ago, many stories ago – I wonder what he'll say about this collection?

While not all my stories literally have a "dad" character, there is often a sense of men struggling in their worlds, universal issues of men, those that love or hate them, and the collateral damage caused and suffered. Hopefully there is often also emotion, honor, and humor. Sarcasm seems to be prevalent, as well, for some reason...

GWS: Do you write every day?

Pretty much, but not always creative writing.

When I do write creatively, like getting this collection ready, I tend to write "new" stuff in the morning hours, and tend to do better with revisions in the afternoons. Often I write both in one day: New creative stuff in the mornings, revisions and judgmental stuff in the afternoon.

I use this metaphor I borrowed from Wallace Stegner to teach my writing students: We all have two people in our heads at the same time, Creative Guy/Gal, and The Judge. You can't get rid of either one of them; in fact you don't *want* to get rid of either of them, because you need them both. But what you need to get good at to write well is calling the one that you need up when you need it, and calming the other one down or making them wait to come forward until you need them. You need both Creative Guy/Gal and The Judge – you run into problems when they both show up at the same time, or when you try to do creative stuff when The Judge shows up, or you try to do revisions or proofreading when Creative Guy/Gal is in the house…

What do I do when I write? I follow my own advice, and cheat just a little. I make sure I have several projects going on at once, all in different stages, so that when Creative Guy shows up but I want to do revisions, I have a choice: Try to squash her down (she is a persistent muse), or simply switch projects for that time and do some creative stuff instead of revisions or proofreading. Mark Twain is an example of a guy that always had many projects going at once; it took him ten years to write *Huckleberry Finn*. But he sure got a lot of stuff right.

GWS: What's the difference between a good writer and a great writer?

Again I'll borrow from Stegner: The difference is the ability to revise. Revise, revise, revise some more. Get it right. Make it the way things are. Make it believable, make it real. That takes hard work, lots of it.

If you are writing mainly autobiographical stuff, and writing fiction instead of creative non-fiction, this is especially important. It might be important for creative non-fiction as well, I just haven't written much creative non-fiction, unless you count my performance reviews and financial projections from my corporate work.

Contrary to popular belief, I think it is harder to write good fiction from autobiographical events. I find that I have to write, write, write to get the real life "out," and to get the literature "in." So what if it didn't happen exactly that way? What's best for *the story*? "Story" should always win. And that's the way it is. And getting that down on paper right is much harder than it sounds.

Another part of this revision process to make a story "great" is time, elapsed time. Use time to your advantage; use time to create distance and space between revisions so you can come back at it "fresh." Some of the stories in this collection have been revised 20-30 times over 10 years or more. I think they're better for it.

Time does some interesting things for you – you are a different person when you come back, you can be a more objective reader and writer. You may know more clearly what you were trying to do with a story, what you intent was – and you're now in better shape to compare that to what is actually on the page.

Finally: A management book out a few years ago called "From Good To Great" talked about how hard it is to take that final step The jist is, many companies say they want to be great, but they really aren't willing to spend the time, effort, and money (in the business case) to get there. F. Scott Fitzgerald, in his famous confessional essay "The Crack-Up," stated that "the price was high." Are you really willing to put in the work and sacrifice and hard cold honesty with yourself that it takes to be great – to follow the story wherever it leads you?

GWS: Why did you put out a collection?

Two reasons. First, I had to do a creative thesis to get my MFA, so I figured, why waste all that effort? Besides, that degree was expensive… expensive, but worth it (as the t-shirt says). Second, I wanted to leave some small legacy of myself for my family. Not that I plan on dying anytime soon, but I mean, it's a little like playing the lottery – you gotta buy a ticket to win, and you gotta get off the porch and play to win. My book is my ticket. If you write, you should put your work out there.

GWS: Why did you want to put out a collection like this, with not only stories but study and discussion questions too?

I thought this was a good way to honor both sides of myself: the writer and the teacher. If my stories are good enough, they'll stand up to some scrutiny by students and/or discussion groups, and just maybe inspire someone else somehow. I'm bridging the gap a little between readers, writers, and learners, I hope, by providing one method to approach a short story through the questions asked (see previous section).

Also: There ought to be a lot more short-story discussion groups as opposed to novel or book discussion groups. The themes and writing in stories are just as good if not better, and a story is much more accessible. People may actually even read them before trying to discuss them.

GWS: Are your short stories autobiographical?

I think all writing is autobiographical, based on personal experience, to a certain extent. A better question is, Which of your stories are the MOST autobiographical?

Either way. it shouldn't matter. Look at the words on the page. If they stand up over time, if they have some meaning and impact on readers, what does it matter how autobiographical they are? Consider the story, stick with the story. In the end, story always wins.

GWS: That begs the question: How much of your writing is autobiographical?

Next question.

GWS: Any advice for aspiring writers?

First, read a lot. And don't read just anything: Read a lot of good stuff. Vince Lombardi didn't say "practice makes perfect;" he said "good practice makes perfect." Read in the genre you're planning to write in. Don't ignore the other genres (poetry, short stories, novels, creative non-fiction) – just read twice as much in the genre you want to write in. Short stories are harder to write than novels, and take different skills or strengths. Poetry is the hardest to get right. Faulkner said novelists are nothing more than failed short story writers, and short story writers are nothing more than failed poets...

Which form of writing calls most to you? Ask yourself why, and try it. Jefferson said, "Read a hundred books, write one." Put your butt in the chair and write – a lot. Writing is mostly a physical exercise. John Irving said writing is one-eighth talent and seven-eighths hard work. Revise. Set your draft aside a few days or weeks or years. Rewrite it again. Set it aside. Repeat until it's done.

GWS: Who are your favorite short story authors?

Ever since I can remember, Ernest Hemingway has been a favorite. Then I went to VCFA and was introduced to Andre Dubus, Amy Hempel, Raymond Carver, Alice Munro, Jane Smiley; to Sherwood Anderson and Tim O'Brien. To Chekhov. Louise Erdrich's short story sequence *Love Medicine* (wrongly tagged a novel) is perhaps my all-time favorite. I think I found Miranda July and Richard Russo on my own (yeah, Russo wrote one short-story collection). Another great Missouri author I found is Daniel Woodrell. William Gay, Richard Bosch, Larry Brown and of course Flannery O'Conn0r gave me a taste of Southern Gothic. And what about Joyce Carol Oates? She is phenomenal. She has to be on the list.

For fun and escape I read good murder mysteries: John Sandford, Michael Connelly, Greg Iles are favorites.

Of course, as long as Louise Erdrich keeps writing, I'll read anything she writes first. Have you read *Roundhouse*?

GWS: Who has inspired you most in your lifetime?

All my heroes are teachers. My wife Linda comes in a close second: She has shown me a different way to be strong, to be courageous, to live. I'm still learning her methods, but tend to fall back to a more primitive "me" most of the time. My friend Mark keeps working to enlighten me, too, over breakfasts at the greasy spoon.

GWS: What are you going to write next?

I like the answer Louise Erdrich gave to this question when asked: "The same story I've been writing my whole life." Fitzgerald said we all have one or two stories in us that we tell in a hundred different ways.

If there is a "next," it'll probably be a lot like these stories -- just told in a different way.

AUTHOR COMMENTARY AND DISCUSSION QUESTIONS

What my stories mean to me shouldn't matter to you, any more than whether or not they are autobiographical or "true." Judge the words on the paper. What's important is what the stories in this collection mean to *you* and how they affect and speak to *you*.

Given all that, it is still interesting and a little fun to reflect, reminisce, and have a short virtual discussion here with the author and his/her stories – I get it. It was fun for me to share the "rest of the story" with you, too.

Don't limit yourself to just what I think. You can do better than that.

The background and discussion questions provide an excellent jumping off point for your Story Circle discussion groups or creative writing classes. Start here, but don't limit yourself to just these points. Go where your hearts and minds and, most importantly, your own questions, lead you. The answer in literature, as is often true in life, is to question. Keep questioning everything.

My commentary and discussion questions are provided below in **alphabetical order by story title** for your quick access and reference.

"Baffled"

"Baffled" is one of those stories based on a "real" event (define "reality," someone). We did go to Summerfest from my Northern Illinois home one summer, we did go to the beer tents and listen to music, we did witness a man strike his kid – and I did nothing, an action that has haunted me ever since.

Have you ever been in that situation, seen something you could fix or do something about, and did nothing? You might also want to think about the title, "Baffled." Who was "baffled" here? About what? (HINT: They probably weren't all baffled by the same thing.)

Baffled

This story, "Baffled," was my Senior Reading just before graduation at Vermont College of Fine Arts. According to David Jauss, my final advisor at VCFA, who introduced me for this reading, "…'Baffled' deals with the complex and difficult relationship of a father and son. In particular, it reveals how a son's relationship with his father can have effects that are delayed, subtle, and indirect… It illustrates…the ability (of a writer) to be simultaneously restrained and powerfully emotional."

How did the father/son relationship affect the main character – what are some of the traces of that impact (name at least two)? What was the *main* effect of that fatherly influence? Defend/support your answer.

How was the story made to be "restrained" (another way of saying "suspenseful")?

"Coming Home"

"Coming Home" is another of my favorites. Originally, this story was conceived as part of a Rockford (IL) Writer's Guild short story contest in the 1990's: You and a bunch of other writers showed up in an auditorium at 9:00 am; they gave you a prompt (word, sentence, phrase that had to be a significant element in the resulting story); you went away for three hours and handed in your story at noon for judging; everyone showed up again at 3:00 pm for the judge's results and a reading of the top three stories. I remember dragging my Apple II computer along in the car in case I couldn't get a computer on campus.

The prompt for this particular story contest was (as I recall): "He tied the dog to the bumper of the car."

"Coming Home" is also the short story that earned my acceptance at Vermont College of Fine Arts MFA in Writing Program. Thanks Doug Glover for seeing some potential in that early draft.

"Coming Home" is about a young man literally coming home to his northern Illinois homestead. Why did he come back? Why did he leave? What did he learn during the raccoon hunt that night he returned? What was his relationship to his father Ike before he left? While he was gone? After that night? What, if any, change occurred in him? Define it. What, if any, change occurred in Ike, the father?

In the scene around the fire, when Jim confronts his father, some of the men look away from them. Do you think the other men already knew the truth about what happened? Or are they still unaware? What does it say about them if they all knew? Explain your answer.

Like the story "Garage Sale," perhaps (depending on your interpretation), this story deals with (SPOILER ALERT!!) euthanasia. What value does the story place on euthanasia? What do *you* think of euthanasia?

This story could also be read as an *initiation* story, a prevalent archetype in Carl Jung's beliefs (see Jung's *Man and His Symbols*, among others). If so, what was Jim's journey, and how did he "triumph"?

Or did he?

"Famous"

Yes, as a trucker as in all things, my father's nickname really was "Famous." This was back in the days of CB radios and nicknames and "handles," back in a *Smokey and the Bandit* world. The relationship between fathers and sons LOOKS less complicated than that between mothers and daughters – but is it? Why? Explain your answer.

Think about the main scenes in this story. How are decisions made in this seemingly average, middle-class family? What does that say about the family/individual relationships? Who is "in charge" here?

How does the family handle a crisis? How does this crisis affect the father? The mother? The son/daughters?

What (if anything) is the connection between "Buddy," the grandfather's dog, and "Ginger," the family's dog? Why use a dog at all in this story – why is she/are they there?

This story too might be seen as a sort of initiation story, a "coming of age" story. Who came of age? When? How? Explain your answers – use examples from the text.

"Garage Sale"

Originally, this story was one of three conceived as part of a Rockford (IL) Writer's Guild short story contest in the 1990's:

You and a bunch of other writers showed up in an auditorium at 9:00 am; they gave you a prompt (word, sentence, phrase that had to be a significant element in the resulting story); you went away for three hours and handed in your story at noon for judging; everyone showed up again at 3:00 pm for the judge's results and a reading of the top three stories. I remember dragging my Apple II computer along in the car in case I couldn't get a computer on campus.

The prompt for this story contest was (as I recall): "He wiped the water from the glass."

"Garage Sale" is on the surface a story of a garage sale, of course, but it is also the story of two marriages, and it is also a story of at least two lives, one ended prematurely in war, one yet to start. What do the two main couples in the story have in common? What do the two husbands have in common, how are the different? What do the two women (wives/mothers) have in common, how are they different? Do these comparisons/parallels add to the story, yes or no? How? Why? Be specific.

Tension is key in this story, too. What is the initial tension between the young couple? Is this tension resolved? How? What techniques does the author use to build tension in the story (look especially at why and how Jeff goes in the house)? Do they work? Why or why not? Explain, using one of the techniques/sentences as an example.

On one level "Garage Sale" also addresses (SPOILER ALERT!!!) euthanasia and suicide. How? To answer, you probably have to decide whether the woman dies from natural causes, euthanasia, or is part of a double suicide. Does it matter? How is the story different depending on which method you determine? What does the story have to say about euthanasia or suicide – is it good or bad? Or doesn't the story place a value on them? What do *you* think of euthanasia or suicide?

"Showtime"

The state of reality TV today is not far from this scenario – true or false? Some inspiration/influences from Kurt Vonnegut here (hopefully). One side of this story is about commercialism – what are the advantages of the State for this show? For the producers? What is with the knitter? Where else in literature have we seen a lady knitting through violent circumstances (hint: check out Dickens)? What else does this story have in common with that one? Look up the movie reference, "High Plains Drifter" – what was that show about? What does that story have in common with this one?

Take a look, too, at the character names here. In some ways, the character names give the story an allegorical feel. Look up "morality plays" of the Middle Ages. Any relevance to this story? What is the lesson being told?

Originally, this story was conceived as part of a Rockford (IL) Writer's Guild short story contest in the 1990's: You and a bunch of other writers showed up in an auditorium at 9:00 am; they gave you a prompt (word, sentence, phrase that had to be a significant element in the resulting story); you went away for three hours and handed in your story at noon for judging; everyone showed up again at 3:00 pm for the judge's results and a reading of the top three stories. I remember dragging my Apple II computer along in the car in case I couldn't get a computer on campus…

I don't remember what the contest prompt was.

The real take-away for writers here, however, is to not stop at the first version. Many writers and teachers of writing, among them one of my favorites, Wallace Stegner, founder of the Stanford Creative Writing program, have voiced my belief that the difference between a good writer and a great writer is the ability to revise. Stegner's advice the beginning writer? Create, yes – but don't stop there. "Revise! Revise! Revise!"

"The Sum of All Fears"

"The Sum of All Fears" is a story of a young family where suppressed events from the past catch up with them, and must be faced and dealt with. For the wife, the event is being left behind, being different, not having any friends growing up. For the husband, the catalyst is the idea that he is doomed to repeat his parent's history of divorce and destruction he experienced as a child. A third party enters the picture bringing a suppressed dynamic of his own, and eventually brings events to their dramatic head.

What do you think? Does history repeat itself? Have you ever felt this way? Did you feel doomed or did you feel happy? If history does repeat itself, how does one ever break the cycle?

Can a couple be happily married and still have friends outside of the marriage? How – what are the guidelines, the rules? Be as specific as possible. Use personal examples.

There is also an element of naivety in the characters here – or is it innocence? Explain which you think it is, and why. Where was Doug naïve or innocent? Where was Wendy? Was Tony naïve, yes or no – what makes you say so?

I don't often get hung up on names, or put hidden meanings in them (with few intentional exceptions – see "Showtime") – but look up the name "Wendy." It comes from the story *Peter Pan* – what does it mean there, how did the name come about for that author?

One of the struggles I had with this story was how to present it. I settled on a "conversational" format that, except for the opening and closing (third person), switches back and forth between the two main characters as a dialogue of sorts. What does this do for the story? How important is it that each person narrates their own story – what does the reader learn about each character that way? Does the reader learn things about the character that the character doesn't know about himself or herself? If yes, give an example.

The intent of this approach was to mimic diaries, or at best perhaps a couple's counseling appointment/session or series of sessions. Was this "dialogue" approach successful to you? Why or why not? What was good about it? What was a weakness to this approach? If it was told from one point of view or the other, how would the story be the same? Be different? Whose point of view would it best be told from?

Finally: Which is more "distant," first-person or third-person? What are some of your favorite first-person stories? What are some of your favorite third-person stories? Why was each story told in the point of view it was? What does switching back to third-person do to/for this story in the end?

What will happen next? Do you think this couple will stay together? Why or why not? Explain/support your answer.

"Throwing Snowballs At Cars"

I spent many thrilling nights throwing snowballs at cars from behind the hedgerow on Custer Avenue in Rockford with my buddies – like the baseball games of summer providing fodder for winter conversations, throwing snowballs at cars gave us something more to talk about in the summer – and, of course, kept us in baseball shape. It was a rarity to get chased by a driver, but it was a real rush when we did – whether we got caught or not. While the main dynamic here is (perhaps) the relationship between the three boy characters, there are lots of other relationships to explore for enjoyment and understanding: family relationships for each; brother/sister, father/son, mother/son; drivers to throwers; "haves" to "have nots." Explore and define the key relationships you see. Do these relationships support or distract from the story?

Can you see/imagine/consider "Throwing Snowballs At Cars" as a metaphor for other life situations, or perhaps life itself? What dynamics are present when you throw snowballs at cars? Are these same dynamics present in life? Present in *your* life? What is the role of the Hurst Olds 442 in the story? Define what this repeated image means, and explain its significance in your own words.

What is the relationship between Mr. Holland and the main character? What do you think about the main character's decision in the end about the scholarship – why did he make the decision he did?

An influence/inspiration in this story in the form of "Hurst Olds Guy" was John Irving: First his ever-present, ever-ominous "undertoad" in *The World According to Garp,* and then the "mystery Mustang" in *Last Night at Twisted River.*

"Trinity"

"Trinity" is an attempt at a linked short story with the stories "You Just had To Do it," "The Wait," and "Dreamer." My main influence here is Louise Erdrich's wonderful short story sequence *Love Medicine* (if you still think her book is a novel, we're going to have to have a talk); but more specifically in this case, with the three stories in my "Trinity," the influence/inspiration was Stuart Dybek's story "Nighthawks" in his collection, *The Coast of Chicago*.

I'd always thought of a short story sequence as being a collection of stories, i.e., a linked "book." Until Dybek I'd never considered that one could create a sequence/links within just a few stories, as well – and create some of the same dynamics. In Dybek's case, the nine stories within his story "Nighthawks" are sub-sections of a larger short story sequence about Chicago, the place, and the neighborhood characters, and still stand as a sequence of stories under "Nighthawks" as well.

Stories serving double-duty – like overtones in music.

In a short story sequence, you have not only the stories in the sequence themselves – you also have the space and time between the stories. As Robert Luscher said in his seminal essay "The Short Story Sequence: An Open Book," a short story sequence balances the separateness and diversity of a short story with the unity of a novel. The result is something like eating mixed nuts with jelly beans (my favorite gourmet snack) – salty and sweet, combined, with each taste still separate and distinct, but each "flavor" blended together to create *another* entity – the combination itself. In this combining of short stories under a related story arc, the author creates another story or two or three, through her balance of independence and unity, through her linking or sequencing devices: plot, character, symbols, and/or place or time.

How many stories are in "Trinity"? Explain. Which of the stories is your favorite? Why? Which of the stories is your least favorite? Why? How many years are between each story? What year does each story happen in – and what do you notice about these dates? What *happens* between each story (define)? What characters, places, situations appear in all three stories? In more than one?

Where else have you heard about a "trinity"? Is there a similar though perhaps not "holy" trinity here? Identify it. Do we all have a trinity? Explain, be personal and specific. In the end, what is the total effect of these three stories together? Could each story stand on its own? Do you think they are more powerful together, or would they be more powerful standing alone (separate)? Explain your answer, be specific.

"Turnabout"

"Turnabout" is about the trials, tribulations, and choices in one man's life in one fateful evening. The setting is a music fair in Rockford IL on a Labor Day weekend. Yes, "On The Waterfront" *was* a "real" festival (sadly cancelled a few years ago). Yes, I attended with my family for many years. Yes, the band "Cheap Trick" really *is* from Rockford.

What are some of these "trials, tribulations, and choices" the main character Jack experiences in "Turnabout"? What about other characters (such as the protagonist, such as the security cop, such as the home-schooling mother on the blanket, such as the mother on the bus)? List these situations and results. Do they add or detract to the story? How (be specific)? Do these other situations/choices add or detract to the main character's situation – how?

What did you think of the ending – is it believable? Appropriate? Telling? Explain your answer.

"Why I'm Here"

This story is perhaps my favorite story. I really had an English teacher like Mr. Stokes, and yes, there really was an *Ideas of Man* class – but does that matter to the story? Explain your answer.

Re-read the story and look for words associated with the concept of violence. List them. Where was the earliest reference? Where is the latest? How many references were there? What do they mean? Is the story "just" about a high school English teacher – yes or no? Explain your answer.

For a long time, this story had the title 'Commencement," and ended after the stair scene. How would this have been a different story? Would it have been better or worse? Why was the story continued – does the continuation add or detract from the story? Explain your answers; be specific, give examples from the text.

This story is also intended as a companion piece to "Wrestleback," a story that on the surface is about going to high school in Rockford IL in the 1970's. John Updike's "early stories" were an inspiration/influence that gave me permission to write these. Some of the characters/themes are in both stories ("Why I'm Here" and

"Wrestleback") – who are those characters? What other themes are present in this story? Does the idea of a "companion story" add or distract from this stories impact/meaning – why or why not? Be specific.

An influence/inspiration here (at least a book I recall reading around the same time as I was revising this story) was John Irving's *Last Night At Twisted River* – the far-reaching impact the "Kennedy Rule" (married men were exempted from the Vietnam draft) had on lives at the time, similar to the far-reaching effect of the draft lottery on the high-school seniors in "Why I'm Here."

"Working Class"

I took on a personal challenge with "Working Class" – I started out to write a (SPOILER ALERT!) story with a happy ending. You decide if I accomplished that or not. Not many of my stories have happy endings.

It's harder than it looks, even though happy endings are a lot easier to sell to publishers, or so I've heard. George Lucas said a happy ending adds millions to the box office. But then again, Ernest Hemingway once said: "Happiness in intelligent people is the rarest thing I know." Who do you think was right? Why or why not?

An interesting struggle for me, with this story, was the title as the story progressed. I had to write my way into a good title, so to speak. The story started out as "Father's Day," later changed to "Lessons," and finally settled on "Working Class." The title "Working Class" has at least two meanings – what are they? How do these definitions relate to the story? Is "Working Class" a good title or not? If not, what title would you give this story?

One of my VCFA advisors (Ellen Lesser) called "Working Class" a "tale of tension and redemption along a father/son paper route." Where is the tension? Identify, define it. How was the tension created by the author – what are one or more of the important writing elements used? Where is the "redemption" in this story? Identify it, define it. Who is being redeemed? Is more than one person redeemed? How? If people are being redeemed, what are they being redeemed *from*?

An influence/inspiration for this story for me was a session at a VCFA residency on happy endings, and Richard Russo's writing -- his novels of course but also his short stories in *The Whore's Child and Other Stories*. Another collection I recall reading around that same time was Miranda July's wonderful *Nobody Belongs Here More Than You*, especially her story "Birthmark."

"Wrestleback"

"Wrestleback" is a phrase used in some high school/college tournament formats for wrestling: Even if you lose a match, you are still "alive" in the tournament until you wrestle the person who also lost to the same person, and lose to him – or, until the person that beat you loses. It is perhaps a more fair and just system than the simple single or double elimination formats found in most tournaments. Does this idea of "wrestleback," of a sort of "ultimate fairness," have anything to do with this story? What? Explain your answer.

What did you think about the "decision" for the wrestling match? (In wrestling parlance, "decision" means "outcome.")

This story is also intended as a companion piece to "Why I'm Here," another story about going to high school in the Rockford IL in the 1970's. John Updike's "early stories" were an inspiration/influence that gave me permission to write these. Some of the characters/themes are in both stories – who are those characters? What other themes are present in this story? Does the idea of a "companion story" add or distract from this stories impact/meaning – why or why not? Be specific.

Is the story "just" about a high school sports assembly – yes or no? Explain your answer.

*I write for the same reason I breathe –
because if I didn't, I would die.*
– Isaac Asimov

FAILED POET'S SOCIETY

Why do people today write short stories? Do short stories have any more value than as warm-up exercises in Freshman Creative Writing courses to "making it" and writing a novel? Most writing craft books can't even define the essence of a short story, other than through some weak definition of length ("shorter than all those other forms of writing"). There is no market for short stories; the market that there is is for novels, and maybe not even novels – creative non-fiction sells better. Sure, there are exceptions to the rule: Dubus and Monroe and Carver, authors that write short stories and novellas exclusively – but these exceptions are few and far between. Short stories now, it seems, are used as filler in between magazine revenue, as e-zine spacing surrounded by interactive ads. Creative writers in this scenario are "content providers," low on the totem pole in this configuration. Don't let the stories get in the way of the marketing.

Yet short stories prevail. Short story writers write short stories because they want to write short stories. Or perhaps, like Asimov, they have to or they'll die. At best, they respect the form and try to get it perfect. It can be done – look at Chekhov, Anderson, Hemingway, Carver, Hempel, to name a few. Benjamin Percy summed it up in Esquire: "The short story can be perfect; the novel cannot." Contrary to popular belief, people do not write short stories just because they can't think of enough words to write a novel. If you do it right, short stories are harder to write than novels, those "great baggy monsters" per Hemingway. Ask Fitzgerald ("The price was high."). And no, as Wallace Stegner's agent remarked, making him pull back on short stories to write more novels – short stories don't take away all your best beginnings and endings. So keep writing them.

Asking "Why do you write short stories?" is a little like asking a major league shortstop why he dedicates his life and career to a game where they hit their weight, if lucky, and fail at the plate two-thirds of the time if they're great. They can, so they do. But it is deeper than that: They respect the game, they play for the moments of perfection possible in the game, they play for the potential of "getting it right," of getting just one play or story "the way it is."

We write what we write because we believe it; more, we think what we write is true and we strive to make it real. How we do that, "make it real" on paper, is at best also a reflection of that story, of that truth, of that reality. How we handle that truth in time plays a big part in that reality.

Now we're getting closer to what I think is true. I like what Faulkner reputedly said: "A novelist is nothing more than a failed short-story writer. A short story writer is nothing more than a failed poet." To all appearances, we have time, plenty of time. But as Albert Einstein said, "To us physicists, time is an illusion, albeit a useful one." Time *seems* endless – but in reality what we have is the present moment, the one we're in, the ones we remember, the ones we create.

That's it. There is no more.

A short story captures and builds on these significant moments, the significant few among the trivial many – turning points, perhaps, "epiphanies" sometimes, as Joyce said, more often tragic realizations or, even more poignantly, when the moment passes without any realizations made.

Short stories are crafted moments, consciously or (mostly?) unconsciously, laid bare for the taking. The compressed space and time, like poetry, adds to the sense of urgency and intensity in the present moment.

Take a moment. Read short stories. The good ones will stay with you for the rest of your life. If one you read looks easy to you, take a moment, try to write one yourself, as Flannery O'Connor said. Then go back and thank those authors that showed you what was possible in the form. They're here for the taking, these moments. These short stories. The form persists. Short-story writers persist.

Maybe the moments themselves persist? Maybe that's just the way it is. Maybe the moment is all there is. Maybe short story writers get it right.

Not bad for a bunch of failed poets.

Gary Lawrence
Phoenix AZ
June 2013